1996

eskimo kissing

By the same author

Becoming a Mother
An Essential Guide to the Facts, Feelings and Emotions of
Pregnancy and Childbirth

The House
Inside the Royal Opera House, Covent Garden

KATE MOSSE

eskimo kissing

Hodder & Stoughton

Copyright © 1996 by Kate Mosse

First published in Great Britain in 1996
by Hodder and Stoughton
A division of Hodder Headline PLC

10 9 8 7 6 5 4 3 2 1

The places in this novel are places I know well – although
certain liberties have been taken – but the story and the
characters are entirely imaginary. Any similarities to real
events or real people, alive or dead, are coincidental. And
should be ignored.

A CIP catalogue for this title is available
from the British Library.

ISBN 0 340 64950 X

Typeset by Palimpsest Book Production Limited,
Polmont, Stirlingshire
Printed and bound in Great Britain by
Mackays of Chatham PLC, Chatham, Kent

Hodder and Stoughton
A division of Hodder Headline PLC
338 Euston Road
London NW1 3BH

To my sisters, Caroline and Beth, with love

But we have different voices, even in sleep,
and our bodies, so alike, are yet so different
and the past echoing through our bloodstreams
is freighted with different language, different meanings—

Adrienne Rich, 'XII/Twenty-One Love Poems',
The Dream of a Common Language, Poems 1974–77

part one

The joys of parents are secret, and so are their griefs and fears.

Francis Bacon, 'Of Parents and Children',
Essays

Green is the colour of history. Not the black and white of books or photographs. Not the frozen grey of tombstones and cathedrals. It is green that is the colour of time passing. Olive moss, sable in places, covering the crow's-feet cracks in the wall. Like fur. Emerald weeds that spring up along a path long unused.

The gabled house stood alone, shabby and still, as if holding its breath. Nothing moved. For two days and nights, rain had fallen from the unbroken sky and melted away like snow into the ground. There was no wind, no frost. More like an endless April than the tail-end of winter.

The house looked as if it had been waiting in its cypress silence for years, patient and unblinking. No lights were on, only a weak gleam from the dirty bulb in the porch. Mid-afternoon was starting to creep up on the four irregular walls and the complicated sloping roof, turning the greens and naked browns of the garden to black.

In the tiny box-room under the eaves sat a man. Striped South American rugs, an empty amber vase, woodwork painted cream, it was a room of life and colour. Cheap gold hooks on the back of the door, an unpolished brass ashtray and a couple of wine bottles for candlesticks. Someone – not him – had lovingly melted wax over the necks of the bottles. He stared out of the window, watching the light fade. His face was troubled.

'They'll be back soon,' he whispered.

The words crackled softly in the air for a moment before the silence closed back over them.

'I must go.'

Her breathing was soft. She lay sleeping on her side, head balanced on the white underside of her right arm. Her left arm rested over her pale body, as if draped there haphazardly by somebody else. She looks so young, he thought, so perfect. Love twisted in him. He felt drugged and infatuated, tortured by a passion that swamped everything in its path. Desperate to close out the world, he tugged roughly at the homemade curtains. The material dug its heels in and stuck halfway along the tiny rail.

'I should go,' he whispered again.

In the darkening afternoon light, he traced the outline of her shoulder blade with his knuckles. His man's hands seemed so clumsy to him, so big. Like a bear caressing a dove. He ran the tips of his fingers down one of her cheeks, then dusted over the flickering lids of her eyes. In her sleep, instinct turned towards the familiar touch.

He touched the printed cotton bedspread, unconsciously pulled up to her waist to keep out the draught. Bold, Aztec triangles. Its folds looked like a voluminous skirt, a dirndl in which a girl could dance and spin.

With the backs of his hands, he brushed the delicate hairs on her arms, a hypnotic and rhythmic pattern. His fingers skated on to the blue–white skin of her breast, without warning, just glancing the nipple. Her breath was coming faster now. She shifted, rolling the flimsy material over with her. He could see the outline of her legs, distinct one from the other. There's so much noise, he thought to himself, as the little room filled up with the sound of his blood beating, thick and heavy.

Trying not to trap the cover under his leg, he knelt on to the bed. Skin and bone touched the top of her thigh, intimate and startling. As he shifted his weight from the floor, the bed rocked like a raft. She opened her eyes and held him in her gaze. Eyes the colour of autumn, he marvelled, of chestnut tumbling into brown.

They looked straight into one another's faces, unblinking and focused. He breathed out. She lifted the bedspread to let him under, watching his red mouth as he carefully lowered his body into the triangular space between her bare legs. Still they stared. The room waited. Pushing gently, he eased himself inside her, little by little, until he could go no further. For a moment he lay still, as if resting.

The hairs on the back of her neck prickled, alert, as warmth seeped through her body like blotting paper. She felt she was being swallowed up. Very full, very powerful, as if her body had grown and grown. A giant woman, one hundred feet tall now. She had no sense of time, of space, just those two blue eyes watching her in the black dusk.

Slowly, he began to move.

'My love.'

The words slipped from between his lips.

She caught her breath. And allowed her weightless eyes to close. Neither of them heard the slam of the front door, nor the radio being turned on in the kitchen two floors below. Cliff Richard and the Shadows. Like smoke, the sound of 'The Young Ones' wound its innocent way up the stairs.

1975

CHAPTER 1

A November morning, sunny after dawn, mist and fog patches, about fifty degrees Fahrenheit. East wind, cloudy later. A pleasant enough modern estate on the outskirts of a pretty mid-Sussex town, no more than fifteen minutes from the city centre. Two-, three- and four-bedroomed terraced houses, staggered to give the illusion of privacy, designed with a touch of variety for the families of teachers and accountants and junior IBM executives.

'Nineteen down,' said Tom Whittaker, scratching his beard with the end of his biro. "They've had it as storytellers". Four, three.'

Sam scowled at her father's paper. *The Times. Wednesday November 12 1975. No 59,551. Price ten pence.* Boring. A photo of two men smiling. The one with the silly name had resigned. Who cares, she thought, banging her right heel over and over against a leg of her chair. She twisted her head slightly to read the man's name. Gough Whitlam. Goff like cough? Gow like bough? It was night in Australia. If they were Australian, their birthday would almost be over.

'Dead men,' said her sister Anna.

'Sorry?'

'"They've had it as storytellers". Dead men.'

'What a brilliant daughter,' muttered Tom, counting out the spaces. 'OK, twenty-four across: "The habit of girls in the swim". Seven letters. B something K something, something, something . . .'

'What *is* Mum doing up there?' interrupted Sam. 'Can't we start without her?'

Anna smiled. The clock above the kitchen door tapped out the time. Tick. Tick. Nearly eight o'clock. Tom folded his paper in on itself, then flapped it down in the middle of the table.

'No, PB2, we can't,' he said firmly. 'Why don't you go and see if she's coming? Or has the shock of turning thirteen taken away the use of your legs . . . ?'

'Ha. Ha,' grimaced Sam, shunting back her chair and sloping out into the hall.

'Mu-um! Mu-um!' she bawled up the stairs, as if she'd been a teenager all her life. 'What *are* you doing? I'm really, *really* bored of waiting.'

'Twenty-four across is bikinis,' said Anna, tucking her hair back behind her left ear.

A blob of marmalade, its five-minute journey down the side of the jar over, oozed onto the face of the dismissed Australian Prime Minister.

Anna and Sam were not identical twins, although physically they were alike. They both had blue eyes, paddling-pool blue, and British mousy-blonde hair. Anna was slightly the taller, all skin and geometric bone to her sister's flesh and curves. Her hair was cut into a symmetrical bob and a precise fringe. It did not hide her crimson birthmark, which splashed across the right side of her forehead and eyebrow. As if someone had thrown red wine in her face. It was the first thing strangers noticed. The second was that Anna was beautiful. Actually beautiful, the lines of an adult rather than a pretty child.

Everything about Sam, on the other hand, was round. Her shoulder-length haystack hair filling the air around her head like a wiry halo. She already had the body of a young teenager. The navy-blue school skirt strained slightly across her tummy and hips, and the second and third buttons of her yellow shirt gaped under pressure. She was emotional, impatient and energetic, a passionate yo-yo of a girl zooming from one obsession to another.

The twins fought and competed and bickered like any other sisters. But beyond the tick-list characteristics, Sam and Anna felt that being one of two was special. If they'd been asked to put their feelings into words, they'd have said that having a twin was like having a lucky angel. Anna would always be there for Sam, and Sam for Anna, come what may. Their love for one another was unconditional, even when they didn't like each other very much.

Their mother, Helen, had never dressed her daughters in the same clothes when little, avoiding the same colours even. The only exception to the rule was bridesmaids' dresses and, as twins, they'd been greatly in demand. It was at their first wedding reception, swathed head to satin toes in peach, that Sam announced she was going to marry Anna when they grew up. All the grown-ups had smiled.

Their childhood nicknames were still used too. For their sixth birthday, Tom had come home with two Paddington Bear toys, one under each arm. Nobody could remember how or when the girls started to be called PB1 and PB2. But the pet names had stuck. Seven years later, Sam's bear still sat propping up her growing collection of singles, preventing Leo Sayer, David Essex and Slade from tipping over like dominoes and crushing the Osmonds. Anna's sat more primly on the little shelf above her bed, next to her complete collection of Paddington Bear books arranged in chronological order. She was PB1, by virtue of having been born twenty minutes before her twin. Sam didn't think it was fair.

Tick. Tick. Twenty past eight. The arrival of their mother had been the catalyst for an orgy of present- and card-opening, Helen suggesting in vain that they should check the envelopes for postal orders before slinging them on the floor.

The girls opened presents like they ate. Sam devoured everything in double-quick time, finishing up with indigestion and a sense of having been slightly let down. As if she'd nearly – but not quite – got the perfect present. Anna savoured everything, jotting down who'd sent what on her thank-you letters list. The girls were united, though, in despising those relatives and family so-called friends who sent a joint card. Even though they always thought of their birthday as a shared celebration, with the graceless hypocrisy of youth they hated anyone else lumping them together. Auntie Joy – humiliated for ever on Anna's list – had only sent one present. A single copy of the *Junior Pears Encyclopaedia* inscribed to THE TWINS. Like they were still children. God, thought Sam, how mean. And boring. She looked at the four waxy colour photos on the front cover, a collage of 1975 so far: some politician – ugly – holding up a little red case; Mohammed Ali, quite dishy; a train, yawn, yawn. The last photo was more interesting, though. Sam frantically tapped the top of Anna's hand, just in case she hadn't noticed the totally nude statue, penis and everything hanging out. Peering more closely at the photo, the two mousy heads shook, giggling with embarrassment at the ways of the world. Thirteen today.

Spotty wrapping paper, striped wrapping paper, pink bows lay discarded like husks on the floor. Green and white and fuchsia envelopes. The kitchen looked shocked. Despite the paper mountain, though, there was an air of unfinished business.

'Dad?' whined Sam, fanning herself with her new LP. 'I don't want to be rude, but . . . well, is this my *main* present?'

'*Captain Fantastic*,' read Anna, thinking that Elton John's silver boots looked like the top of the kitchen taps.

Sam twisted the record, front, back, front, back, looking for an answer to her question in their father's eyes. Anna saw there were sludgy paintings of frogs that turned into flights of stairs and octopus legs and skulls. She wouldn't want something so creepy in her bedroom. She glanced down at the benign profile of Yehudi Menuhin on her birthday album, violin under his chin.

'This record is really *fantastic*,' Sam ploughed on, wondering if Tom would get the pun. 'And I really wanted it. But . . . well, you know what I mean.'

The sun was just edging its way into the kitchen, weakly lighting the wall yellow.

'No, darling, I don't think I do,' replied Tom, trying to keep a straight face. 'I think you've both been very lucky.'

Anna knew what Sam meant, of course, because they'd already talked about it for ages last night before going to bed. After the hair drama, that is. Too impatient to wait for her hairdresser's appointment after school on Friday, Sam had set about her frizz with a pair of nail scissors in the bathroom yesterday evening. Imagining herself as the dark one from Abba. But neither the raw material nor her skill had lived up to her vision and the result had been a tragedy. Reflected in the mirror was not a sophisticated flicked fringe but a hacked and lopsided edge. She'd panicked. Tears in her eyes, she'd scythed on. I'm thirteen tomorrow, she'd mourned, and I've got tragic hair. Everything's spoiled.

Sensing the crisis next door, Anna abandoned her homework and managed to persuade Sam to unlock the bathroom door where both Helen and Tom had failed. Things are always happening to you, PB, she said affectionately, straightening out the line as best she could. You're that sort of bear.

A few hours later, after their parents had gone to bed, Sam had crept across the landing into Anna's bedroom. Ever since their ninth birthday, the girls had exchanged presents in secret the night before their birthday proper. This is our last night as children, really, Sam'd said portentously. A sense of occasion appealed to Sam as much as a sense of order appealed to Anna. It made her feel she mattered, as if one day she would be famous. She tried to make every little thing significant, conducting her life in technicolour, an emotional soundtrack swelling in the background. Important moments should feel important *at the time*, Sam stressed. Not just when you look back.

With less than an hour of being twelve to go, Sam was sprawled like a starfish on Anna's bed, under the illusion that she looked slimmer lying down. Anna was perched on her dressing-table stool. The oldest, it was tradition that she went first. Her tidy fingers prised open a scruffy package that looked as if it had been lassoed by sellotape. The gold caught the dim light of her bedside lamp. It looked exotic, like something a woman would have. Anna stroked the delicate chain and cross across her palm, reading aloud her name engraved on the back.

For Sam, Anna had bedded down a silver locket in cotton wool in a proper little jewellery box. Peacock blue, Anna's favourite colour. There had been room for SAM LOVE FOR EVER ANNA on the back. As the girls hugged, Anna's cross got caught in Sam's hair. Siamese twins now, joked Anna. Giggling gave way to laughing gave way to shushing gave way to loud, loud whispering as they tried to untangle.

With only twenty minutes to go before they were teenagers, they had come to the big question. What would they get from their parents? Record tokens? Too, well, granny-like, said Sam. Money? Too impersonal, said Anna. Tickets to a concert, to the theatre? It's important being thirteen, Sam had said firmly. We'll get something special.

Tick. Tick. Twenty-three minutes past eight. Anna looked at her mother, then her father. They both looked smug. Sam sat peering out from under her cock-eyed sproutings of fringe. It was Tom who gave in, unable to keep it up any longer.

'Why don't you try looking in your bedrooms . . . ?'

Immediately the heavy thump of two pairs of school shoes pounded the blameless stairs. A moment or two later, shrieks and thank-yous came tumbling down from upstairs.

'I expect we'll live to regret this,' muttered Tom happily,

imagining night after night of decibel warfare between rival music centres. Half-standing, he stretched across for his paper, holding his tie against his shirt to protect it from coming to a greasy end in the butter. Fifteen minutes or so were enough to bury one or two more clues, even without Anna. His thumb squelched firmly into Gough Whitlam's marmaladed jaw. He groaned.

'Can you bring mine up with you when you come?' yelled Sam as Anna reappeared downstairs.

'It's wonderful,' kissing first her mother, then her father.

'Eight down,' he said. 'Nine letters. "Getting on, may be seen to sniff".'

Slipping her LP out from her pile of birthday presents, Anna then rooted around in the mess under the table for Sam's record. Trying not to look at the illustration.

'We're just going to quickly try them out, Mum,' she said, escaping towards the hall. 'I promise we'll be quick.'

'Ten minutes,' stressed Helen to her daughter's disappearing back. 'No more.'

There was no reaction.

'Anna? Tell Sam that you've both got to be ready to leave in ten minutes. Otherwise you're all going to be late for school. Do you hear me? Yes?'

There would be a rush, thought Helen with resignation as she started to clear up the breakfast things, there always was. Time ambushed them on Mondays, on Tuesdays, Wednesdays, Thursdays and Fridays, regular as clockwork. God knows what it would be like if Tom taught at a different school and there were two ports of call. She glanced at the time. Mechanical morning actions. Dirty plates to the sink. Milk to the fridge. Jars to the cupboard. Orange marmalade, black marmite, yellow butter, brown toast, white sugar. Upstairs, Mr Menuhin's gentle strings were already losing the battle to the Brown Dirt Cowboy and his acoustic piano.

The taps begrudgingly spat water into the sink. Froth, the lap of china and metal as the water got deeper. Helen looked out over the rows of frosted green postage-stamp lawns, all the same. Front doors, porches, paths. The rituals we surround ourselves with, she thought, just to give an illusion of control.

Abruptly, she turned off the spluttering taps and stretched over to the window-sill. She cupped her hand over a box of matches balanced on a nearly-new packet of Silk Cut. Her thin fingers

14

eased out a cigarette, flipped the lid shut and tossed the box back on to the ledge. Sliding the cigarette between her lips, she struck a match. Inhaled. Bliss. Two flicks of the wrist and the flame died, one more thin, black-tipped stick to join the others in the varnished clay ashtray. MUM was scratched four times round the edge. Surprisingly resilient, smiled Helen, given Sam had made it at junior school and for two weeks had insisted on washing it up herself. MUM. MUM. MUM. MUM. The smile did not reach Helen's eyes.

Tom felt the change of atmosphere in the kitchen and looked up. The happy birthday mood had melted away, leaving something sharper in its place. His wife was half-hugging her long body, left elbow tight in against her ribs, arm crossed over her waist. It's as if she's protecting herself, he thought. He watched her mouth pull again on the cigarette.

'What's up?'

Wrapped in solitary thoughts, she did not hear him.

'Helen?'

Her name floated between them for a moment. She didn't own to it. Tom unwound himself from his chair and came over. Over six foot by the age of fifteen, he had the apologetic stoop of someone used to being taller than everyone else. A scrawny, bearded question mark of a man. Helen held her cigarette away from her body, so as not to brush it against his checked shirt. He carefully threaded his fingers through her greying short curls, as if untangling spaghetti.

'What's up?'

She squeezed the filter between her lips, unwilling to give it up, then folded the stub over in the ashtray. Helen had been awake since half past five, lying in bed waiting for the central heating to start cracking its bones. Dragging her emotions to the surface gave her the upper hand. She was in control, couldn't be taken by surprise. But naming them somehow shifted the balance of power back again. Spoken out loud, the fears seemed more real.

'Everything changes today, Tom,' she said carefully. 'I know you think I'm blowing it out of all proportion and worrying unnecessarily . . . It doesn't make any difference to what we tell the girls, I know that. But I just can't face telling them yet. Not today.'

Her voice tapered off. 'I know we agreed . . .'

Helen looked into Tom's eyes, expecting to see exasperation. There was only concern. He doesn't understand why I'm worried, she thought. He just does not understand.

She could feel the hard edge of the draining-board pressing into her back. A dribble of water seeped through the sleeve of her white blouse, a sudden prick of cold against her arm. Tom leaned across and waved her Silk Cut packet hopefully. Helen handed him the matches in answer and watched as he tapped the bottom of the packet over and over until one cigarette worked its way loose.

One second. Tick. Two seconds. Tick. Three seconds. Neighbours would have seen that nice Mr and Mrs Whittaker, framed in their window. Just another Wednesday morning in November. A car engine spluttered into life next door. Buses, jobs, classrooms were waiting to be filled. Upstairs, two thirteen-year-old girls hummed along to the music that spoke to them. Downstairs, Helen and Tom stood suspended in time and space and silence.

Tom snapped them out of it.

'Right-oh,' he said, turning back into the room. 'We'll wait until we've got the dreaded party out of the way at the weekend.'

His voice sounded as if it was coming from a long way away, a grating, breezy sound. Abandoning the poached cigarette, Tom gathered up his jacket from the back of his chair and stuffed his newspaper into the pile of marking in his briefcase.

'But,' he added gently, 'we've got to tell them sooner or later. Might as well be sooner.'

Helen watched him walk into the hall, knowing he was right.

'Anna? Sam? I'm going in two minutes,' he shouted up the stairs. As he always did. Louder today, to beat the massed orchestras. Muffled protests. As always.

'Tough. If you're not both in the car in two minutes, then I'm leaving without you. Yes, I do mean it . . .'

Upstairs, an explosion of activity. Automated arms lifting off black vinyl, human arms pulling on sweaters and grabbing bags. Thump, thump, thump down the stairs. Anna picked up her violin and brown music case in one hand, then lifted her beige duffle coat from the pegs by the front door with the other. Sam wrenched hers down with both fists. It's amazing that those hooks stay up, thought Helen. As she always did. Then, in a volley of see-you-laters, they were gone. A gust of cold air leaped mischievously into the warm hall and wrapped itself round Helen's stockinged ankles.

16

From the kitchen window, she watched her daughters hurl themselves bottoms first into the back seat of the car. Sam's mouth was still moving, but soundless now behind the glass. Tom reversed the car down the drive into the road, paused, changed into first gear, then pulled away. He honestly doesn't think that it will change anything, she thought as she wandered back into the kitchen. The ashtray was still smouldering. Helen shivered. It wasn't the smoke that was making her feel sick.

'Remember, remember the twelfth of November,' she muttered. The house was not listening. She turned on the little transistor radio on the sill for company, plunging her hands into the lukewarm washing-up water. A burbling *a cappella* version of 'The Way We Were' assaulted her ears.

'God bless Radio 2,' Helen snorted, saluting the irony of the title. 'If only . . .'

CHAPTER 2

'*Tempora mutantur,*' read Sam, '*nos et mutamur in illis*. Which means,' she shouted from the sitting-room, 'the times are changing and we with them.'

Helen was in the kitchen peeling the potatoes. She gave no sign of having heard.

Sam had discovered, sort of by accident, that the *Pears Junior Encylopaedia* was not as boring as she'd assumed. Pinching it back from Anna's bedroom, where it had been ever since Wednesday afternoon, she had been seduced by the joys of the *Dictionary of Foreign Phrases and Classical Quotations*. Not yet intimidated by the balancing act between erudition and pretension, Sam had driven everyone mad for days. She practised upstairs in her room in front of the mirror, then sprinkled every conversation with as many as possible – more often than not, inappropriate – *bons mots*.

It was Sunday morning, the day after the birthday party. Sam was lying on the sofa, knees hooked over the purple end, banging first her right calf, then her left calf, against the side. Right. Left. Right. Left. Beside her on the floor lay an empty four-finger Kit-Kat wrapper. Sam felt a bit flat this morning. Thirteen years and four days old, she calculated. Today was a bit of an anti-climax. Mum was even quieter than usual, Dad had taken Anna to pick some music thing up from somebody or other and there was nothing on the television. Typical. Just the end of *Morning Worship* from Birkenhead, wherever that was, or *Bellamy on Botany*. God. She let the encyclopaedia fall forward. It rested on her chest like a chunky tent. Twizzling the chain of her locket, Sam squirmed to make her jeans a little less tight around her knickers. Right leg, thump. Left leg, thump.

She always felt like this straight after birthdays. And Christmas. Easter too, when she was younger. Anticipation, the build-up, then

18

it was all over for another year and everything felt samey. Like a shrivelled balloon, sighed Sam, looking over at the shiny carriage clock on the mantelpiece. The smells of lunch started to filter through from the kitchen.

She let her mind stray. After Wednesday, the week had passed quickly, funnily enough. The usual round of school, homework, crisps, arguments about who wanted to watch what on the television, playing records – although now, of course, she could do it in her room like a real teenager. Sam had chosen toad-in-the-hole for her special birthday dinner, Anna spaghetti bolognese. In the end, everybody had ended up having a bit of both. The only out-of-the-ordinary thing was that Helen had gone up to London with a friend first thing on Thursday. It had been planned for months, shopping, then Frank Sinatra. But from the second they'd dropped Helen off at the station on their way to school, Anna had been upset.

Less interested in television than Sam as a rule, Anna was none the less addicted to the news. It fuelled the fatalism in her, her essentially pessimistic view of the world. Every evening she absorbed the chaos like a junkie. Experiencing each bomb scare, every hijacking and plane crash through the filter of the reporters, Anna reacted as if each incident concerned them personally. She was word-perfect on all the year's tragedies and saw London, in particular, as a city of death. And London was where her mother was going. Anna was convinced that Helen would be taken hostage over lunch or be burnt to death on the Underground or that the London Palladium would be the bombers' next target.

Tom's joke – after they'd dropped Helen off – about it being a good thing if someone blew up Frank Sinatra, was met with a withering silence. Although sympathetic to a morbid imagination in theory, in practice Sam actually thought Anna was posing. Nothing exciting happens in real life, she'd said. Not to ordinary people. It's always the same old thing, day in, day out. Anna had ignored her, staring stonily out of the car window for the rest of the journey to school.

Feeling rather daft not to have seen it coming, Tom had allowed Anna to stay up on Thursday to watch the nine o'clock broadcast as well as the six. Helen was not due back until after midnight and he hadn't been able to think of how else to reassure his anxious daughter. The train could still crash, was Anna's only comment as she went up to bed half an hour or so later. Tom hugged her hard, full of useless love. Sam squeezed his arm encouragingly, understanding that he felt he'd failed Anna.

Friends again, Sam snuggled into her sister's bed in the dark. She threaded a protective arm uncomfortably under Anna's neck, for once the comforter, then immmediately dozed off. Anna lay flat and still with her eyes wide open, feeling her sister's numb arm sliding away as Sam turned on to her side. Dead weight. It was only when she heard familiar murmurings in the hall, the sound of the front door closing and the chain being slipped on, that Anna finally let go her demons and fell asleep too.

Mum had been funny since then, reflected Sam. In fact, she'd been funny all week, now she came to think of it. Sam continued to bounce her legs rhythmically against the side of the sofa. I was here this time yesterday, she thought. But yesterday I was only thirteen and three days old, with a brilliant birthday party to look forward to. Excitement, churned up with nerves about people not turning up, had made Saturday morning drag too. Sam had practised walking in her new platforms. She'd washed her hair – with shampoo *and* conditioner. And they'd laid out what they were going to wear before Anna had gone off to orchestra at nine o'clock. Nothing to do but wait. It was just a matter of surviving the next few hours until guests started arriving at four.

By half past five, it was freezing outside. The whole estate looked miserable, the pale brick and white slatted houses shrouded in drizzle. Inside Number 208, it was boiling hot. Every window dripped with condensation as the pack of twelve- and thirteen-year-old disco queens danced to the tunes of ace DJ Mr Tom Whittaker. Brilliant, Sam reflected. Not like a dad at all, Katrina had complimented. Flushed and sweaty, they'd gulped Coke while he changed the records. Jumping and swivelling, elbows flapping, legs apart, faster and faster and faster until someone lost their balance and the whole line collapsed into a giggling heap. Deeper and down. Even Anna had sung along with Rod Stewart, all hands clasped above heads as they swayed in an emotional circle. The music made them feel heady. And Katrina had bought 'Space Oddity' for Sam. They were the only two who knew all the words, even though it'd been at the top of the chart for a week. A re-release, or so Katrina said.

'I'm floating in a mos-t pec-ul-iar way,' she chanted as she lay on the sofa, spelling out the words like David Bowie. She loved the clipped, arrogant sound.

Sam flattened out the silver foil of the Kit-Kat between her fingers. Empty. She couldn't be bothered to go and get another one from the kitchen. Letting the wrapper float down to the floor, she sighed dramatically. It had been a brilliant, brilliant party. The best.

Bang. The front door slammed. Sam registered the bustle in the hall as Anna and Tom hung up their chilly coats, eased off their boots. She swung her legs off the sofa and sat up. The encyclopaedia slid from her chest to the floor, folding itself shut in the process.

Everyone else was already in the kitchen when Sam appeared. Helen, as usual, at the sink. Dad hovering.

'Everything fine?' she asked Tom.

'Yes, thanks,' he replied. 'Any coffee going?'

Helen nodded, shook her damp hands, then rolled down her sleeves. Unplugging the kettle, she prised off the silver lid and turned on the cold tap. Water sprayed up. Lid back on, flex in, switch pushed, Helen tapped her hand along the window-sill for her cigarettes. Tom threw over a box of matches from the top of the fridge as he took the milk out of the door. Muttering about lung cancer, Anna frowned at them as she went off to practise her violin before lunch.

'About an hour and a half,' Helen said to Sam, who was peering through the greased-up oven door. Sam drifted away, bored. A couple of seconds later, another set of thick-socked feet could be heard tramping slowly up the stairs. The listeners heard Anna's door open, a slither of an arpeggio, Anna's door shut, then Sam's door slam.

'Three, two, one,' counted Tom, 'and . . . here's Elton!'

Helen smiled as the music started, bang on cue. 'She'll be sick of him soon,' she replied.

Taking a sip of coffee, she pulled the ashtray towards her from the middle of the table. Then wearily closed her eyes.

'Tired?' Tom said softly. 'Why don't you go up and lie down for a bit? I'll tidy all this lot up.' He gestured towards the evidence of a Sunday roast in the making.

Helen pulled on her cigarette.

'I'm fine, Tom. Really.'

She rubbed her eyes, pressing her forefinger and thumb over the bridge of her nose, then blinked hard.

'Have you said anything to either of them, about us wanting to have a proper chat later?'

He shook his head.

'I thought it would be better to just do it,' he explained. 'Perhaps straight after lunch?'

Tom looked at his wife's grave, green eyes. Like cat's eyes.

'Don't worry,' he said, emphasising each word reassuringly. 'Everything will be fine.'

By ten past two, all the bowls had been cleared. Anna put what was left of the cream back in the fridge and pushed the salt and pepper into the cupboard. Sam had eaten too much. She was acutely aware of her bloated stomach. It felt revolting, like a big flabby monster with a life of its own. She undid the button of her jeans and eased the zip down, untucking her crimson jumper so that no one would see. Tom was making coffee, having managed to knock most of the dirty cutlery off the draining-board. Spoons, forks and knives had clattered into the sink. Helen sat at the table, an almost empty wine glass in front of her. Her apron hung over the back of her chair.

'Is it OK if I go round to Katrina's?' asked Sam, wriggling uncomfortably in her chair.

Tom answered. 'Maybe a little later,' he answered, silencing her protest by holding up a hand. 'We want to talk to you both first.'

'God, what've I done now?' moaned Sam, her face a picture of penitence and cheek. Another family joke. Everyone smiled.

'No, it's not you,' Tom responded. 'For once.'

'I promised Katrina . . .'

Tom surprised Sam by getting up and walking across the kitchen to where his briefcase was sagging against the door jamb. Crouching down, he fished around until he found what he was looking for. Anna tucked her hair behind her ear. Three faces watched him as he came back to the table holding two white A4 envelopes.

By now, the twins had been caught by their parents' sense of purpose and were intrigued. Sam even stopped fidgeting.

Tom threaded his tall body back under the table.

'As you know,' he began, 'you two are adopted.'

The girls exploded, Sam's honking laugh drowning Anna out.

'Da–ad . . .' giggled Anna.

Sam pretended to faint.

'If only you'd told us sooner,' she shrieked, pressing the back of her hand to her forehead. 'The shock, the shock . . .'

'Yes. Thank you very much,' smiled Tom. 'If you'd just let me finish . . .'

Helen flicked ash into Sam's work of art. MUM. MUM. MUM. MUM. Now the time had come to get it over and done with, she actually felt quite resolute.

'What your father is trying to say,' she said firmly, 'is that this seemed the right time – now you're thirteen and old enough to understand – to tell you what we know about your natural father and . . .'

Helen faded out, unable to bring herself to say the word. She took another drag of her cigarette.

'And your natural mother.'

There, she'd said it. Mother.

Neither Sam nor Anna knew what to say.

'Lots of it you know already,' Tom continued. 'But we thought that you could have a look through these bits and pieces. *Quietly* . . .'

Both girls grinned as he looked pointedly at Sam.

'Then you can ask us about anything you don't understand.'

'If there is anything,' added Helen, as Tom slid one envelope across the table to each of his daughters.

Anna and Sam had always known they were adopted. It was what made them doubly special. They were twins. And they were adopted. When little, the explanation of how they had been *chosen* by Mum and Dad – rather than just turning up in the usual way – had been their favourite bedtime story. Once upon a time, so the fairytale went, there was an ugly old wicked witch who put a spell on Mummy so she couldn't grow a baby in her tummy. Then along came a beautiful good fairy. She felt sorry for Mummy and Daddy, so she promised she would take them to a magic cave where they could choose a baby of their own. When they got there . . . At this point, she was always interrupted. Anna wanted to know how they had been able to fly with the fairy. Magic, answered Mum. Sam, on the other hand – already more interested in fashion than science – wanted details of the fairy's wardrobe. Was her dress pink? Was her wand silver? Did she sparkle? Yes, yes and yes, replied Mum. Anyway, there were millions and trillions and zillions of babies in the magic cave. But tucked in a corner were the prettiest, most intelligent twins in the whole world. Tom and Helen asked if they could be greedy and choose two babies. And the good fairy, who knew that Mummy and Daddy would be the best parents in the world, said of course and that twins were special. So they took Anna and Sam home to their house to be their daughters and everybody lived happily ever after. The end.

When she was three, Sam had gone through a phase of approaching random women in the street and asking if she had grown in their tummy. Not the sort of question that ladies in Chichester were expecting. By the age of six, Sam had become more sophisticated, sidling up to pregnant women and enquiring if they were going to keep their babies or have them adopted. Tom had thought it hysterical. Helen claimed she was rarely able to finish the shopping because she was forever having to apologise and hurry away.

Every now and again, a new neighbour who didn't know the girls were adopted, would speculate as to whether Anna or Sam would grow as tall as their parents. Given that Helen was five foot eleven, and Tom several inches more, it seemed unlikely. Especially since the twins were two of the shortest girls in their class. But speculation about them turning overnight into giantesses had become another Whittaker family joke.

Another bonus about being adopted was that, like Paddington, they got two birthdays. They had one on the actual day they'd been born and one six weeks later, Thursday, 27 December, the day Helen and Tom had brought them home. '"Monday's child is fair of face",' Helen would quote. '"Thursday's child has far to go." You can choose which you want to be.'

But, for the most part, nobody thought about it at all. Mum and Dad were Mum and Dad. Anna and Sam were their twin daughters. Being adopted was as irrelevant to their day-to-day lives as the name of the hospital in Oxford where they'd been born. Which is why, thought Sam in passing, it is odd that they're making such a big deal of things now.

She glanced at Anna, sensing it had crossed her mind too.

'There's nothing to worry about, PB1,' Tom said. 'It's just facts. You don't even have to look at it if you don't want to.'

Sam was excited. She'd always been more bewitched by the idea of their natural parents than Anna who didn't seem interested at all. But to Sam, those two shadowy figures were quite divorced from her real life. From school and home and loving Mum and Dad and

Anna. She enjoyed weaving stories. And what more fertile subject could there be for her over-active romantic imagination?

Sam's fantasies were based almost exclusively on her blood-mother. In her favourite version, the wicked man – that was their father – seduced the innocent and very beautiful young girl. When she told him she was expecting a baby, he abandoned her to her fate. Even though her heart was broken, she nobly struggled on until she gave birth to perfect twin girls. Then she gave them up, so the babies could find the happiness she had been denied. A true tragic heroine. Sam intended this to be the plot of her first novel. That the fantasy was better suited to the 1860s than the 1960s did not concern her.

Although Sam rarely thought of her biological mother as a contemporary flesh-and-blood person, from time to time she did wonder what she looked like. She had spent many fruitless hours trying to persuade Anna to join in the game. Sam was quite pretty, but she desperately wanted to be beautiful. Like Anna was. By imagining their natural mother to be the most beautiful woman in the world, she was giving herself the possibility of a genetic leg-up.

She had gone through a phase of being convinced that she had seen their blood-mother without knowing it. Perhaps she was famous? On the television even? Or perhaps she was someone they passed in the street every day? That, too, would be in her novel.

Sam wanted to be popular, cared about it a great deal. When they'd started secondary school – Dad's school, as they'd always called it – Sam had found it hard at first to adjust to being a small fish in a very large and choppy pond. So she started to tell the girls in their form that she was adopted, as a way of standing out. Eight weeks into term, a spiteful girl – who was in the process of stealing Sam's new best friend – shouted that everyone hated Sam and her mother obviously hated her so much that she'd given her away. It had been the most shocking moment in Sam's eleven-year-old life. She would never forget how she'd felt then. The smell of the hot autumn classroom, the embarrassed silence of the other girls in their navy uniforms, the sensation that the blood was freezing in her veins.

Until that very second, Sam's belief that everyone was jealous of her and Anna had never been challenged. They were special, so obviously people were jealous. It had genuinely never occurred to her that others might see things differently. She felt humiliated, as if the world was laughing at her behind her back. It was Anna who helped Sam regain her self-confidence, encouraging her to worry less about other people's opinion. It's what you think, PB, that matters, she'd said. Only you.

Although very sorry for their crushed daughter, afterwards Helen and Tom teased that it was the quietest three days the Whittaker household had ever known.

Twenty past two.

'*Nil desperandum*,' said Sam, breathing in and pulling up the gaping zip of her jeans. 'We will go forth unto the hills and read and return armed with questions.'

Tom rolled his eyes at Sam's ornate sentence, watching as she scooped up her envelope, pulled at her sister, then set off towards the kitchen door. Anna followed. Helen glanced up at the ticking clock, its white face ringed in pine.

'That wasn't so bad?'

Helen smiled at him. Like a great big friendly dog sometimes, she thought. Blundering around, missing the point. She was twitchy about how her daughters would react to some of the information they'd just been given. Of course she was. But that was not the reason that she had woken early for the last few mornings, nervous and unable to sleep. A tight control of her head, she could manage. But her body was soaked in a pure, visceral fear, far stronger than common sense or logic.

Helen knew – legally, logically – it could not happen, but subconsciously she was waiting for the knock at the door as they came to take Sam and Anna away. In June 1963, standing in that courtroom, she had thought that the insecurity was all over. That their children were theirs, once and for all. All she had wanted was to be allowed to get on and live their lives like any other family.

Then the law had been changed. Just like that. Wednesday, 12 November 1975. All that life-long secrecy and confidentiality they had been promised thirteen years ago, stolen away from under their noses. That it also happened to be the girls' birthday was simply one of those painful coincidences. After all, every day is somebody's birthday. But the echo had made everything worse.

Helen looked over at her husband, fiddling around with more Sunday afternoon drinks. Her unhappiness upset him, her sombre moods beyond the comprehension of his sunny, optimistic nature. Not wanting to worry him more than she already had, she chose her words with care.

'I feel betrayed, Tom. As if they've moved the goal-posts.'

He nodded. Uncomprehending. She tried again.

'I know I'm being silly. But the whole business of Wednesday brought back all those feelings I used to have.'

What obsessed Helen was not the vision of her daughters finding their natural mother one day. It was the fear that they would love the woman who had given them life more than her. The tortured thought that novelty was more exciting than day-to-day familiarity. A mum versus a . . .

The girls spent a couple of seconds at the top of the stairs, unable to decide whether they should go straight into Anna's bedroom or whether they should open their envelopes privately, then rendezvous ten minutes later.

'Your room, I think,' decided Sam, bundling Anna through and kicking the flimsy door shut behind them. Sam knew there was no hope of her concentrating if she was on her own. She flung herself on to Anna's bed. She felt excited, almost as if it was their birthday all over again. Immediately realising that she'd be sick if she tried to read lying down, she propped her body up against the wall instead. Then, sticking her flared denimed legs out in front of her, Sam shook her envelope so that everything fell out on to the blue bedspread between her knees. There was less than she expected.

At first, Anna just watched her twin. Then, positioning her envelope slap bang in the middle of her dressing-table, she spun round on the stool and threaded first one leg, then the other, under the glass top. As she stared at her reflection in the mirror, she saw her fingers automatically reaching up to touch her birthmark. It looked very red against her winter skin.

Neither girl was aware of the Sunday sounds in the road outside, the occasional car, the shout of children out riding their bikes before it got too dark. Anna's bedside alarm clock insistently tapped out the seconds double-quick, like a foetal heartbeat.

Time passed.

27

CHAPTER 3

Not knowing how long their daughters might be, Tom and Helen felt at a loose end. Helen put her apron back on and started washing up, Tom tried to organise his marking into piles according to urgency. Nearly Late, Late and Desperate.

He was not an organised man. Nevertheless he loved devising complicated systems which he hoped would help him achieve his goal of every class getting their homework back, marked, the next time he took them. It was Tom's bad luck that Fridays and Mondays were his busiest days, eight full lessons with no free periods to catch up in. As a result he spent almost every Sunday night sitting at the kitchen table, red pen in hand. As his crooked pile of grainy yellow exercise books shrank, the heap of cigarette butts and matches grew.

Helen heard Anna's door open. That was quick, she murmured to herself.

'That was quick,' she repeated, louder than she'd intended, as first Sam, then Anna, appeared in the doorway. Both were holding their envelopes. Sam's looked scruffy already, Helen noted with amazement. Anna was pressing hers firmly against her chest with both hands, clean and white against the heavy chestnut wool of her jumper.

Tom immediately shuffled the half-formed piles of books back into his bag.

'OK, PBs 1 and 2,' he said, in his best bad imitation of John Wayne. 'Fire away.'

His daughters, each practised in her own form of crucifying look, stared at him in such a way as to make him feel foolish. No, worse than that, pathetic.

'Anyone want a cup of tea?' he asked lamely, accepting the rebuke. Sam honked at his hang-dog expression.

'I'll do it,' smiled Anna, going towards the counter and shaking the heavy kettle to see if there was enough water for four.

'Mum?'

'Coffee, please, sweetheart.'

'Dad?'

'Tea would be lovely.'

Sam, making herself useful for once, reached down the mugs and the teapot for Anna before sitting down at the table. Her fingers played absent-mindedly with her locket, whizzing it up and down on its chain. Everyone was aware that making yet more drinks was a delaying tactic. But no one was quite sure how to start.

Five minutes later the four Whittakers sat facing each other round the table, armed with hot and familiar landmarks. Tea, coffee, Mum's Silk Cut, Dad's Rothmans. Helen and Tom took deep breaths and started to speak in unison. They stopped, they laughed, tried to persuade the other one to go first. When the unrehearsed *pas de deux* was over, Helen took charge.

'Why don't you get the things out first?' she said. 'Then we can go through the bits and pieces one by one.'

Sam turned her envelope upside-down. A silver christening bracelet clattered on to the formica table-top. It looked huge next to the tiny pink plastic hospital bracelet: *Sam 12.11.62 5lbs 6oz.* The handwritten sheet whooshed on to the table, sending up a spray of ash. Sam put her hand inside to dig out her birth certificate, its thin edge caught in the folds of the envelope. She smoothed it flat.

In the top left-hand corner were the words *Certified Copy of an Entry in the Records of the General Register Office.* In the middle was a Crown crest, then *Given at the General Register Office, Titchfield, Fareham, Hants.* The first column was tiny, the number of her entry on the Register: *201061.* Anna was 201060. The next column was fat enough for *Twelfth November 1962 England* to have been written on two lines. In the third box was *Sam Mary Claire Whittaker,* then *Female* cramped in the fourth skinny gap. Seven lines of spidery writing filled the widest column: *Tom Charles Whittaker, 12 Harley Road, Abingdon, Oxon Teacher and Helen Patricia Whittaker his wife of the same address.*

'This is the only thing we didn't get from the Adoption Society,' said Tom, fingering Sam's birth certificate. 'The rest – the bracelets, the hospital tags, our official case notes – came from them.'

Anna was studying her certificate with great concentration. The lines, the symbols, the curves and twists of the letters. Adult systems in black and white to be absorbed by her young mind. The sixth box was headed *Date of adoption order and description of court by which made*, official language designed to deaden any spark of interest: *Thirtieth June 1963*.

'Why doesn't it say the twenty-seventh of December?'

Tom rubbed his beard, craning his head to see where Anna was pointing.

'Ah. Yes,' he said in his classroom voice. 'Now, we got you, as you know, when you were tiny. In December. But you didn't officially become Whittakers until the Social Services people and the court people had done all their checks and written all their reports. And for all sorts of reasons, legal and so forth, problems over signatures, it took longer than expected. Hence June.'

Tom was suddenly pierced by the memory of what it had meant to cradle his daughters in his arms for the first time. Anna first, then Sam. Ever since they'd been rung by the adoption people to say that they had suitable babies for them, Tom had worried that he would feel like an impostor after so long as a father-in-waiting. People met, fell in love, got married, had children. But that wasn't how it had been for him and Helen. For eight years they had tried to live the conventional life they had expected, courteously deflecting well-meaning questions about when they were going to start a family.

They concealed their grief from outsiders, from each other too, as expectation turned to hope, hope to disappointment and disappointment gave way to despair. All that blood, Helen once said, all that blood. But when Tom had stood in that cold house in Oxford in December 1962, and the woman from the Adoption Society had put Anna into his arms, it had felt like the most natural thing in the world. As if everything in his entire life had been leading to that one, precise moment.

Helen watched the emotions flitting across his face and guessed what he was thinking.

Tom felt her green gaze upon him. 'They were awful months, though, weren't they?' he murmured.

Sam watched them. With the arrogance that is the preserve of youth, she never thought of her parents having hidden lives, secret landscapes of passion and doubt. To her, being grown-up seemed to be mainly a matter of practicalities. Sorting freshly washed socks into pairs, rushing from arrangement to arrangement, worrying about food and shopping and running out of loo rolls, nagging. No room for reflection or intimacy. She was thrown off balance, embarrassed almost, by this sudden glimpse of emotion she'd never imagined.

'Sorry,' said Tom, suddenly realising that their daughters were staring at them. 'Off in a world of my own. The point is that it was one of the worst winters on record. It started snowing on Boxing Day, which was the day before we were due to go to pick you up, and didn't really stop again until March, April. Something like that.'

Helen picked up the box of matches.

'All you could think about on the way,' continued Tom, looking at her, 'was that we'd get snowed in and the social workers would think we weren't coming and would strike us off their list.'

She shook her head at the memory, smiling.

'On the way back, I was convinced that we'd get trapped in our car and all be found frozen to death in the morning.'

She paused as she lit her cigarette. Sam's eyes flared wide at this shy confession from her quiet, down-to-earth mother.

'It's all I thought about,' Helen added, 'all the time. I kept prodding you to check you were still breathing. Mind you, your father was just as bad . . .'

All four of them were aware that they had skippered the conversation into a safe backwater. The girls had heard the story of their first winter many times before. It was an unthreatening reminiscence of their common history, the family they had been since December 1962. By common consent, it was usurping the rawer business of talking about those lost first six weeks of Sam and Anna's lives. The delivery room, the post-natal ward, the foster-home.

Attempting to steer things back on course, Tom picked up Sam's handwritten sheet.

'This is all the Adoption Society jotted down for us about your natural mother and father,' he said. 'It's not much. We always assumed that the christening bracelets were family heirlooms, as it were. From her side of the family perhaps?'

The official version was brief and Helen knew it off by heart. So far as the Society was aware, neither biological parent had a family history of heart disease, diabetes or asthma. The father was twenty-five, a graduate of the University now working in Oxford. He was married to the mother, who had attended music college in London but had not completed her studies. She was twenty-one and had certain health problems. The decision to offer the children for adoption had been made before the birth and appeared to have been entered into willingly by both parties.

A rather indiscreet woman at the Society had fleshed it out a little, off the record of course. Rumour, slightly nasty hearsay. Helen had tried – and failed – to put it out of her mind. It haunted her right up until the adoption order was stamped, sealed and signed in June. She'd felt as if she was locked into a grotesque duet with this woman she had never met, experiencing loathing and guilt and overwhelming gratitude in shifting measure. In the end, it was one of the main reasons she and Tom had decided not to change the names that the girls had been given at birth. By keeping them as Sam and Anna, Helen felt like less of a thief, as if she had paid her debt to the woman who had borne her children. Their real mother, as Helen thought of her in her blacker times.

They had contented themselves with choosing middle names. On their honeymoon – twenty-one years ago now – they'd planned four children, two of each. Lying in the seaside hotel bedroom, they tried out the sounds of their favourite names, flirting and happy. Claire and Rosalind both sounded good with Whittaker, so that's our daughters sorted out. What about Simon and Andrew for boys?

But as the years went by and there was no pregnancy, the game fell out of favour. It was not until the winter of 1962 that Tom and Helen remembered their initial excitement and dusted the names down. So plain Sam became Sam Mary Claire Whittaker, Mary after Tom's mother. Anna became Anna Louise Rosalind Whittaker, Louise in memory of Helen's mum. Both girls were proud of having three names and covered their books with initials. Sam signed herself S. M. C. Whittaker with a great flourish. Anna neatly printed A. L. R. W.

'We thought there'd be more than this,' said Anna.

'The idea in those days was that everything was kept secret,' Tom explained. 'We weren't given any details that could have helped us guess who your natural parents were – that includes your original birth certificate, with their name and address and occupation – any more than they would have been given information about us. The hospital must—'

'What I don't understand,' interrupted Sam, 'is why she didn't want to keep us.'

This was a question that Helen had asked herself for nearly thirteen years. In those days, so-called respectable society was unyielding, quick to judge. No legal abortion then. For a young woman who was unlucky enough to fall pregnant without a husband on the horizon, there was little choice. Helen had read all about it. The girls disappeared into a mother and baby home for nine months, their babies were taken from them by the Church or the Social Services to be given to a couple considered decent enough to give them a decent life. Circumstance, not love, was all. Occasionally, one or two of the girls rebelled and kept their sons and daughters. But the majority understood that their reward for not stigmatising their child with the burden of illegitimacy was the promise that their slate would be wiped clean. Most believed that it would.

This was the blueprint to which Sam and Anna's natural parents had not conformed. The unorthodoxy of the situation was one of the catalysts for Helen's anxiety. In the beginning, she and Tom had speculated endlessly. Why would two adults, married to one another, decide that they didn't want to be parents to their babies? It was like a thorn in Helen's side. She had been unable to imagine how any woman could give up her babies. To carry them for nine months, to endure the pain of labour, the exhilaration of birth, just to hand them over to . . . to whom? And forever. To never see them again.

Tom spun convincing stories to back up his theory that Anna and Sam were the innocent result of an extra-marital affair. Helen thought it more probable that the husband had not been prepared to share his wife, so had forced a choice. Him or the twins. She was more circumspect, keeping her thoughts to herself. It was less of a game to her than to her husband, randomly curious about everything.

As the sixties became the seventies, Tom gradually stopped talking about it. It still crossed Helen's mind every now and again, but usually only on the twins' birthdays in November and December or the anniversary of the adoption order. Significant dates, as Sam would've put it.

Although Anna was a worrier, like her, Helen knew her elder daughter was capable of accepting life's subtle uncertainties.

She had always felt confident that Anna would be capable of understanding that their adoption was the result of adult pressures and adult mistakes. That it had nothing to do, as such, with her and Sam, the people they were. But Sam? For all her outward sound and fury, Sam had a rather fundamentalist approach to life. Everything was black and white, with Sam in the centre of things. So Helen had always worried that Sam would feel personally rejected when she found out the facts of the matter. The issue was, whether or not Sam would be able to assimilate the information without experiencing too much damage to her self-image.

Helen sighed and looked down, realising she was drumming the kitchen table with her nails.

'Does it upset you, sweetheart, that they were married?'

Sam shook her head, unconvincingly.

'It's just not what I'd imagined,' she said miserably, 'that's all.'

The kitchen fell quiet. The November afternoon had robbed the rest of the house of its light. Outside, cold shards of drizzle danced orange around the bulbs of the streetlamps.

'Why don't we carry on this conversation another time?' said Tom, taking in his family's drained faces. Helen looked tired, Anna was too quiet and Sam was clearly losing concentration, fiddling with the locket on her chain again.

'The most important last point to make,' he added gently, 'is that we love you both very much. And when you're older, if either of you feels you would like to trace your natural parents, then we want you to know that we will give you all the help and support we can.'

He leaned out and placed one of his hands on Sam's shoulder, the other on Anna's.

'Once you're eighteen you'll be able to get hold of copies of your original birth certificates. That's the law – as of four days ago. Anything is possible.'

Helen marvelled at how easily Tom gave this information. Anything is possible, she repeated in her mind. She looked at her daughters. They haven't even registered the words, she thought wryly. Not even the date. Normally, Sam would have been the first to read something into a coincidence like that. She could see that Tom was weighing up whether or not to say more. Discreetly, she shook her head.

'The worst thing,' she added quietly, 'would be if you felt you had to keep things secret from us. Or that you couldn't come to us with any questions. You mustn't worry that we'd feel hurt. We won't.'

Liar, liar, the voice in her head taunted.

Tick. Tick. Five past four.

Helen suddenly slapped her hands firmly on the table and stood up. Sam, Anna and Tom were all taken by surprise. Jolted out of their private thoughts.

'Enough of all this,' she said. 'Time for homework. Before tea. Come on. Chop, chop. Otherwise there'll be no *Poldark* . . .'

The room seemed to spring into life, rustling and humming with the sound of joints stretching and paper being gathered up.

'What time's tea?' asked Sam.

Eleven o'clock on Sunday, 16 November 1975. A pea-souper tobacco fog had settled over the kitchen. As always, by this time in the evening. Visibility was poor as Tom continued to smoke and wade through his mountain of marking. He scratched his chin through his beard with the chewed end of his biro.

Anna and Sam had gone to bed over an hour ago. The house was still. Helen sat alone in the sitting-room, unable to summon the energy to drag herself upstairs too. For want of something better to do, she picked up the copy of the *TV Times* and opened it. Flicking through, she noticed that London Weekend Television had a late-night programme about adoption. Unbelievable. No escaping the subject. She glanced up at the clock on the mantelpiece. Not on for an hour. She slid her eyes down the page to see if it was being shown on Southern as well. It wasn't. That's the end of that then, she said to herself, relieved to have been let off the hook. She tossed the magazine back on to the coffee table.

It really is time for bed, she thought, pulling herself to her feet. She ambled over to the door, gave one last look around the room, then killed the lights. The colours flooded away, leaving only the black outlines of the sofa and chairs and books.

1979

CHAPTER 4

Shit, thought Sam, I'm going to be sick. She blundered through the sea of flashing red, yellow and green lights, towards the fire exit. Made it.

Sam clutched at the damp wooden rail around the crowded platform at the top of the stairs that led up the side of the dark village hall from the car park. She leaned her dizzy head into the sub-zero January air, willing it to make her clean. A couple of boys and a girl turned to go back inside, the girl flicking her burning cigarette butt over the edge as she went. Sam saw it flare orange on the gravel below, then slowly fade away.

Tonight she'd had her first joint, a landmark of sorts. Illicit between her fingers. The thin, needle-sharp white paper, tiny cardboard roach. Sam had felt sophisticated. Bright girls like her were not expected to experiment, so she felt wild and rebellious. As if she was asserting her individuality in some indefinable way. Anna would be outraged. But when she swallowed the smoke it felt as if someone had smashed her in the face. She was convinced she was going to pass out as she doubled over, coughing and embarrassed as the burn hit the back of her throat. Now her mouth felt filthy, her teeth as if they'd been scorched. And she could still taste the sweet sherry, proudly smuggled in under their coats, on her puffy tongue. Please God, she muttered into the night, don't let me throw up. The insistent beat of 'Picture This' pounded through her stomach.

Sam couldn't face going back in. For a couple of hours, she'd had a good time, dancing and dancing, feeding off the crush. Julia had promised sixth form boys in general, Phil in particular, so Sam'd spent even longer than usual getting ready. Rejecting jumper after shirt after skirt, she'd ended up back in the Cadbury-coloured baggy man's polo neck she'd tried on first. Stripy pyjama bottoms she'd got at a jumble sale, camel-coloured desert boots, hair loose, the perfect designer look for a winter party. A smear of cherry lip-gloss, a slash of eye-liner. She had felt brilliant. Six feet tall. As the music throbbed through eight o'clock, nine o'clock, half past, every now and again she'd let her eyes stray ostentatiously to the door. She wanted her friends to notice she was looking out for someone.

By ten, Sam'd had to bow to the intimidating heat and take her jumper off. Things had started to go downhill. Although fascinated by her appearance, Sam was rather self-conscious about her weight. The topic of pounds and ounces was the great leveller at school, an initiation into the cliquey society of girls where the talk was of diets and hipbones and who could squeeze into a size 10. Sam was pretty and plumpish and hated it. Camouflaging her curves with sloppy tops and Indian print wrap-round skirts, she hungered to be as slim as Anna, now two inches taller and three-quarters of a stone lighter. Like so many of her friends, Sam half-envied and half-admired the girl in the fourth year with anorexia. Although not enough to stop her eating crisps, Minstrels and Toast Toppers.

The relief at air tingling on her sweaty skin had been accompanied by the unpleasant suck of confidence draining away. Draping the jumper over her shoulders, Sam untucked her whitish T-shirt, now damp and crumpled around the waist. For the next fifteen minutes she'd twitched, flapping the T-shirt around her, pulling obsessively at it, panicking that the thin material would touch her somewhere embarrassing. Anywhere like her thighs or her tummy or bra. By twenty past ten, she'd accepted that she'd rather be hidden and broiling than cool and dancing. Back on had gone the scratchy brown wool, charging her frizzy hair with static electricity.

She was glad of the warmth now at least, as she leaned against the freezing outside rail feeling a mess. Ugly and lumpy and disappointed. Only three-quarters of an hour to go and no sign of Phil. No sign of anyone in fact. All that build-up for a completely crap evening, she thought, already aware that it was another one of those nights that was only worth it to boast about afterwards. Retrospect, coloured by a few judicious untruths, would make it worth remembering . . .

Inside, everyone was camping it up to 'YMCA'.

Julia's father dropped her off. Sam let herself into the quiet house, colourless in the blue moonlight. She carefully pressed the front door shut. Now the chain. Porch light off.

The kitchen hummed with the sounds of night. The fridge buzzed and the hands of the clock clipped their way through the early hours. The cold tap, still not fixed, dripped and dripped and dripped, water bouncing with a metallic twang into the empty sink.

Sam clattered around making herself a drink, dropping a tea-bag into her favourite mug, heaping in sugar, then drowning it in milk. The only recipe. As she leaned against the counter waiting for the kettle to boil, she absent-mindedly ate digestive biscuits.

For a couple of months, Sam had felt as if she was on the verge of something. Something just around the corner. It was as if there was a voice at her shoulder saying 'On Your Marks, Get Set', but never quite getting to 'Go'.

In November she'd thought it was the build-up to their birthday. Then she'd put it down to Christmas and an entire holiday wrecked because of having to revise for the exams in January. But the exams had been and gone and there were five clear months before O-levels started for real. Yet Sam still felt on edge. It wasn't all the usual things that teenagers were supposed to feel. She loved her parents. She loved her life. She wasn't miserable or at odds with the world or suffocated and over-protected. But something was coming. Something big.

The kettle boiled and switched itself off.

'Hi-yah.'

Sam jumped a mile, splashing water everywhere.

'Fucking hell,' she said to Anna, who was standing in the kitchen doorway in her nightie. 'You scared the shit out of me.'

'Sorry. I heard the door.'

'Want one?' Sam asked, gesturing at her mug.

'Tea, please,' Anna replied, pulling out a chair and sitting down at the table. 'Good time?'

'Brilliant,' she replied automatically, then stopped. This was Anna. She didn't have to lie.

'No, actually, not really.'

'No Phil?'

'No Phil,' confirmed Sam. She brought the two mugs over to the table, dangling the biscuit packet between two pinched fingers. Unloading her hands, she brandished the red wrapping at Anna, who shook her head.

'I did try some grass though . . .'

She left the words dangling in the air, watching Anna's expression.

'Sam!' Anna exploded. 'Why?'

'Why not?'

The twins sat in silence for a couple of seconds, Sam smug, Anna shocked. And cross. She didn't like being forced into the role of the judgemental parent, not at all. The fridge rattled in the corner.

'So,' Anna said finally. 'Why no Phil?'

Sam shrugged, genuinely not bothered. It was the idea of Phil – rather than the reality – that had attracted her. The possibility of Phil had given the party a focus. Now the party was over, he was no longer needed.

At sixteen, Anna and Sam had no friends in common, even though they were in the same form at school and did most of the same subjects. They'd constructed their social lives along wholly different lines and spent their time and pocket money in ways incomprehensible to one another. Anna cared about her violin and her exams, in that order. Boys and discos and trendiness seemed as pointless to her now as they ever had. She knew she was considered a bit of a boffin, but she saw no point in pretending. She disapproved of Sam smoking or drinking or doing anything stupid like that. And she was irritated by her swearing as often as possible and showing off. It seemed too much for the benefit of an audience, rather than herself. Unnatural. But because she loved her sister, she treated seriously Sam's intense attraction to these abrasive teenager things.

As for Sam, the post-mortem afterwards was integral to her enjoyment. Anna was an appreciative listener and a willing sleeping partner in her exploits. And because she wasn't in Sam's circle, there was no edge like there was with, say, Julia. Chalking up her seamy underlife experiences, however insignificant, with Anna made them more special. Seamier. Sam felt glamorous, more than just another schoolgirl living a respectable middle-class life in a respectable middle-class town. That Anna might not actually be impressed did not cross her cocky mind.

'Why are you awake anyway?' Sam asked, taking her seventh biscuit. 'I thought you were knackered.'

'I was thinking about my results, so then I couldn't sleep.'

'God, Anna,' snapped Sam affectionately. 'You're the last person in the entire world who's got anything to worry about. What about me? I bet I've failed half of them.'

Another front, thought Anna. Even though Sam was not preoccupied with her grades, Anna knew she'd be mortified if she'd done too badly. She'd heard Sam boasting that she'd done no work over Christmas, a sort of competitive laziness with the repulsive Julia and cronies. In Sam's case this macho bravado was false. She'd worked very hard during the three-week holiday. Most evenings she'd disappeared upstairs to revise – albeit with the very vocal support of Elvis Costello – reappearing several hours later muttering about what a shame it was that revision wasn't set to music. Lyrics, after all, were so easy to learn off by heart without even thinking about. *This Year's Model*, for example . . . This, added to the expression of agonised martyrdom Sam wore for the entire Christmas break, had amused Helen, Tom and Anna no end. Their teasing had made Sam scowl.

'You'll be fine,' Anna smiled. 'You always do better than you think you will. You're that sort of bear . . .'

Lying in bed later, Sam wondered what it would be like if there was someone next to her. She stretched, long and hard, breathing in to make her stomach as flat as possible. A little self-conscious, guilty even, she slid her hands under her nightshirt and put a hand firmly on each of her breasts. She lay there in the dark, completely still, trying to imagine what it would feel like if they were not her hands. Would she feel sexy, like people said? She couldn't believe it. Her breasts felt nice and soft, but somehow childish. When she squeezed, they felt squidgy. Like warm playdough.

Sam wriggled slightly, shuffling herself into a more comfortable position. Orange light from the streetlamps in the road outside shone through the curtains. She tried to imagine herself into the head of a boy, fantasising herself balanced on the narrow bed. Sam's heart started to beat faster. She licked the tips of her fingers, then methodically circled each nipple in turn, slow, lazy, warming movements as she encouraged her mind to do the work.

What would it be like . . . she breathed . . . to do this . . . to someone . . . else. Her body felt as if it was getting bigger and bigger, as if every nerve tip was standing on end. She was hot now, dizzy, like at the beginning of feeling drunk. Instinctively she let one hand slide down, over her ribs, over her pale stomach, down to the hardness of her pubic bone. Then, as if on tiptoe, her inquisitive fingers snuggled themselves further down into the prickly hair until they gently nestled into her vagina. Sam lay stock-still. It felt warm and wet and familiar, as if she had slipped her fingers into her mouth. Not wanting to break the spell, she slowly pulled down her right hand to join them. Easing her forefinger on to her clitoris, she slowly and carefully began to move her sensitive flesh backwards and forwards. She became entranced with the rhythm, with the sound of her blood pumping red inside her head. It was as if she was walking, faster and faster and faster, but now it was painful to walk and she could not stop herself from running, faster and faster and faster. Now she was spinning, high in the air, faster and faster and faster, faster, faster until she was soaring up and up and up over the edge, weightless up and up . . .

Sam opened her eyes. Blinked. She felt as if she'd been on a fairground ride that was gradually, gradually slowing down. Her arms and legs felt unusually heavy, tender all over, as if the slightest touch would be too much. She felt cold. Perhaps she'd fainted? She couldn't believe that Anna or her parents hadn't heard anything and come to see what was going on. But the house was silent, her bedroom looked exactly the same as always. As if nothing had happened. Only Paddington Bear stood watching in his blue duffle coat and cock-eyed red hat. He looked as if he was winking.

Sam rolled on to her side. Her clammy fingers smelled of green apples, slightly metallic. She wiped them on the edge of her bedspread. Then, curling her knees up to her chest, she tugged her nightshirt down over her bare legs and tumbled asleep. Like a baby.

Sam was self-conscious at breakfast the next morning. Convinced everyone could tell, she kept peering at her nails. Looking for stains. She felt as though there must be a flashing sign above her head, betraying her nocturnal solitaire.

But Sunday passed as every term-time Sunday did, the same as always. Breakfast, errands, coffee, roast, more coffee, television, tea, homework, the screech of Anna's violin. Sam had originally decided that what had happened was too private to share. Even with Anna. But discretion was proving too much of a let down, so by the time Sam was lying in the bath at half past six, listening to a crap Top 40, she had changed her mind.

Pulling the plug out with her toes, she resolved to engineer a girls' heart-to-heart after supper.

'Can I come in?'

'Sure,' Sam replied, as Anna opened the door. Sam was surprised. It was usually her bugging Anna, rather than vice versa.

'You OK?'

'Sort of.'

'What's that supposed to mean?' pressed Sam, as she continued threading her beads on to a leather thong. 'You're not still worrying about your results . . .'

It was more a command than a question.

'No. Well, yes. But that's not it.'

Sam's necklace was not shaping up quite as she'd imagined. She continued fiddling, waiting for Anna to elaborate.

'I don't know why,' Anna said hesitantly, 'but for some reason I've been thinking a bit about our mother. Our natural mother, I mean.'

Sam was stunned. She could not remember Anna ever initiating a conversation about their biological background, not ever. For a few weeks after their parents had given them the copies of their birth certificates and notes, Anna had talked a little, on and off, about the adoption. Or rather, she'd been prepared to listen to Sam talk. The only thing that had really sparked Anna's interest had been the fact that the law had been changed. She'd quizzed Tom about it for a while. But it was a pragmatic rather than an emotional interest, so once she knew the facts, the questions had stopped.

Sam, on the other hand, had been profoundly shaken. Betrayed by fact and by her own sense of theatre. All the years she'd imagined their blood-mother as a delicate angel, broken by the cruelty of a world in which a marriage licence was more important than anything. Once Sam knew that documents and notes did not bear her imagination out, she'd been devastated. All wrong. The angel became a witch, a selfish and unnatural woman who'd abandoned her children. Sam felt tainted by association. The more Mum had tried to convince her that it wasn't her – Sam – who had been rejected, the more angry she'd become. And however much Dad warned her against jumping to conclusions, Sam's unforgiving thirteen-year-old mind judged harshly.

Over the next couple of years or so, Sam's views had mellowed only slightly as a plan of attack took hold. Then six months ago, when subjecting Anna yet again to a long and rambling complaint, Sam had declared her intention to track down her natural mother when she turned eighteen. Sam would give her the chance to account for herself. To right the wrong. Replacing one set of fantasies with another, Sam now imagined a woman bowed down by guilt. In her new mind's eye, their mother was suffering the constant grief of having abandoned her daughters. She was desperate to atone. The pain was particularly bad on their birthday and other family occasions, such as Christmas or Mother's Day.

This statement of intent had been the cause of the twins' first adult row, painful and raw and fundamental. Anna could not believe that Sam would be so self-absorbed, so arrogant, as to make – *unilaterally* – a decision that affected both of them so deeply. *Your* natural mother, she'd shouted. What about me? It has to be a joint decision, you can't just do what *you* want. In her bones Sam knew that Anna was right, so had retaliated all the more vehemently. Guilt made her spiteful, screeching that she'd do exactly what she wanted and there was nothing Anna could do to stop her.

The argument had shaken both of them to the core. This was uncharted territory. Sam felt bereaved, somehow, as if her life-support system had been severed. But neither girl knew how to cope with their feelings of loss, obscured, as they were, by a poisonous and self-righteous anger. They had remained trapped in their entrenched positions.

After nearly two weeks, Sam apologised. She no longer cared about who was right, who was wrong. All she wanted was for them to be friends again. Rendered nearly inarticulate by her tears, Sam had promised that she would do nothing without discussing it with Anna first. Not now, not ever. Not just discussing, Anna insisted, but *agreeing*. Sam had cried and cried. I promise that we'll either trace her together or not at all. I promise. The summer had given way to autumn, and autumn to winter. The subject had not been raised since.

But here was Anna. Now. In her bedroom. Wanting to talk. Sam put the beads and strip of leather down on her desk.

'What it is . . .' Anna tried again. 'What it is, is that I've been wondering about where she went to college.'

Sam looked blank.

'On the Adoption Society note it said that she went to music college,' reminded Anna. 'Remember?'

'Of course,' Sam replied vigorously, in an attempt to disguise the fact that she had forgotten.

'You know I've been thinking about auditioning for the Royal Academy? Either this September or after A-levels, like Mum and Dad think. Well, I found myself wondering if the Academy was where she went. Out of the blue.'

Anna looked at Sam, already half-regretting the impulse that had brought her across the landing to her sister's bedroom.

'It would be odd to go to the same place and not know it. That's all.'

Sam pulled her jumper away from her body, the pit of her stomach fluttering. Anticipation banged against her ribs.

'It would be odd,' she agreed, stressing each word ponderously. 'But there isn't any way of finding out. Is there?'

Sam let the sentence peter out, willing Anna to take the bait. Anna smiled, reading her sister's transparent thoughts without effort. The cogs in her brain were almost visible when she was plotting something. Aware of Anna staring, Sam blushed and started to pick at an imaginary thread on her skirt. In the end, she had the grace to laugh.

'Yes, well . . .' she laughed. 'But is it important for you – I mean *really* important – to know about the college?'

'I don't know. Maybe. It seems such a little thing, so trivial really. Too trivial to make it worth going through all the stuff you have to go through. I don't think I want to know anything else about her.'

Anna looked over at Sam's enthusiastic face.

'You might get sucked into looking for her, Sam, but fail. Have you thought about that?'

The answer was no. Anna knew it, Sam knew it. Not for one moment had Sam considered failure. The equation in Sam's mind was simple. Effort and dedication equal success. She knew they could get copies of their original birth certificates when they were eighteen. Dad had told them that ages ago, although not the hows, whys and wherefores. It had fleetingly occurred to her that their natural mother might not still live at the address on the certificate. But since Sam was not really interested in the process of searching, her imagination had always leap-frogged the middle bit and gone straight to the mother-daughter reunion.

Sam visualised herself standing at the door of a picturesque old cottage. As she raised her hand to knock, the door would open – as if by magic – to reveal a slim and beautiful woman, the spitting image of Sam in twenty-five years' time. They would talk for hours and hours, like sisters. Sam would forgive her, explain why Anna was not yet ready to meet her.

Sam had never been able to imagine her mother having a name, somehow. Nothing sounded quite right. Perhaps Sam – as opposed to Samantha – was a family tradition, passed on from one generation to the next? Perhaps their natural mother was called Sam too . . . ?

Despite her promise to Anna, Sam had always assumed that she could persuade Anna to change her mind about tracing when the time came. Or, at least, that Anna would not stand in her way. Sam felt the ball was in her court. She could choose to search for their mother, or she could choose not to.

'The thing is, PB,' Anna said firmly, 'I'm not saying that I *do* want to trace her. This is not a green light. It's more that I *might* want to one day.'

Sam jumped up and hugged her cautious twin.

'I understand, I understand. We can't do anything until we're eighteen anyway. We've got ages.'

Anna wriggled out of the cuddle.

'I mean it, Sam. I'm not going to let you bully me . . .'

'I promise I won't,' Sam joked, slashing two diagonals on her chest with her forefinger. 'Cross my heart and hope to die.'

Anna grimaced, kissed Sam's cheek, then opened the door. Sam waited for it to click shut, then punched her empty bedroom air in triumph, swallowing her whoops of delight. Victory. She sensed victory. No physical gesture was big enough to do justice to her excitement. Hurling her body on to her bed, ramming it against the wall in the process, Sam rolled up on to her shoulders. Supporting her back with her bent arms, she started to pedal an imaginary bicycle faster and faster above her head. Brilliant, she thought as her knees pumped up and down. Fucking brilliant!

*   *   *

Across the hall, Anna stood in the centre of her room. She felt all knotted up. Anxiety gave itself away in her shoulders, just as it did in Helen. Tense, angular bones. I'm not going to let Sam bully me, she thought. I'm not. She suspected her sister was already embroidering their conversation in her mind. Ambivalence would be rewritten as assent, she knew it. By the morning, their entire exchange would be unrecognisable.

Anna sighed. Sam was so unstoppable once she got an idea into her head, a genius at seeing only what she wanted to see. She'd ignore the nose on her face if it suited her to do so. Anna smiled. It was her own fault, really. She knew what Sam was like. It was stupid to have said anything before she'd worked out what she wanted for herself. Stupid. She wrapped her arms around her waist, realising she'd have to talk to Sam about it tomorrow. Make sure she was not intending to *do* anything.

Resolved not to brood about it now, Anna walked over to the music-stand in the corner. Its thin metal arms and legs dominated the room. She took her tall manuscript book from the overcrowded ledge. Its thick blank cream sheets felt comforting between her fingers, all those precise black staves waiting to be marked with bowing and semibreves and dynamics. She found a rubber, searched out her yellow orchestra pencil, stubby now after months of use, then carried everything over to her desk.

Smoothing the paper out, Anna tucked her hair back behind her ear and began to write. Her own private diary. A treble clef, one flat, six–eight time. Concentration melted everything else away. No more worry, no more headstrong sister, as notes started to fill the page.

Later that night, Anna dreamed she was standing on a concert platform in a flowing dress. Anna Whittaker, composer and soloist, vivid against the black and white of the ladies and gentlemen of the orchestra in their bare shoulders and pearls and bow-ties and penguin suits. Everything was ready. A world première. But as Anna lifted her violin to her chin, the silence behind her was shattered. Cymbals and triangles and drumsticks slapped against the floor, in slow motion. Unscored sound, everything falling.

When Anna looked round, there, behind the shiny rubble of the percussion section, was Sam. No more than three years old, in a ruffled party dress, clumsy and apologising. In her sleep, Anna smiled. The indulgent look of a mother for her naughty child.

CHAPTER 5

Rows of old wooden regulation desks, regimented in long aisles and scattered with exam papers, sweltered in the June heat. It was boiling in the gym, even though every single one of the high windows had been tipped open. A rippling lake of yellow school shirts. The sun was in their eyes in the afternoons, the beam hitting Sam at about half past two. Like a spotlight suddenly being turned on her.

For more than a month, various squadrons of fifth formers had reported to the gym corridor a.m. and p.m for their O-levels. Clutching pencil cases and each other, they whispered and hissed and flexed their intellectual muscles. Today, Thursday, was the last day. Being Whittaker, Anna and Sam were near the end of the very last row, with only Wood, Wylie and Zaptcek after them.

'You have five minutes left to finish the question you are working on. Five minutes.'

Sam watched the gold chain glinting at the nape of Anna's neck as she scribbled and scribbled. Sam had finished. Her exam paper was shut, ready for collection. Her pens were zipped away in their tartan case. Her watch was back covering the tell-tale white patch on her wrist, evidence of revision attempted in the garden.

She ran her hot fingers through her sticky peroxided crop, gelled into spikes. She'd heard Dad describing her on the phone as looking like a straw-coloured hedgehog. Smiling, she glanced up at the clock again. Twenty-five minutes past three. Nearly over.

Freedom, sang Sam in her head. Freedom. For all of July and for all of August, until everything started up again in September. Unless she'd really fucked up. She didn't think she had. Sam flapped her shirt away from her chest, trying to cool herself down, as she rounded up her wandering thoughts. *If* she hadn't really fucked up, then next year would mean A-levels and the sixth form and no uniform. She underscored the last two words in her mind. No more blue skirt, no more blue jumper, no more washed-out-banana shirt. They might have Dad as a form teacher. Shit. That'd be bad news for skiving off . . .

'Will you now please stop writing and put your pens down,' said Miss Wilson. 'Do not leave your seat until all papers have been collected. No talking until you are outside the examination room.'

A rumble took hold of the gym like a Chinese whisper, as examination papers were swished up from each desk and taken ceremoniously to the invigilator's desk at the front. Miss Wilson turned round to face them.

'You may go now. *Quietly*. Please make sure that you take all your belongings with you.'

The last sentence was drowned by the sound of chairs being grated back by the backs of sweaty legs. One or two chairs toppled over, smacking the wooden gym floor with a sharp clatter, as the sea of teenagers bobbed and jostled towards the doors. In the corridor outside, gabbled post-mortems were punctured by sudden shrieks and elaborate embraces. By the time the girls had bundled their way through the school to their lockers, the noise was building to a raucous crescendo. As if the carnival had arrived.

Anna and Sam had decided to mark the end of their exams with a meal, to touch base with each other before going off to celebrate in character: Sam at a party with friends, Anna with a book at home. Helen had reserved a table at Chez Gaston in the centre of town. Tom was acting as chauffeur. They'd all four first eaten at the restaurant in February 1973, for Mum and Dad's twentieth wedding anniversary. The girls had chosen it for family treats ever since, but they'd never gone alone before.

By nine-thirty, Sam and Anna had talked and drunk and eaten themselves to a contented standstill. Leaning back into her chair, Sam undid the safety pin masquerading as a button at the top of her skirt. For a few minutes, she even toyed with the idea of going straight back to her comfortable bedroom with Anna rather than hitting the crowd at some old barn in the back of beyond.

'Taxi,' said Tom, appearing at their table having settled the bill. 'Had a good time?'

Two satisfied daughters smiled up at him.

Sam was still in two minds about the party as they gathered up their things, said goodnight and walked to the car. But as Tom

pulled up outside The Three Crowns, where she was meeting Julia
– the ghastly Julia, as Anna always called her – the butterflies in
Sam's stomach started to flutter. Waving goodbye, she reassured
her father that, yes, she'd get a lift home and, no, she'd not make too
much noise when she came in. In the loo of the pub, she transformed
herself from smart grown-up to homespun cool. It was going to be
a great summer, she promised herself, putting the finishing touches
to her face. There. Perfect. She could just feel in her bones that it
was going to be a fucking brilliant summer.

By the time Sam got home the following morning, the estate was
bathed in a purple light. A sparkling dawn. Everything looked
scrubbed, the glistening green lawns, the pale bricks and white
boards of the houses, the red, yellow and beige family cars standing
in the drives. There was no one about. Sam strolled along the
pavement towards home, baggy blue dungarees, black T-shirt and
bare feet. Her sandals dangled from one finger, swinging gently
to and fro. She felt like the queen of a wide, wide world.

Rummaging for her key amongst the crumbs and grit and tampons
at the bottom of her bag, Sam carefully let herself into the sleeping
house. She dropped her shoes with a quiet thud by the front door.
Quarter past five. The kitchen was tidy, ready and waiting for the
day ahead.

Exhaustion crept up on her. Adrenalin stopped pumping and she
realised she was running on empty. Sam looked down at her feet.
Filthy. Can't be bothered to wash them now, she thought to herself,
as she padded slowly up the stairs. On impulse, she pushed open
Anna's door a fraction, as quietly as she could. Her sister was fast
asleep, lying neatly on her back in the quiet room. Sam smiled,
shutting the door carefully with both hands.

Her room smelled unslept in. It's a Friday and I don't have to
get up, was the last thing Sam remembered thinking as she crawled
under the duvet.

The next couple of weeks passed lazily, as June turned to July. Anna
got up in the morning as usual, followed the same routine as usual.
She read and practised her violin and thought about her orchestra
tour. Ten concerts and two inter-county competitions in two weeks.
With Sam's encouragement, she even bought a new white blouse
and long black skirt. The uniform of the professional musician.

Sam, on the other hand, hauled herself out of bed when she wanted, ate when she wanted, dressed how she wanted. And because she always missed family breakfast and because school didn't break up until the end of the month and because Helen now worked part-time four days a week, some days Sam did not see her parents at all until the evening. She sunbathed in the garden, listening to Tubeway Army and the Boomtown Rats on Radio 1, and dreamed about love. The summer of '79, she decided, would go down as the summer of sleeping, shopping, socialising and sex . . .

Sam'd had one or two rather repulsive, sub-sexual experiences during the last six months or so. Clumsy wet tongues and slimy gropings in the dark were part of the reason for going to parties in the first place. Something to talk about afterwards. But Andrew was different. They'd met at a party in May. The year above her at school, he was the spitting image of Gary Numan and he had his own car. What girl could ask for more? He always wore a cotton handkerchief, sometimes checked, sometimes spotty, stolen from under the noses of pensioners at Saturday afternoon jumble sales, tied back to front round his neck. Kissing him made Sam feel hot, a bit out of breath. She felt physically involved. They had, she admitted to Anna, already gone as far as a sort of mutual masturbation, semi-clothed. At parties, in the car. Back-seat love. Anna had opened her eyes wide. Don't get pregnant, was all she'd said.

Sam was actually sensible enough to realise that it would be pathetic to embark on the loss of her virginity – however much of a burden it was – just before the most important exams of her life. Her sense of occasion also insisted her first time should be special, her mind filled with romantic images culled from every romance she'd ever read. Cascades of white muslin in candlelight, yellow and red rose petals, crimson blood on lace. I want it to be unforgettable, she'd confided in Anna during one of their late-night heart-to-hearts. I want it to be making love, *not* having sex. Anna had rolled her eyes at the cliché and pretended to throw up.

Now the exams were over, Anna suspected that the last barrier to Andrew and sex had come down. She was properly worried that Sam would get carried away and do something stupid. Forget to use contraception or something. So as the entire Whittaker family congregated in the school car park at the end of July – waiting to wave off Anna and the orchestra – she whispered in Sam's ear to be careful. Sensible.

'You too, PB,' joked Sam, nodding her head towards the spotty boys of the brass section.

Anna grinned as she climbed into the coach, violin clasped to her chest. Tom was confirming the coming-home arrangements with the Head of Music. For the third time.

'August 9th. Eight-thirty. Here,' he shouted through the glass at Anna. She gave him a thumbs-up sign before settling herself in a window seat.

'See – you – in – two – weeks,' mouthed Sam.

'O–K,' Anna mimed back.

Sam and Helen and Tom stood waving on the shimmering tarmac with the other parents and friends. The antique coach coughed, then lumbered into life, exhaust belching. It crawled off across the car park at about ten miles an hour in a black trail of carbon monoxide.

'I'll lay a tenner that it doesn't make it round Sussex,' spluttered Tom, waving his hand melodramatically in front of his mouth. 'Let alone Hampshire . . .'

Sam linked arms with her parents, one on either side.

'Andrew's picking me up in fifteen minutes,' she announced bossily and started to frog-march them back to the car.

Anna rang most days to give a progress report, from Billingshurst, Crawley, Portsmouth, wherever. With Anna gone, Sam was spending more and more time with Andrew. She learned that he was a Taurus, born on a Monday like her. She memorised his favourite songs, could recite the bands he'd seen and where, she knew which were his most treasured memories. In return, Andrew listened to what Sam wanted to do when she left school, discovered that she was a Scorpio, the sort of girl who saw symbolic significance in almost everything. She told him about being adopted and how she planned to trace her natural mother when she was eighteen. If Anna agreed.

As the hot and sunny July gave way to a heavy and sweaty August, Sam and Andrew moved beyond simple trading of their life histories into more intimate waters. Not close to his parents or step-brother, Andrew was attracted by Sam's close-knit family. In particular, he was inquisitive about what it was like to be a twin, one of a pair. Is it like having a soulmate? he asked. Someone who knows what you're thinking before even you do?

Sam was torn. She wasn't sure if she was ready to cope with the idea of a third party being as important to her as Anna. The fact of men was inevitable. Both girls had always assumed they would grow up and get married, like everyone else. The natural course of things was that parents, sisters – even twin sisters – would be dethroned in time by someone special. But the timing was not right.

The second dilemma battering her sixteen-year-old head was altogether more subtle. Too often in the past Sam had squandered her emotions, offering little bits of herself to many people, giving away too much. And she always ended up feeling tawdry, a bit dirty. But despite her big mouth about everything else under the sun, she had never shared the intimacy of her relationship with Anna with anyone. Not ever. What they felt for one another had remained private. It would be like I was being unfaithful, she'd tried to explain to Andrew when they first started going out together. I'd feel disloyal, talking behind her back. He'd smiled, sympathetic but out of his depth.

But as Sam increasingly felt like a proper girlfriend, she started to want to demonstrate her commitment to Andrew. Proof of how much he meant to her. Bit by bit, she wore down her own resistance, an anecdote here and a memory there. Anna featured more and more in their conversations. And by the beginning of August, without Sam having decided as much, the two of them had become three.

With this last emotional barrier fell the remaining physical one. Andrew's mother, step-father and step-brother all worked, so his house had become their *de facto* base during the day. Like most parents, they worried about their younger son getting up to sexual mischief at night. Like most parents, they rarely gave the unsupervised nine to five hours a second thought.

One lunchtime, Sam and Andrew decided the time had come. Very seriously, they sneaked up to his bedroom. As if the house would tell on them. There were clothes and records everywhere. Apologetic, Andrew cleared a space on the bed. They perched themselves down on the edge, feet on the floor, legs touching, like they were on the sideways seat of a bus.

They started to kiss, both concentrating very hard. Sam's mouth felt dry. With one hand, she fumbled with the button on

Andrew's fly, then juddered down the zip. He yanked his jeans off, half-standing, then slid down his pants. His penis sprang out, like a crazy purple jack-in-the-box. Sam giggled, embarrassed and very self-conscious.

As Andrew groped in his bedside table for the condoms they'd bought together, Sam slithered off her skirt and knickers. She heard the dull rip of the Durex packet, registered the unpleasant smell of functional rubber. Usually enthusiastic and active, Sam lay awkwardly on the quilt, watching Andrew's shoulders moving as he unrolled, pulled and pushed the Durex.

In all, the whole business took no more than about ten minutes. Andrew did have an orgasm. Sam didn't. Didn't even come close. They both felt rather detached from the experience, as if they'd stepped out of their skins to perform a compulsory ritual. A sterile rite of passage best got out of the way with as little fuss as possible. Sam shuffled back to the edge of the bed, ruffling up the covers. Tucking one bare leg underneath her, she let the other dangle down. The top of her big toe just reached the carpet. Andrew held up the mucus-coloured condom. They both peered at the rubber bubble of semen with a clinical interest, tempered by relief. It all appeared to have gone according to plan.

By half past one, the pair of them were back in their usual positions at the formica breakfast bar, listening to the radio. They drank Coke to celebrate, sharing a cigarette and a plate of toast. In her mental diary, Sam was scribbling a note: Wednesday, 8 August, Had Sex. She underlined the last couple of words four times. Thank God Anna's back tomorrow, she thought. I've got so much to tell her.

Having dreamed of blood and babies, Sam was woken earlier than usual the next morning by the sound of torrential rain. She squinted at the digital watch blinking on her wrist: 8.15. Swinging her legs to the floor, she pulled on a long T-shirt and peered out of her bedroom window. The trees in the road were plunging and rearing like unbroken horses in the wind. The undersides of their leaves looked white, like back-combed hair, as if they were cowering from the violent rain. She let the curtain fall back, then padded downstairs.

Her father's expression as she appeared was one of pure surprise.

'Good God,' he joked, glancing up from his crossword. 'To what do we owe the pleasure?'

Sam pulled a face and ambled over to give her mother a kiss on the cheek.

'What's all this?' she asked, gesturing at the weather.

'Tropical storm, so the weathermen say. Gusts of up to eighty miles an hour in some places.'

Helen turned back to look out of the window, cigarette in hand. 'I expect it'll blow itself out.'

Sam nodded as she put the kettle on, then padded over to the table in her bare feet.

'Tea? Coffee?' offered Helen.

'Coffee, please,' answered Sam. 'Dad? Can you give me a lift into town?'

'If you're ready by quarter to,' Tom replied, scratching his beard with his pen as he struggled to get another clue without Anna's help. 'No Andrew?'

Sam shook her head. It would be the first day for over a week that they had not seen each other. Off visiting his Essex granny, or something like that. Today of all days, thought Sam. What shit timing.

Helen put a blue china mug in front of her on the table. Sam ladled in sugar and milk, then stirred so ferociously that coffee slopped out over the table.

'Sam!' said her mother reprovingly.

The rain did not stop, cascading black lines from the granite sky. By the time Sam had trudged back from the shops, wind smashing into her ears and nose and neck, she was soaking wet and cold and pissed off. No one she knew was in town, so she'd only managed to kill an hour and a half.

The house seemed very empty. No Andrew, no Anna, Mum at work, Dad off somewhere. Running herself a bath, Sam felt restless and bored and abandoned. She wandered from room to room in a towel, trailing talcum powder. She picked things up, put things down, ate chocolate. She even watched *Houseparty*. Twenty-five minutes of sneering at the simpering housewives and their handy household hints didn't cheer her up as much as she'd expected.

Helen found Sam asleep on the sofa when she came home at three o'clock, television still blaring. Turning it off, she went back into the kitchen to unpack the shopping and to wait for the silence to wake her daughter.

Wide-eyed at this extraordinary natural disaster on their doorstep, the BBC devoted the entire evening news to the tropical storm. Winded reporters, deep-throated voice-overs and ominous pictures of the carnage. Bushes had been torn from the earth, trees were lying dead across roads, their brown limbs ripped apart. Even more dramatic was footage of cars crushed like cardboard boxes and green–black walls of sea breaking against the coast. All ferry sailings had been cancelled. Cowes Week was under attack.

'I bet Anna's glued to this,' commented Sam, after a roll-call of deaths and devastation. 'It's the worst news in ages.'

'They'll already be on their way home,' Tom said. 'And I very much doubt if their coach has got a functioning radio!'

Sam laughed.

'Can I come with you to get her? I'll be so bored waiting.'

Tom glanced across at his wife. Anxious at the best of times when either of her daughters was out, Helen, he suspected, would worry about Anna and the weather until they were all safely tucked up in their beds.

'Actually, I think it'd be better if you stayed put, PB2. They're bound to be late, in any case. Then we'll have your mother upset about all three of us.'

Sam humphed but couldn't be bothered to argue.

Just before *Citizen Smith* finished, Tom pulled his long skinny body out of his chair, kissed Helen on the top of her head and announced that he was off. By the time the news was over, Sam was brain-dead, bloated by hours of junk food and television and indolence. For the third time, she decided to check that the phone was on the hook. Andrew had said he'd call when he got back. And he hadn't.

Just as Sam got into the hall, it rang. She grabbed the receiver, heart pounding. Helen heard the tone of her daughter's voice change, then the sound of the handset being clunked down with disappointment on the hall table.

'Some woman for you,' she said from the doorway.

'Who is it?'

Sam shrugged her shoulders in response. 'Didn't ask.'

As Sam got to the top of the stairs, she heard her mother

settling down to a tedious conversation about cakes, flowers and Sunday school.

It was not until eleven o'clock that the front door slammed. Sam knew she was being childish, but the later it had got, the more aggrieved she'd started to feel at Anna's non-appearance. She should have been home over two hours ago, Sam muttered to herself. I've been waiting up specially. In the end, Sam decided she would not go down to say hello but would wait for Anna to come up to her. Cutting off your nose to spite your face, Helen would have said.

This resolution lasted only five minutes. Sam couldn't bear to be ignored in her room any longer, left out when everyone else was downstairs. She flung herself off her bed, threw open her bedroom door and stomped aggressively down the stairs.

In the kitchen, Tom was standing with his arms around Helen. Statues. Sam looked at their fixed reflection in the window. Mum's place, as she always thought of it.

'What's going on?'

Tom jerked his head up at the sound of her voice.

'What's going on?' repeated Sam. Her voice reverberated in her head, loud and distorted. 'Where's Anna?'

A sob escaped from Helen's lips, buried against the blue of Tom's shoulder. He was still wearing his coat. Panic hit Sam in the chest, stealing her breath.

'Where's Anna? Mum?'

It was Tom who answered.

'Sam,' he said quietly. 'There's been an accident . . .'

Tom uttered the words as if they were in a foreign language. Meaningless, nothing words. Sam's head started to shake from side to side, denial crouching in her throat.

'There's been an accident,' he repeated. 'I'm . . . She's dead, Sam. Anna's dead.'

Sam heard the screaming. Pain tore the air, slicing through bones and blood and muscles and teeth. Someone was crying. Louder and louder. No – no – no – no. Like bullets, over and over and over again. Sam didn't realise that it was her mouth giving birth to the violence.

CHAPTER 6

Sam heard the thud of the newspaper landing on the mat, the tap of the letter-box as it clipped shut. The same metallic sound every Monday to Saturday. No different today.

It was six-thirty in the morning. Friday, 10 August. They had sat in the kitchen all night, listening to the wind die. Three white faces with bruised eyes. Midnight, two o'clock, four o'clock, five, when the streetlamps switched themselves off. They had not been aware of colour draining from the sky. Ebony to peacock blue to dirty alabaster, as night gave way to the dawn.

Grief and disbelief had hollowed them out. The aftermath of trauma lay about them. Stale mugs, a crushed cigarette packet, ash, matches. Sam felt sick and cold, shrunken by hours of crying. No tears left now. Nothing left. She could not stop shivering.

Tom ran his fingers through his hair, over his beard, then scraped back his chair and walked out of the room. Helen turned from the window at the movement, but said nothing. A few minutes later, mother and daughter registered the normal whoosh of the chain flushing, the slow tread coming back down. Tom hesitated at the bottom of the stairs, then bent to pick up the concertinaed paper lying by the front door. As he did every morning. The *Telegraph* now, not *The Times*. The *Times* lot were still on strike. Had been all year. The comfort of routine.

Tom dropped the paper on to the kitchen table, the debris of a world that no longer made sense. Sam's eyes took in the gothic patterns as the paper sprang open like a pop-up card. Ireland. A photo of a hooded man. Sam put a hand up to her cheek. Her skin felt tight and dry, not enough of it to cover her face.

The police hadn't known much about the accident. For seven hours, Tom had recited the bare bones of their report in an unreliable monotone, unconsciously mixing his words with their

60

official language. Bad driving conditions had forced the coach from the road. Only about fifteen miles away from here. They weren't sure why it had happened to that particular coach on that particular stretch of road. No sharp corners, no other vehicles involved. The coach hit trees, ripping the roof off, flinging glass like confetti over the wet grass. One of the worst road disasters he'd seen in thirty years, the ambulance driver said apparently. Bodies everywhere. Never seen anything like it, he said, except on the news.

There was quite a crowd of us at the school, said Tom. Men mostly, since it was late. Gone ten. Friendly atmosphere. We were tapping our watches, joking about it being a father's lot to spend his life waiting for teenage daughters. You know how it is . . .

We heard the sirens before we saw the blue lights. We didn't worry. Knew they weren't for us. In passing, we felt sorry for somebody else. Then we saw little orange lights blinking, police cars indicating and turning into our car park. Silence covered our mouths with its hand. No noise, just the slam of car doors one after the other, like a macabre round of applause. And the wind, of course.

The officers walked towards us, military steps of black shiny feet. The superintendent was holding his hat. Ladies and gentlemen, he said, I regret to inform you there has been a serious accident. There are some fatalities. That's how he put it, Tom broke in. Fatalities. He read out the details as if he was calling the register. Make sure everyone is accounted for. Driver killed, tick; teacher killed, tick; four girls killed, tick, tick, tick and tick; one in intensive care, two in a critical condition, five in a stable condition; the remaining twenty-three in hospital being treated for shock, as we speak, prior to being released. Tick. Please give your names to Woman Police Constable Avery, he said. Then we can make our way to the hospital, as appropriate.

Please God, let it be other people's children who are dead. That's what I thought, said Tom. Only four girls out of thirty-five. Pretty good odds. Why should it be Anna? Then I was at the front of the queue. She had a nice voice, WPC Avery. Mr Whittaker? She ran her eyes down her list. She paused. I'm sorry, Mr Whittaker, your daughter . . . No, I'm afraid there's no possibility of a mistake. Kind. Everybody was very kind. They drove me to the station. Tried to ring here, but the line was busy . . .

Here Tom faltered. His conscious mind wasn't working properly. It was going blank with the struggle of preventing the images from leaping out of his mouth. He knew he couldn't change what had happened. But instinct told him he could protect Helen and Sam by not telling them what he had seen at the morgue. He heard the white lies crawl out from between his lips, into the ears of his wife and daughter. Anna looked peaceful, he said. She can't have felt a thing . . .

The police had done their best to minimise the extent of Anna's injuries, of course they had. They had warned him. But in the everlasting seconds while her face was not covered by the clinical sheet, Tom understood that he would have to live his life knowing that his daughter had died in agony. Vicious lacerations on her pale skin, as if her unique birthmark had spread to cover all of her face. Her matted hair. Her slit lip. The jagged choker around her neck. For Anna there had been no dignity in dying. Just a head near-severed from her young girl's body. Tom had thrown up.

Everybody was very kind, he kept repeating over and over. As her father's voice rose and fell over her, Sam knew that she would never stop hating those who had survived the crash.

Friday, Saturday, Sunday. Funny how the days kept coming, just the same. The phone, the post, the doorbell. Boys and girls delivered cellophaned flowers. Black-edged condolences flooded in. Dear Helen and Tom . . . Dear Mr and Mrs Whittaker . . . Dear Whittaker Family . . .

No death is higher in the pecking order than the loss of a child. Tom and Helen spoke to everyone they knew, or so it seemed. All those family friends and neighbours keen to be involved, offering help and support in exchange for a role in the tragedy on their doorsteps. Terrible thing to happen. Such a nice couple. One or two people asked how Sam was taking it. Nobody thought to ask her themselves.

The business of death is all-absorbing. It sucks you in, leaving no time for reflection or grief. Like a frantic children's game, it's a race against the clock. Decisions to be taken, arrangements to be made. What's the time, Mr Wolf? Quarter to six. What's the day, Mr Wolf? Tuesday. What's the time, Mr Wolf? Half past two. What's the day, Mr Wolf? Friday. Lovely day for a funeral, Mr Wolf. Coffins and graveyards, invitations, car rotas, *vol-au-vents*. Mushroom and prawn.

Sam watched the haphazard parade from a distance, as if looking up from the sapphire bottom of a swimming-pool. Although familiar, everyone was distorted. A malicious penstroke here, a charcoal line there. Friends, relations, Andrew, even her parents. All sinister caricatures of themselves. She didn't want to face them. She didn't recognise herself any more, so how could she recognise anyone else?

Sam found that she thought only in clichés, no appetite for first-hand emotions. It's like someone's stolen my shadow, she said to herself. Life is pointless after a death, she said to herself. That's what they say. And that's what I feel.

Friday, 17 August. A week had passed. The Whittaker family led the congregation through the dark summer afternoon, wind and rain mocking their efforts to bury Anna. The little graveyard was crowded, formal black and grey and isolated pockets of white obscured by umbrellas. Women pressed their new hats to their heads, some with gloved hands.

Sam walked with her parents, the adagio strings of the music still humming in her mind. Slow and sad. Her clothes scented by the dank and musty smell of an English church. Bitterness and rage gnawed away at her. She'd caught the tail-end of the lunchtime news just before leaving the house. The main story was the memorial service for those killed by the storm during the Fastnet Race. Sixteen, seventeen dead. The worst disaster in the Race's history. Wall-to-wall tributes from the rich and famous, and hundreds gathered at Plymouth Church for a memorial service. How come these deaths matter so much, the voice in Sam's head blasted. The more the merrier? Anna died too. My sister died too. Why is no one telling that to the world? She wanted to kill every journalist and reporter who had not considered their tragedy good enough copy.

Anna's death had, in fact, made the front page of the *Chichester Observer* two days after the accident, but only as a statistic. A tabloid headline – 'Six Dead in Horror Coach Crash Tragedy' – perched above a grainy photo of the wreckage. You could just make out the smashed body of a double bass, lying on the ground. Its snapped strings were jutting out like four arthritic fingers. Beyond repair.

The priest struggled against the gale, mouthing the half-familiar passages. I know this from films and books and plays, Sam muttered to herself. How strange. I've never heard the words in real life.

'Forasmuch as it hath pleased Almighty God of His great mercy to take unto Himself the soul of our dear sister here departed, we therefore commit her body to the ground; earth to earth, ashes to ashes, dust to dust; in sure and certain hope of the Resurrection to eternal life, through the Lord Jesus Christ . . .'

His vestments flapped theatrically in the wind. Sam flinched at the sound of the mud thudding down on to the lid of the coffin. Her eyes moved like a camera, slowly tracking everything, recording everything, but reacting to nothing. Passive, unemotional. Over there were Anna's friends, weeping and huddling into one another for support. Frame One. Close-up. Pan behind them, the parents of the other dead children. Solidarity. Frame Two. Close in to that bandage. She must be a survivor. Sam felt her eyes narrowing to slits. I hate you, she thought. Frame Three. Full-length on Andrew, awkward in his borrowed tie. She felt him wondering at her dry face, but didn't linger. Frame Four. Wide. At the back of the sombre crowd their next-door-neighbours-but-one, sour as always. Cut.

'. . . who shall change our vile body, that it may be like unto His glorious body, according to the mighty working, whereby He is able to subdue all things to Himself.'

Sam felt her father start beside her, as if the vicar's words were dredging up memories best forgotten. She glanced at him out of the corner of her eye, registering his tall, stooping body and bony fingers intertwined with those of her mother. She looks so smart, Sam thought, so long and thin. It was a detached judgement, no longer meaning anything.

Sam felt weightless, as if she was floating high above the ant-sized people, the scruffy tombstones, the younger children scuttling in and out of the graves like rats. The heavy perfume of the honeysuckle. This is all happening to someone else, she thought, someone who looks like me. Someone else's sister is suffocating in that wooden box down there. Not mine. A wave of nausea swept over her head. Sam swallowed hard.

For six days, Sam continued to hold grief at arm's length. Helen had begun to cry the night of the funeral, her body releasing huge, primaeval sobs for hours on end. It was the only time that Sam had ever heard her mother cry. Her father broke two days later. Speaking to no one, responding to no one. Sam felt she was sleepwalking, protecting herself as best she could. An emotional limbo where she barely shut her eyes, barely drank. If she couldn't feel, then she couldn't hurt. If she didn't accept that Anna was dead, then the parody of a day-to-day life without her sister could be kept at bay for just a little longer.

She made pacts with herself. Just one more day, then I'll believe Anna's never coming back. She wandered into her sister's empty bedroom and felt nothing. She brushed her hand over Anna's clothes, stealing her smell with her fingers. Her heart did not crack. Sitting at Anna's dressing-table, she tried to conjure up her twin's face. Her own washed-out eyes and cropped hair looked back at her, roots showing. Only you here now, the image jeered. No one else. Just look at you.

On Thursday, 23 August, two letters came in the post. One was addressed to *Miss S. M. C. Whittaker*, the other to *Anna Whittaker*. Sam's hands started shaking as she looked at her sister's tidy handwriting. Anna always printed her name with such care. Sam slid her numbed finger under the flap, cutting herself in the process. She did not notice she was bleeding. The typed letters on the flimsy blue and white sheet danced in front of Sam's eyes: *English Language (A), English Literature (A), Music (A), French (A), German (A), Biology (A), Chemistry (A), Physics (A), Maths (A), History (A)*. Anna, you've done it, she started to yell, but the words disintegrated in her throat. Horror punched her in the stomach. Anna would never know. All that work and she would never know.

Helen and Tom heard the noise, like the keening of an animal caught in a trap. From the upstairs landing, they saw their daughter collapsed against the front door, her body jerking like a puppet. They ran down the stairs, Tom jumping from halfway. He stumbled as he landed, clipping his head against the edge of the bannister. Helen saw the bruise later.

It was a disturbing tableau. Lifeless and silent. A mother cradling her grown-up child's head in her lap. A father arching his anguished arms over them both. Two envelopes. One empty, spotted by rust-coloured blood. Tiny red polka dots. The other unopened, twisted under Sam's bare feet. *Miss S. M. C. Whittaker* inscribed in green ink.

*   *   *

Sam was in bed for four days. Shadows came and went, faces, the light. She called out from time to time, half-aware that time was passing without her. Burning up one minute, she was sweating cold and chill the next. It was as if her body was purging itself.

On Sunday evening, her temperature dropped. At twenty past eleven, her eyes opened. They registered the dimensions of her familiar bedroom, the colours and shapes. Stiffly, she turned her head on her pillow to see her mother dozing on a chair.

'Mum?'

Her voice sounded tiny, shrivelled up.

Helen jolted awake.

'I'm here, sweetheart,' she soothed, reaching out a hand to Sam's forehead. It felt cool. 'There's nothing to worry about.'

'What time is it?'

'Nearly half past eleven. Sunday night.'

'Sunday . . .' Sam whispered under her breath.

'We've been very worried about you,' Helen whispered, stroking Sam's cheek.

Outside, someone turned off their ignition, slammed their car door and walked up the path towards a house. Stillness closed around them again. Helen wondered how much her exhausted child remembered of the past three days and three nights.

'I think I'd like something to eat,' Sam said suddenly, her voice almost normal. 'And a drink.'

'I'll get you something straight away,' Helen replied. 'And tell your father you're awake. He's been so worried.'

Pulling herself out of the chair, Helen planted a kiss on the top of Sam's very greasy hair. Ill hair, sticking up in tufts all over her head.

'I love you, Mum . . .'

'I love you too,' answered Helen, trying not to cry.

Sam heard her mother walking down the stairs, imagined her turning left into the kitchen. Hearing the familiar murmurs filtering up through the floorboards, Sam propped herself against her pillows and smoothed down the edge of her duvet. So tired.

Sam didn't understand what had happened to her on Thursday. She could remember picking up the letters, then nothing. She had only half-memories of what she'd been through since then. But her head was clear, as if she'd experienced years in those few days, learned everything, from the safety of her sick-bed. She no longer felt sixteen but like an adult, responsible and facing a bleak and uncompromising world.

Two things. Since Thursday, her unconscious mind had forced her to accept two things. First, that Anna was dead and was never coming back. Second, that she had a duty to tell their natural mother. She had no choice. However long it took, however difficult it might be. And when she'd hunted her down, Sam would tell her – somehow – that her elder daughter was dead. The knowledge that Anna was still flesh and blood in her mind was unbearable, the idea of her continuing to picture her twins growing up side by side. Turning eighteen, twenty-one, thirty, getting married and having children of their own. Anna would never grow up.

The sound of her father's size thirteen feet bounding up the stairs three at a time shattered Sam's thoughts. She quickly rubbed her eyes, wiping her wet hands on the corner of the duvet as Tom burst into the room.

'Welcome back,' Tom cried, hugging her tight in his arms. 'We thought we were going to lose you too.'

Sam noticed that his eyes were red.

Wednesday, 5 September. For the first time in six years, term started without the Whittaker twins. Sam could not face going back to school. Not straight away. Possibly not ever.

Tom took his register. A promising new sixth form group, but what did it matter? No Anna, no Sam. During the day he looked out over the sea of faces in his history classes. Ever since the twins were eleven, his teaching days had been punctuated by sightings of one or both of his daughters in amongst the hundreds of other girls. It had made all the difference to his day. Now the overcrowded school seemed empty. He felt the eyes of pupils and colleagues on his back, when he turned to the blackboard, when he walked into the staff room.

He took one day at a time, wondering what the point was. He smoked more, socialised less, stopped putting on silly voices. Now he impersonated himself, the man he had been before Anna's death. But he didn't try to persuade Sam to come back to school to keep him company. Neither did Helen. They understood her refusal to confront Anna's ghost head-on.

Sam did go in to school for the memorial service at the end of the second week of term. A kindly intended arrangement for

Anna and the other pupils who had been killed in the crash. As she walked into the dappled hall, stuffy in the hot autumn sun, Sam felt everyone's tongue-tied look on her. She was surrounded by whispers and hushed voices, like a swarm of bees round her head. Everything reminded her of Anna. The smells and squeaks of the polished floor, the blues and yellows of the uniform. The pain made her giddy.

She couldn't go back to her old life, as if nothing had happened. That much was clear. School was over and done with now. She'd never stop expecting Anna to appear at break, she'd never not look for her in that special corner of the library. Sam didn't want even to catch sight of any of the people she'd known before, not even Julia, not even Andrew. Especially not Andrew. Somewhere buried very deep down, Sam blamed him for Anna's death. She had chosen sex over her sister and the price had been paid. Sam couldn't bear to look at him.

The strength Sam had felt immediately after her illness proved to be illusory. It was as if she'd just been surfacing for breath before plunging back down. Everything was a struggle, even the mundane things like talking, brushing her teeth, putting her clothes on. She was not ready to do anything yet. If she felt better by Christmas, then perhaps she would go to the local College of Further Education in January instead. No one knew her – them – there.

Somehow the weeks passed.

11 November. The eve of the first solo birthday. Just the first of forever. Sam said that she didn't want any fuss. No presents, no cards. There was nothing to celebrate now. If Anna would never be seventeen, then neither would she.

Sam had spent the whole day stopping herself thinking about the fact that this was what every birthday would be like now. Year after year of just her on her own, getting older, leaving Anna further behind. She'd tried to blank out the date in her mind, a thick black line ruled through 12 November . . .

Just before midnight she'd woken from an uneasy sleep, startled, her heart hammering like a panicked bird. As the room slowly came into focus, her terror evaporated. Shoving her wrist up against her nose, she squinted at the flashing green numbers on her watch: 11.53. Sam swung her feet out of bed and pulled on a baggy jumper over her baggy nightshirt. Light from the landing flooded her face, reflecting off the jaundiced ends of her limp straw hair. She screwed her eyes up and reached out blind for the handle of Anna's door. With one hand on top of the other she slowly pressed it down. The radiator inside had been switched off. She didn't know why she was sneaking into Anna's untouched room like a trespasser. But this was where she had come, every eve of birthday for as long as she could remember. In some fundamental way, Sam felt honour-bound to observe their shared ritual.

Her parents found her on the floor in the morning, slumped against the side of the bed. She was clasping Anna's Paddington Bear, knees drawn up to her chest. The fingers of her left hand were tightly fisted around her locket, as if she'd feared that someone would rip it from her in the night. She'd protected herself from the inhospitable cold with Anna's blue bedspread, but her skin felt chill to Helen's touch.

'This can't go on,' she whispered to Tom.

He looked down at his sleeping daughter, thinking how strangely peaceful she looked. As if some personal rubicon had been crossed.

'No,' he replied. 'I'll ring my mother.'

part two

There is no erasing this:
the central memory of what we are
to one another, the grove of ritual.

Robin Morgan, 'The Child', Part IV of
The Network of the Imaginary Mother

White is the colour of leaving. Oyster corridors, dirty round the edges. The milky wings of the planes queuing patiently against the wintry skies. The cups and chalky saucers in the cafeteria. The white of space and time and distance, bleaching everything it touches.

The woman stood alone in the gift shop, a fake Afghàn coat slung over her arm. With its variegated speckled cream fringe and caramel skin, it looked like an exotic ice-cream sundae. The blurred wreckage of the Manchester to Euston express dominated the racks of newspapers. Eleven dead, forty injured. In her hand she was holding a carrier bag, concealing a pearly I LOVE LONDON mug. An impulse goodbye present to herself.

Seven years ago she had stood here, or hereabouts. Fewer shops then, of course, but somehow more colourful. Everything bright, so very English. The uniforms of the air hostesses, pillarbox red and royal blue. The youthful head of Queen Elizabeth, on money and postage stamps the colours of the English countryside. Everybody so polite, so attentive. Seven years ago. She had been young then.

The woman squeezed her bag, reassuring herself that everything was still there. Passport, boarding card, dollars. She thought of those she was leaving behind, the few friendships that would struggle to survive without day-to-day contact. Maybe it was crazy to go back. To the snow and the politics and the war? Perhaps it was naive to hope that thousands of miles could erase memories carved in her bones?

Inoffensive, characterless vowels floated out over the tannoy. You could hear the plastic smile.

'Would all remaining passengers travelling on BOAC flight 742 to Washington please make their way quickly to the departure lounge. This is the final call for passengers travelling to Washington on BOAC flight 742. Thank you.'

73

A flesh-and-blood voice right next to her cut gently across the tannoy's next announcement.

'Ready?'

She nodded, hitching her Indian bag up a little higher on her shoulder to stop it from slipping. The two tiny brass bells jiggled, anachronistic in the controlled modern environment. They began walking, perfectly in step. The garish nylon carpet with its aggressive symmetrical pattern gave way to a rubber conveyor-belt floor. They felt the change of surface through the soles of their shoes, but didn't look down. The woman was aware of the smell of the airport, the muffled roar of engines behind the glass, the sleet on the sweeping windows.

Luminous posters advertising Scotch, cigarettes and perfume twinkled down at them as they passed by. The whisky was the colour of the woman's eyes. She blinked.

This is it, she breathed. No turning back.

1981

CHAPTER 7

Television gets more ridiculous every day, thought Sam, watching the newly-released hostages being paraded through the freezing New York streets in open-topped cars. From Tehran to this, just to be showered in ticker-tape? Mad. Completely loony. She flicked the remote control, drained the tepid instant coffee from the bottom of her mug. She could taste limescale from the furred-up kettle on her teeth. Silence, thank God.

Nearly a year and a half after Anna's death, Sam looked more like her twin than ever before. She'd let her hair grow back to its natural colour and had it styled properly. A fringe, a bob and no split ends. She was slimmer too, although with curves rather than Anna's boyish angles. She still dressed from jumble sales, having no money, but she'd replaced the vomit-and-pus chaos of her Two Tone days with an eclectic sort of period look. Sometimes she even looked stylish.

Sam was very nervous and had run out of ways to kill time before the appointment at three. She'd written out her final list of questions for the counsellor, settling it in her bag with her copy of the Adoption Society's notes and the information Dad had given her – given them – on their thirteenth birthday. She'd checked her bag four times, just to make sure.

At dinner last night, Tom had tried to hammer home that this meeting was only the first step in what could be a very long and possibly frustrating process. Don't feel let down, he said, if the answers aren't all there staring you in the face. I know, I know, Sam'd snapped back. Dad was spot-on, though. She knew she was hoping for too much. Knew she was bound to be disappointed.

Sam looked at her watch. Twenty-five past one. By the time she'd been to the loo, touched up her make-up and got into town, it would be just about time. She stood up, swivelled her polka-dot skirt straight, so the button and zip were at the back, then shovelled her feet into her black twelve-hole Doc Martens. Fifteen minutes later, she clicked the front door behind her and set off into the murky January afternoon.

'Three sausages or four?' asked Helen.

No answer. 'Tom?'

'Sorry?'

'Do you want three sausages or four?'

'Sorry. What are we having with them?'

'The usual,' she snapped.

'Right-oh. Four then, please.'

With a fork, Helen squidged them on to the grill pan. Then, after a moment of hesitation, added four more just in case Sam arrived home within the next ten minutes. She glanced up at the clock. Five past six. She'd expected her back by now.

Until a few days after Sam's eighteenth birthday in November, Helen had thought she'd come to terms with it all. It was the weekend, Helen remembered – a beautiful, crunchy, copper and gold Saturday – when Sam came into the kitchen and told them that she'd written to the General Register Office. Posted the letter that day.

As Tom listened with unselfish interest to Sam's sensitive pre-pared speech, Helen was hit by the extent of her own self-deception. She had been unable to hear a word, every syllable drowned out by the familiar malignant fears flooding her mind. How could she have deluded herself that Sam would never actually *do* anything? Talk, yes. Act, no. She had continued to be as outwardly supportive and loving as she ever was, in her usual calm and quiet way. It was an act, though. Inside she felt as if Strewelpeter had chopped her into a thousand pieces.

Helen turned the grill off, asthmatic with worry, stabbing the eight charred sausages to let the fat drain. One daughter gone, one to go, chanted a vindictive internal voice. You're going to lose her too, you're going to lose her too.

As she undid the strings of her green and white striped apron and folded it neatly across the back of a chair, a phrase came to her mind. 'Love casts out fear.' St John? She snorted. In her experience, it was exactly the opposite way round.

*   *   *

By ten past six, Sam was actually sitting in The Bell, swirling a gin and tonic in her hands. She'd never been in the pub before, but it was the nearest to the Social Services offices, and Sam had reckoned she was unlikely to run into anyone she knew. It had a hushed crimson and gilt atmosphere, like the inside of a seaside Victorian theatre down on its luck. A couple of men, regulars by the looks of things, straddled stools at the bar. Three lads were playing pool, pairs of silver ten pence pieces lined up along the wood claiming the next three games. Their big-haired girlfriends fed the juke-box. Everything looked, smelled, a little dingy.

For once, Sam was not brooding about all the things she'd meant to say at the time but had forgotten. She wasn't quite sure how she felt about how the meeting had gone, hence the pub. The dust needed to settle in her own mind before she swirled it all up again going through things for her parents. Sam glanced over at the greasy hood of the payphone by the front door. Perhaps she should ring? She didn't want to.

'Not worth it,' she muttered to herself, louder than she intended.

One of the girlfriends glanced over, critical mouth sneering. Self-conscious, Sam mucked about in her basket until she felt the eyes turn away.

She took a gulp from her lukewarm gin. The counsellor – feel free to call me Pat – had not been too bad. Squat plywood office chairs with green seat and back, spindly-legged desk, DHSS posters, two straggly spider plants on the window-sill, the room looked much as Sam had imagined. Pat, too, if she was honest. One of those mildly annoying, good-natured people who have a habit of repeating your name at the end of every sentence. The introductions and awkward business of melting the ice were, again, no worse than she'd expected. But Pat's first question was a shock, it had somehow winded her. And to Sam's embarrassment, she'd started crying and been unable to stop.

Usually she could survive questions about Anna. Most of the time, at any rate. Sam could only suppose that the camphor of tension and nerves had somehow short-circuited her self-defence mechanisms. Ten minutes and half a loo roll later, Sam felt drained but curiously relaxed too.

When thinking beforehand about the meeting – the compulsory counselling meeting – Sam had assumed that the point was to hand over a copy of her original birth certificate. It had become clear within minutes that there was more to it than that, as first one leaflet, then two, then three, had crossed the desk. Sam had shovelled them straight into her bag without looking.

The whole two hours had in fact felt more like a sort of cat-and-mouse vetting session. At first, Pat's job seemed to be as discouraging as possible, as nicely as possible. Why do you want to trace your natural mother, Sam? Do you think you understand what could be involved, Sam? She strongly recommended an intermediary rather than a direct person-to-person approach, to save any possible distress. After all, Pat had added, we are unaware of her current circumstances.

Sam had nodded, as if taking notice, but was thinking only of herself. If you do find your biological mother – emphasis on the if – she might not want to meet you. What would you do then, Sam? If you find her, you might not like her. Yeah, yeah, yeah, Sam had blahhed to herself, I'm not a complete moron. If she'd appeared a total psycho, would Pat have tried to dissuade her from going further? Refused to hand over her birth certificate? Sam smiled at the implausibility of good-hearted Pat writing anyone off. Anyone at all.

Pat had smiled sympathetically as Sam had hooked out a gritty tampon from the bottom of her bag together with the list of things she wanted to ask. The sort of hideous girls-together smile that Sam most hated. But after the worst-case scenarios had been dispensed with, Pat had actually been clear and helpful about the next steps Sam should take and what sort of support she could expect from the Social Services. Between them, they worked their way down Sam's list until all her questions had been answered. If only with other questions.

I suppose that's how I feel really, she murmured, tucking her hair back behind her ears. She was not aware she'd inherited Anna's gesture, although others had noticed. I feel pretty positive, like at last I have a blueprint of what to do and who to ask.

For fifteen months after Anna's death, Sam had simply stopped living. It was as if she was diseased, rotting from the inside out. When Helen and Tom had found her cold body curled up on Anna's floor, they had decided to send her away from the raw landmarks for a while. This is the hardest time, everyone told her. Birthdays, Christmas. Time is a great healer.

For nine weeks Sam had convalesced with her grandmother in her kind, irritating world. Sleeping, eating, steeped in the smell of wet fern and Yardley. Sam heard the wind whipping the rigging on the sailing boats in the harbour with unhearing ears. With her blind eyes, she saw the white and grey backs of the gulls diving. She wasn't lonely because Anna was always with her. Untouchable and mute, but at her side all the same.

Helen and Tom drove down to Devon every weekend. Four hours there, four hours back, depending on the traffic. Every Friday night, Sam was aware of her grandma's hushed bulletins whispered behind the door, immediately her son and daughter-in-law arrived. Every Sunday afternoon, Sam took in the sight of her grandmother waving away their thanks as her parents took their leave. Thinking of it now, she could not bear to imagine the pressure they must have been under. Grieving for one child, terrified for the other.

In January 1980 Sam came home, numb but determined in the cold new decade. She would enrol at college, she would set things in motion once more. Shit, mumbled Sam into her gin, this time last year. She'd thought she was better, that she was mentally capable of functioning as she had in the old days. So she had written to the address at the top of the Adoption Society notes. Only to find it had been closed down in 1969 and that most of their records had been lost.

Sam felt as if she'd been physically attacked when the letter was returned. Victimised. Perhaps you should give yourself longer to get back on your feet, sweetheart, Helen had said. Wouldn't it make more sense in any case, Tom had added, to put things on hold? Wait until you're eighteen and can apply for a copy of your original birth certificate? Sam had waited.

January became February, February slid into March. Unwilling to inflict more pain on her parents, Sam sucked herself dry struggling to seem normal. Disguising the scar tissue. She went to college, like any other student. She handed in homework, like any normal student. She moaned about the price of filled rolls and the taste of the canteen coffee, but made no friends. Winter, spring, summer. Thursday, 7 August, Friday, 8 August, Sunday, 17 August 1980. A sunny day for a funeral, not like last year.

Pound by pound, Sam's body thawed. At first she felt guilty at being able to think about Anna without breaking down. Part of her resented the fact that time was making things easier. She wasn't sure she wanted to be healed. Sam almost missed the gnawing pain, as if her sister was slipping away from her. Day after day, she had woken suffocated by sadness, as if someone was kneeling on her chest. Then one morning it wasn't there. She no longer cried in her sleep. She no longer woke wet with overnight tears, skin taut like a face mask. She could say Anna's name in a sentence now and yet carry on talking.

Not this afternoon though, Sam thought wryly, draining her glass. The limp crescent of lemon slapped down on to her top lip. Time to go. She wriggled her arms into her fake fur coat – mole with a hint of pony, as her father described it – grabbed her purse and inched along the spongy red bench, dragging her wicker basket by its thin handles. As Sam wrenched the sticky saloon bar door towards her, she registered John Lennon vibrating from the juke-box for the third or fourth time. Nothing like a death to boost record sales, she muttered, and let the door swish shut behind her.

About half an hour later, Sam was putting her key in the lock. Her hands were frozen.

'Only me,' she shouted from the hall, slinging her basket over the end of the bannister with her coat.

'We're in here,' Helen called back from the sitting-room, gesturing to Tom to turn off the television.

'Whatever's happened?' demanded Tom, as she appeared. 'Are you all right?'

'What?' replied Sam, confused. 'Of course I'm all right.'

'You've been crying,' he said accusingly, as if it was evidence.

Sam looked over at her mother for some help in this bizarre exchange.

'Your eyes . . .'

Sam charged up to the bathroom. Two black, smudged patches looked back at her defiantly. Fucking hell, said Sam under her breath. She tore off a wad of cotton wool, stuck it under the tap, then started jabbing away at the offending eye-liner smears. Thanks a lot, Pat, she grouched to her reflection in the mirror. You could've bloody well said something.

The next morning, Sam went straight back up to her room after breakfast. Thin leaflets of lime, turquoise, rose, official attempts at design and accessibility, already covered her desk. Flicking on the radio, she pulled out a piece of writing paper from her stationery tray. It was so white it almost smelled laundered. Sitting herself down, she picked up her new pen, cerulean ink ready to shape itself into whatever letters Sam wanted. She needed a heading. Thought for a moment, then pulled the lid off and wrote 'What I Know About My Natural Parents' in the middle of the page at the top. A slight pause, then Sam underlined it with a ruler. One minute passed, two, three. Her mind had gone completely blank.

Patience, she sighed. And I need to be methodical. Yesterday Pat had impressed upon her how crucial it was to keep accurate records. Otherwise you'll end up duplicating your avenues of research, she'd warned. Of course it made sense. Sam was the first to admit that she could be a little haphazard at times. But she didn't want to spend her morning compiling yet another list. She could do that later.

Instead, she found herself turning again to her new – her original – birth certificate. She pretty much knew it off by heart already. Less than twenty-four hours in Sam's possession and already there was a greasy thumb-print on the top right-hand corner. At last, she had a name. Names, in fact, addresses. *Julian Samuel Driver, Bookshop Assistant, and Gayle Driver (née Faye), Housewife.* Wincing at the word housewife, Sam's eyes continued to scan the columns. *When and where born: Twelfth November 1962 St Saviour's Hospital, Oxford. Signature, description and residence of informant: J. S. Driver, Father.* He lived at the same address as Gayle, according to the certificate. Sam frowned.

Yesterday, she'd had to stop herself snatching it from Pat in the office. Her gut reaction was to head for Oxford, like an amateur detective living off instinct and clues. Don't forget, Pat advised, that it is a trail already more than eighteen years old. It is unlikely, although possible, that your natural parents still live at the same address. It is not uncommon, in cases where a couple appears married, for the pregnancy to be the result of an extra-marital affair. One of Pat's official-speak sentences still rang in Sam's ears: You should proceed with extreme caution.

The idea of her biological mother's husband not being her biological father had never occurred to Sam, any more than the likelihood of him not being the villain of the piece. Julian. Shit-awful name anyway. She smiled to herself at the cumbersome euphemisms her mind was churning out. Biological this, biological that.

She decided to lose Pat's affair comment under 'Unlikely' in her mental filing system. It was easier to concentrate on Pat's suggestion that Gayle and Julian – as she already thought of them – might have divorced. If this is the case, Pat had spelled out, your natural mother might well have reverted to her maiden name. Or, of course, remarried. Parallel lines. Sam's romantic imagination wanted to discover similarities, however tenuous, between her life and that of the mother she had never met. It was a disappointment to have been given Julian's middle name, rather than something of Gayle's. As if they'd expected a boy. She had hoped for a female family tradition, all the girls called Sam or something like that. She rolled the sounds over her tongue. Gayle Faye to Gayle Driver back to Gayle Faye. Perhaps? And she had gone from Sam Driver to Sam Whittaker. There was a pattern of sorts . . .

Sam's fingers automatically started to unwrap her Double Decker, still chilled after a night in the fridge. Still thinking, she vaguely dropped the orange and purple paper in the vicinity of the waste-paper basket squashed under her desk. It missed. Pat had suggested her starting-point should be the Electoral Register people, to find out if anyone else had lived at Raphael House with Julian and Gayle in November 1962. I *will* do that, Sam promised herself. But it is loony not to try a direct approach when I've got an address right here in front of me. She sank her teeth through the squidgy chocolate to the biscuit below. Perfect.

After a moment's indecision, Sam took another sheet of paper and started to write. *Mrs Gayle Driver, Raphael House, Boar's Hill, Oxford, Great Britain*. Half an inch space, then the date. Then . . . well, what? Sam pressed her spine into the wooden struts of her chair. How should she begin?

An hour and a half later, and a floor full of crumpled false starts, Sam had a letter she was satisfied with. With immense care, she folded it three times and slid it into an envelope. She looked at the photo of herself and Anna she'd intended to send. They were both laughing, making dummy rabbits' ears with Victory V fingers above one another's heads. June 1979, just after the end of their exams. Anna's crimson birthmark was hardly visible under her fringe. Sam contemplated the plump, peroxided version of herself, fingering the photo as if she could breathe life into it. Not true now, she thought. It wouldn't be fair to send this photo.

Downstairs the phone rang in the hall. She heard Helen answer.

For her? Sam waited, but there was no shout. She shivered, suddenly overwhelmed by the enormity of what she was doing.

'Just get on with it,' she muttered to herself, plonking her wicker basket on the desk.

Sam pressed the sticky edges of the rectangular envelope tightly together. Then, licking the fir tree stamp, a leftover from Christmas, she banged it on with a thump of her fist and wedged the letter well down inside her bag. She could put it in the post on her way to college, in time to catch the lunchtime collection. It would be in Oxford by second post tomorrow.

As she walked towards the door, Sam looked at her watch. Just time for a coffee, she thought, walking out on to the landing. Her bedroom was left with only the white noise of the radio for company.

CHAPTER 8

'Two coffees, please,' said Sam, finally at the front of the long Saturday afternoon queue.

'Anyfin kelse?' squawked the waitress.

Sam turned and bellowed at the black polo-necked figure in the window alcove.

'Peter! Do you want anything to eat?'

He shook his head. Sam swivelled back on her flat-booted heels, uncomfortably aware of the wet denim clinging to her calves.

'And a piece of the strawberry shortbread,' she added, holding out a soggy five pound note.

'That'll be two pounds, five pence,' said the sour-faced waitress. 'Have you got the five?'

Sam shook her head and was punished with a collection of slippery coppers in her change. She tossed it all on to the tray and made her way across the steamy, fifteenth-century tea rooms to where Peter had finished rolling her a cigarette and was starting on one for himself.

'Great,' he said, as she put the coffee down in front of him. His soft West Coast accent, short vowels, caught the ear of a couple of girls at the next table.

He was the only friend that Sam had made at college. She hated the girls for not being Anna and despised the boys, with their clumsy chat-up lines. Always after something. Most people thought her surly. Peter, on the other hand, was open and cheerful, courteous to everyone. But he wasn't after a girlfriend to boast about to the lads and he disliked the pack mentality of the sports crowd. And, like Sam, was irritated by the intrusive habits of the other students. Kids, he called them. Floppy black hair, watchful face, Mexican leather bracelet, one pierced ear. Different, not provincial English. His father was dead, of cancer.

86

The Big C got him, was how he'd put it. Only thirty-nine years old.

Recognising the hollowness in one another, they'd started talking. Two outsiders together. Just a little at first, both reluctant to be drawn in. Week by week, the words turned to sentences turned to whole conversations. Neither pressuring, neither feeling obliged to fake intimacy, they found themselves inhabiting a comfortable routine. Sam'd started to take the piss out of his pronunciation, Peter'd taught her to swear in Spanish. Their alliance had been clinched by the confession that neither of them liked lager, Peter because he didn't want to be British blokeish, Sam on the grounds that it tasted like ear-wax.

'So . . .' continued Sam, taking up the thread of the conversation as if there hadn't been a ten-minute break, '. . . I sent it to the address on the birth certificate.'

'What did you go for?' Peter asked, bringing his mouth down to the rim of his cup and sucking up enough coffee to make room for the milk.

'Gayle Driver, in the end,' replied Sam. 'Mrs. I mean, who knows what she calls herself now? She could easily've gone back to her maiden name.'

'Or married again . . .'

Sam sploshed two lumps of sugar into her frothy cup. For the first couple of days after posting the letter, she had mentally followed its progress. Now it was in the postman's grey sack, now at the sorting office, now on the train. She imagined it arriving in Oxford, like a tourist, looking left, then right, before setting off towards Boar's Hill. She tracked it falling down on to a bristly brown brush mat, caught her breath as she thought of Gayle's eyes focusing on the unfamiliar writing, bending to pick the envelope up. Not recognising the postmark. At this point, the scene ended. Just a line of running dots at the end of a chapter . . .

When the twins were little, one of Sam's favourite games had been fantasising their natural mother. A sort of painting by numbers. As she had grown up, individuality crushed by fashion magazines and films, the ideal had become a glossy model type. After the accident, Sam stopped dreaming. All she could see was a ghost tenant in Anna's body. Now Gayle was on the verge of becoming real? Her imagination dropped the curtain. Nothing.

'Sam? Hello . . . ?'

She jumped, blinked in surprise at being back in the wet weekend café.

Peter handed her the cigarette he'd rolled, then pulled a soggy box of matches out of the pocket of his suede jacket.

'Thanks. Now, where was I?'

'Letter. What you called her . . .' prompted Peter.

'Yes,' said Sam. 'So then I wrote to the Oxford Electoral Register people. The social worker, Pat, said they will be able to tell me where the electoral records are kept for 1962 to see if anyone else lived with them. You never know. Hopefully, I should at least get one or two other names to try to track down, if all else fails.'

Peter nodded as he leaned forward to give her a light. He watched Sam pluck the withered strawberry from the top of her shortbread, then drop it into her mouth. Tobacco and fruit.

'I'm going to look in the phone books in the library, just in case she still lives somewhere in Oxford.'

'Or Julian.'

'Maybe,' replied Sam absentmindedly. 'I'm not really that interested in him.'

Peter raised his eyebrows.

'What?' challenged Sam. 'What's that look for?'

'Nothing,' he grinned.

Peter knew Sam had convinced herself way back that Julian was inherently bad and that Gayle was fundamentally good. The prejudice was too firmly rooted to shift. He already knew her too well to try.

Sam scowled out of the window in an exaggerated huff. Silent, flat rain streaked down the little latticed windows. The minutes passed. She tucked her damp hair back behind her ear. Peter thought she looked rather lovely.

Sam's mood evaporated as quickly as it had blown up. Reflective now rather than cross, she twisted the fag-end of the anorexic cigarette round and round in her fingers.

'She hasn't tried to find me,' she said.

'You don't know that,' replied Peter.

'Well, put it like this. She's never contacted the Social Services to ask about us. About me and Anna.'

'Sure. OK. But what about the guys at the Adoption Society? Or maybe she sent something to the counsellor which went astray.'

Peter leaned across the rickety wooden table and put his hands over the top of hers. A supportive, thoughtful gesture. Sam grinned at him with affection. Secure in their friendship, the two of them flirted shamelessly all of the time. And she loved the fact that no one at college could quite figure out their relationship.

'OK?' he said softly.

Sam nodded firmly, once. Then, springing back to life, she pulled her hands out from under his and held out her cup.

'Another coffee would be nice,' she said cheekily, 'since you're asking. Tea, actually!'

'Yeah, yeah,' Peter muttered, standing up and taking her cup anyway. He noticed a smear of cherry lip-gloss round the rim, pulled a face.

'Gross . . .'

She beamed and blew him a kiss.

Three weeks later, a letter with an Oxfordshire postmark arrived for Sam. Heart thumping, she ripped it open. From Gayle, despite the typed address label? No. Her pulse slowed down, disappointed. Official maroon and white letterhead. Dear Ms Whittaker . . . She looked at the bottom of the page to see an illegible signature for and on behalf of the Electoral Registration Officer. Thanking her for her letter, he was pleased to inform her that the information pertaining to the year required was kept at the County Records Office, open to members of the public between 10 a.m. and 4 p.m., Mondays to Fridays. Closed on all public holidays. Please do not hesitate to contact us, blah, blah, blah . . . Why *do* they write like that, Sam thought to herself. Perhaps all civil servants are sent to a special tedium course before they're let loose on the public? How To Bore For England, just a few places remaining . . .

Sam looked at her watch, waved the letter at her mother in the kitchen, then headed for the phone. Her fingers dialled Peter's familiar number without conscious thought. Balancing the receiver uncomfortably between her ear and her shoulder, she listened to the ring at the other end.

'Hi. Is Peter there? It's Sam.' A slight pause. 'Yes, fine, thank you. Yes.' Another pause. She never quite knew how to take Peter's mother, who was only thirty-seven and insisted on being called Annette rather than Mrs Newman. Even Peter called her Annette. Sam could hear the faint clip of her shoes disappearing down the long parquet hallway, then the squeak of Peter's trainers.

'Hi,' she said, as he picked up the phone. 'Fancy a trip to Oxford?'

Four hours later they were standing outside the imposing stone facade of the Oxfordshire County Records Office.

'I think we should probably check 1961 and 1963 as well,' Sam hissed as they walked up the steps. 'Just to get a clearer picture.'

'Clearer than what?' Peter teased.

'Just clearer,' Sam snapped, a little over-awed by the building. She was nervous and her orange and silver junk-shop blouse was starting to scratch against the chain of her locket. She wished she'd made a bit more effort to look smart.

A clerk with a voice like a machine-gun explained that the electoral lists were compiled each autumn and operational from the following February. Before 1966, only those over the age of twenty were listed. A 'Y' next to a person's name indicated that the individual was between twenty and twenty-one during the year in question. Sam tried, without success, to catch Peter's eye, wanting to take the piss out of the clerk's friendly nasal rattle.

For the next three and a half hours they searched and scribbled and shuffled papers, sneaking back through the hushed, high-ceilinged rooms every now and again for illicit fag breaks. Each time it seemed to be colder outside, the sickly February sun slanting lower and lower across the steps. Sam produced an enormous bag of Maltesers from her pocket.

'Family size,' she read aloud from the packet. 'Appropriate, in the circumstances.'

Seven o'clock. Having treated themselves to a sit-down pizza (extra mushrooms on one half) with side salad when the Records Office had closed at four, Peter and Sam were now standing in the buffet of a near-empty British Rail train. It was surprisingly quiet, just one or two people fixed mutely behind the long-suffering grey tables watching the dark Berkshire countryside flash by. Change at Reading for all stations to Portsmouth and the South.

They'd pooled their remaining pounds and pence to buy themselves real drinks. A melancholy gin and tonic for Sam, a lukewarm scotch for Peter. Leaning sideways against the bar, heads huddled, they looked almost like an old commuting couple who'd done the same journey, day in, day out, for years. Only their clothes gave them away, the heavy DMs, the frayed jeans, Peter's bracelet, his black pony-tail.

Sam used the sleeve of her synthetic brown fur to wipe down the dribbly, lurching counter before rescuing three grubby bits of paper from her bag. The sum of their afternoon's work.

'So what do we know,' she asked rhetorically, smoothing out the top sheet of notes. 'In 1962, Raphael House was owned by one Pamela Greene . . .'

'. . . still is,' Peter interrupted, 'unless she off-loaded it in the last year.'

With a spurt of lateral thinking, Peter had checked the most recent Electoral Register to find that Pamela Greene was still listed. No other names, though.

'So in November 1962,' continued Sam, ignoring Peter's comment, 'there were five people living in the house. Everyone from 1961 – Pamela, Rebecca Lawson, David Rogers, Julian – and Julian's new wife, Gayle.'

Peter pushed his fingers over his hair, an habitual clearing-out-the-cobwebs gesture.

'I guess it means your parents . . .'

'They're not my parents.'

The words jumped from Sam's mouth, more violently than she'd intended. Force of habit.

'Whoa, sorry,' he apologised, holding up his hands in a conciliatory gesture. 'My mistake. What I was gonna say was, it only gives them twelve months to get married. Between the '61 Register and your birthday in November '62.'

'The notes from the Adoption Society said they were already married when they first approached them. So . . .' Sam counted the months forward on her fingers, '. . . about seven months.'

'Right,' said Peter. 'It should be no big deal getting hold of their marriage certificate.'

'Maybe,' muttered Sam vaguely, following her own line of thought, 'Pamela Greene is still there – I mean, almost certainly – at Raphael House. There's no reason why she wouldn't have kept in contact with Gayle.'

'I guess. But I reckon she'd more likely be in touch with Julian. Remember, they were friends to start with.'

'True,' Sam conceded, 'but my point is that if Pamela Greene *does* forward my letter to Gayle, then I won't have to search any further. She might already have it.'

'Still worth checking out the telephone directory,' Peter said firmly. 'You might find a current address for her, just sitting there. You wouldn't be relying on Pamela being around, knowing where Gayle is and getting it together to pass on your letter.'

He turned to look at Sam, aware that she was no longer listening. She appeared to be in a trance, peering into her empty plastic cup.

Peter drained the last of his scotch. Time for another approach.

'Let's back up a moment here. What were you saying earlier about divorce papers?'

Sam still took no notice. A shiver was slithering down and up her spine as she imagined what Gayle might be feeling at this very moment. Perhaps she was sitting alone in a room, a yellow patch of light in a dark winter house? Perhaps she was thinking about all those lost years without her children? There were tears in her eyes. An elegant pen began to skate over watermarked paper, the hardest letter she had ever had to write.

My dear daughter . . .

Sam sensed trouble as she walked up the front path and saw her mother looking out of the window, shoulders brittle, mouth tense. She did not return Sam's over-enthusiastic wave.

'It's nearly half past eleven,' Tom shouted, flinging open the door. 'Where in hell's name have you been?'

Sam knew she was later than she'd promised. Four hours later, in fact. She had intended to apologise and had been rehearsing a convincing lie about a broken-down train and vandalised phone boxes all the way back from the station. Sam was already on edge because she felt guilty. The success of the day was somehow a betrayal of them. Like she was being unfaithful or something. She felt as if she had the scent of Gayle on her clothes.

Sam's fiery temper, hoping for fun, started to flex its muscles.

'You know where I've been,' she said defensively. 'I told Mum I was going to Oxford with Peter, to the County Records Office.'

'You waved a piece of paper in front of her nose, said you'd be back at seven and charged out the door, more like it,' Tom raged. 'We've been worried sick.'

'God, this is so unfair. I'm eighteen,' Sam retaliated aggressively.

'I can look after myself. It's like a prison, having to clock in and clock out on the dot.'

Anna's death had left a legacy of clock-watching. At first, all three of them had been paralysed by anyone being even the slightest bit late. Time had helped Tom to control his fear. But for Helen, the eighteen months since the accident had made no difference at all. She still became twitchy when anyone was fifteen minutes late, angry after half an hour, worried after forty-five minutes, then sick to the bottom of her stomach as each additional minute ticked by. Private as ever, she concealed the extent of her anxiety from her daughter.

When Sam first started going out again after her sister's death, she had religiously been home when promised. But in the last couple of months, since she and Peter had become day-to-day friends, she'd gone back to her old, sloppy time-keeping ways.

She banged her watch self-righteously. 'Annette didn't hit the roof.'

'I don't care what Peter's mother did or didn't do,' yelled Tom, incensed by Sam's attempt to make them feel over-protective. 'Apologise to your mother at once.'

'God, I can't believe this,' shrieked Sam, storming out of the kitchen and up the stairs. 'I'm not apologising. I haven't done . . .'

Her parting words were drowned by the slam of her bedroom door. Minutes later, the manic trumpets of The Teardrop Explodes blasted through the floor. Her parents looked at one another. Five past eleven. Tick, tick.

Helen pulled out a Silk Cut from her nearly empty packet on the window-sill, put it in the corner of her mouth and lit up.

'I handled that well,' said Tom ironically.

Half an hour later, when they were in bed reading, there was a timid knock at their bedroom door. Sam's sheepish face appeared, followed by the rest of her in equally humble mode. After a certain amount of rather self-indulgent weeping and a sniffed apology, she promised to be more considerate in the future.

Harmony restored, Sam told them everything about her detective trip to Oxford. It was a relief to be honest, made her feel better and more responsible. She felt very safe now, snuggling at the end of her parents' double bed, baggy purple nightshirt stretched over her knees. When they were little, she and Anna had crawled in for a cuddle every morning. While Helen went downstairs to start the breakfast, they dunked biscuits into Tom's tea and brushed the crumbs out of his beard.

Sam wanted to reassure them that searching for Gayle had nothing to do with what she felt for them. That she was doing it because of Anna. Desperate not to hurt them if she could avoid it, she instinctively knew that any words of explanation would be inadequate. The more colourful or emotional, the less convincing she'd sound.

Now she was an adult, Sam felt that protecting her parents was more important than being completely honest. The truth might be too painful to tell. It might not. Whatever, she didn't want to risk it. She therefore decided to keep quiet about the letter she had sent to Gayle. For the time being, at any rate.

CHAPTER 9

Through the grubby windows of the college canteen, Sam watched the woolly March clouds scampering, hustled by the boisterous March wind. Like huge florets of cauliflower. It was so bright out there. An English springtime painted in children's colours, primary reds and yellows and blues.

She turned back to the beige plastic world inside, bored. For the past seven months, this corner was where she and Peter had come to kill time between lessons. An exclusive little club of two. Sam thumped her elbows down on the table and watched him sprinkling tobacco like a stock cube into the orange Rizla paper.

Sam knew she would never have stuck college if she hadn't found him. No way. When she'd come home from Devon in January 1980, it was obvious immediately that she wasn't going to be able to cope with making up the lost A-level term. Her parents had encouraged her to enrol anyway. Five months of retake classes, trying to get up to pass-mark level the three subjects she'd failed the previous summer. Venn diagrams, periodic tables, elasticity.

The results had arrived on Thursday, 21 August. A cloudy day, unremarkable. Thursday, like last year. Helen was smoking at the kitchen window, Tom was struggling with his crossword, both concentrating hard on forgetting what had happened on this day fifty-two weeks ago. Three hundred and sixty-five days ago. The clip of the letter-box made them jump. Sam dragged herself into the hall to pick up the solitary envelope lying on the mat. Black ink, handwritten, self-addressed to Ms S. Whittaker. Inside, the same flimsy white paper and washed-out blue type: *Maths (C), Chemistry (C), Physics (D)*. Who cares, she'd thought. Who the fuck cares.

Two and a half weeks later, Sam had gone back ready for A-levels. English and History. A year behind her peers, but ready.

And three weeks after that, Peter had turned up, doing the same two subjects. Or, as he put it, lit-er-at-ure and the kings and queens of Europe. An alliance was born.

Peter told her how he'd skipped school for a couple of years after his father had died. How he – and his once-English mother – had abandoned debts and trailer in San Diego and headed south, over the border into Mexico. When the money dried up, they'd borrowed enough for two air fares from a friend in Mexico City and arrived in Britain at the end of August 1980. To put down roots with Annette's mother. It all sounded so romantic to Sam. Like someone in a film rather than someone hanging out in the local College of Further Ed.

Sam looked back out of the window. The sky was still unrealistically blue. This time last week it had been pissing with rain. Peter had turned up clutching a squashed doughnut and announced that today was his Paddington birthday. Never having heard of Paddington Bear from Darkest Peru before meeting Sam, he'd thought the idea of two birthdays a year was great. I'm starting a family tradition of my own, he said in a mock English accent as he cut the doughnut in half. Monday, 23 March, 1981. Seven months of being British today. Bottoms up!

Since their cold trip to Oxford, Sam was prepared to admit that she'd needed a lot of cheering up. Doughnuts, theatrical gestures, whatever. Exhilaration at their success at the County Records Office had quickly given way to disappointment when she heard nothing from either Pamela Greene or Gayle. Peter had helped Sam scour the local phone books, turning up three P. Drivers and one G. Not a bad start. But each call had led precisely nowhere. The first number had been disconnected; numbers two and three were six doors apart, answered by a pair of cantankerous brothers who boasted not to have spoken to one another in twenty years. The fourth was a very pleasant-sounding lady, most disappointed not to be able to help.

Next, they'd tried all the other Drivers, the rest of the A to Z, looking for cousins or brothers or in-laws. Again, they'd drawn a blank. Everyone else who'd lived in the house seemed to have vanished off the face of the earth. No Rebecca Lawson was listed for the Oxfordshire area, no David Rogers. The only piece of good news in the past six weeks had been confirmation of a telephone at Raphael House in the name of P. Greene. The bad news was that the number was ex-directory.

When they'd first become close, Peter had read all Sam's adoption leaflets. Under his mellow skin were solid, sensible bones. A realistic optimist, as Sam always called him, rather than a hippy-dippy dreamer. He expected the process of tracing to require persistence, stamina and patience. Most of all patience. Without in any way being discouraging, he'd been trying to help Sam accept it too. With little success.

Demoralised, she mooned around in a listless and apathetic bad temper. At night, her head was invaded by clever and subtle ghosts, jeering at her efforts to hunt them down. She woke up muffled and disoriented, more tired than when she'd gone to bed.

Peter screwed up the empty Rizla packet, shoved his tobacco back in his pocket, then slipped the skinny roll-up between his lips. The end flared as he lit it, orange flame followed by white smoke.

'OK,' he said decisively. 'You're gonna hate this. But we gotta go for Gayle's family.'

He looked over at Sam, who was tipping back on her plastic chair and banging her foot against the thin metal leg of the table.

'Sam?'

Bang. Bang.

'None of them were G,' she said sulkily.

'Sure, but there were only three Fayes listed. It's worth a try.'

Bang. Bang. Bang.

She had what Helen would call her 'Sam-knows-best' expression on her face.

'I don't see why you're so sure Gayle's family live in Oxford.'

Usually Peter liked Sam's spikiness. He'd grown up among bland and acquiescent Californian girls, so her spirit had been one of the things that attracted him in the first place. That, and her laugh. Like a braying mule. But just every now and again, her bolshiness and sneering bugged the hell out of him.

'Jesus, Sam,' he said irritably. 'You're being a total pain in the ass . . .'

Immediately Sam bumped her chair back down to the ground, hating herself for having over-stepped the mark.

'God, sorry. I'm sorry,' she apologised. 'I know I'm being a complete nightmare at the moment. It's just . . . well, all this effort for nothing.'

She reached out her arms across the table in reconciliation, knocking over the salt. 'Forgiven?'

'*Mierda*,' swore Peter, slapping the tops of her hands. Gentle horse-play. 'But quit being so negative. OK? And *listen* to what I'm saying.'

'O–K,' she mimicked in her worst American accent, capping it with an exaggerated jaunty Hollywood salute. 'I'm a-listening.'

'Yeah, yeah,' he responded, wagging his finger. She grabbed hold and shook, turning it into a miniature arm wrestle.

'Go on then,' she giggled. 'Get on with it . . .'

'Right. We know that Gayle went to music college someplace in London. From the notes your folks got from the Adoption Society.'

'Right.'

'And we also know that she flunked out because she was sick. Right?'

Sam nodded.

'OK. So we have Gayle dropping out of school. She's what, twenty, twenty-one years old, stuck in London with no cash, no work, and she's sick. Where does she go? Where all sick kids go. Home to Mom and Dad in Oxford. Where she meets Julian and marries him.'

Sam was sceptical, although she was forcing herself to keep her tongue in check. She was usually happy to trample rough-shod over facts if it suited her. But frustration and boredom were making her pedantic. So. What did they know? Actually know for a fact? One, that Julian had gone to Oxford University. Two, that he was twenty-five at the time of her adoption, living and working in Oxford. Three, that Gayle had not finished her course in London. That was it. Perhaps Gayle's parents did live in Oxford, but she and Julian could just as easily have got it together anywhere. Even if they had met in Oxford itself, Gayle might have been simply passing through, staying with a friend for the weekend or something.

'Suppose your theory is right,' she eventually replied, 'and one of these Fayes does turn out to be related. What makes you think they'd give us her address, just like that?'

Peter pulled a saucer towards him and stubbed out his roll-up. Sam watched one last gust of smoke filter out from his nose.

'Look, we use the same story as before. That we're old friends but we lost touch, that we found some old stuff of hers, photos, whatever. Jesus, Sam. Tell them you got mugged and your address book was stolen!'

'Oh, yes,' Sam retorted sarcastically, 'that's really convincing . . .'

The bell drilled raucously for the start of the next period. The canteen was filled with the grating of chairs being scraped back as students pulled themselves to their feet and gathered up their belongings.

'You can't just sit it out,' Peter shouted over the repetitive vibration, as they joined the shuffling procession heading for the swing-doors. 'Let's make some calls later. Annette's gonna be out.'

In the event, Ronald Reagan was shot. Just minutes after finishing a law-and-order speech at the New York Hilton. Rather than hitting the town as intended, Peter's mother and her West Coast friend had therefore stayed in to watch the fun on the television.

'Nearly a triumph for the forces of anti-Fascism,' Annette announced, as Sam hovered in the doorway of the huge sitting-room.

'Unfortunately,' she added, 'the bastard's not dead.'

Peter grinned as he went to his friend's rescue. He was proud of his unorthodox mother, loved her a great deal, but he knew Sam found her intimidating. It had not taken him long to figure out that Sam was not half so wild as she made out. Despite her men's boots and kooky clothes, the odd joint and occasional tab of acid, Sam was actually a pretty conventional girl.

As Peter steered her towards a chair, Sam peeked at their saggy sofas and Mexican rugs and shells out of the corners of her eyes. She wanted to take the take-it-or-leave-it mess in her stride, but somehow couldn't. The wholefood and wholepolitic leaflets covering every available surface. Even the old black and white television in its own wooden case made her feel uncomfortable, a symbol of quite how different it all was from her own family life.

Annette somehow took over their evening, persuading them into keeping her and Rusty company. And because even Annette had an iron fist when it came to her phone bill and her teenage son, Peter's original plan for the evening was soon forgotten in a haze of grass and Rioja. *Tales from Topographic Oceans* and *Ladies from the Canyon* filled the room. Everything floated in slow motion, shimmering in lavender and lilac round the edges. Sam got stoned and giggled and giggled and giggled.

*   *   *

99

Three days later, Sam turned up for college to discover that there'd been a break-in and all classes had been cancelled. She glanced at her watch. Dad would be taking register at this precise moment. Sam smiled at the thought of a school full of all those little girls in their blue and yellow uniforms. Mum was going up to London for one of her regular lunch and matinée days. Of Peter there was no sign and she didn't fancy the idea of going home on her own to an empty house.

Sam suddenly felt butterflies in her stomach as an illicit plan flashed into her head. London. Sam looked at her watch again. I don't have any of her stuff with me, she muttered. Does that matter? Probably not. If I run, I should just about make it to the station in time for the 9.59. I might even get there in time for Mum to pay for my ticket. While she's shopping and weeping along to *Evita*, I can go to St Catherine's House and check out the marriage certificates. Somerset House too, if it's not too far away.

'Yes,' she said aloud, starting off across the college car park at Scout's Pace. Twenty running, twenty walking. Jacob's ladders straddled her path, strong golden rungs of sun.

Sam achieved a great deal. By the time she arrived back at Victoria to meet her mother, platform 19 for the 18.17, she was bursting to show off. A quick kiss on the cheek, a peremptory enquiry about the show, and Sam was off, yelling her news over announcements for platform alterations and late arrivals and the frantic rush-hour roar. Everybody was hurrying, frowning, rude, clumsy. Helen suggested Sam could perhaps start again, once they were safely settled on the train.

Sam managed to swallow her excitement while they bagged their window seats, unloaded their styrofoam coffees and sugar sachets and packed their shopping on to the grey overhead racks. Two Dickins and Jones carriers acquired by Helen and a tiny Our Price bag belonging to Sam, the words *Remain in Light* just visible through the plastic. The force of throwing herself on to the blue and green seat sent the tape straight through the metal bars and down on her head. Since she was supposed to be saving money, Sam surreptitiously slipped it into her basket, hoping Helen hadn't noticed.

Bubbling with impatience, she watched her mother brush imaginary crumbs from her seat before sitting down. Court shoes, tights, silk scarf, even after an entire day in London, Mum looks immaculate, thought Sam. She looked down at her big sixties floral skirt, cheap because of the stain on the hem that wouldn't wash out.

'Right, sweetheart,' Helen said at last. 'Tell me all about it.'

Immediately words started to tumble from Sam's mouth, information leaping out from every corner. First she went to St Catherine's House. A horrible modern building, just opposite Bush House. There are statues of two naked men, said Sam, sharing a torch that looks suspiciously like a Mr Whippy ice-cream. Helen smiled at the description. Marriages were indexed in alphabetical order and bound in volumes. One for each quarter of the year.

'How did you know where to start?'

Sam doubled-back to explain how she and Peter had worked out a date for Gayle and Julian's marriage. Helen found the jumbled information rather difficult to follow.

'Anyway, I found the entry almost straight away,' said Sam. 'It was amazing. 20 October 1961.'

She paused for dramatic effect. And to open her packet of smoky bacon crisps.

'I didn't get a copy of the full certificate there and then,' she continued, 'because it was *incredibly* expensive. I decided that if they'd stayed married, then I could always go back and get it later.'

'Why did you think they might not have stayed married, darling?'

Helen was pleased that Sam was involving them in the search, rather than shutting them out. But none the less she found herself flinching at the ease with which she uttered the names Gayle and Julian. They sounded like friends.

'Pat told me . . .' continued Sam, off at another tangent.

'Pat?'

'The social worker I saw in January. You know, the one who didn't tell me I'd got eye-liner all down my face.'

'The eye-liner,' Helen smiled. 'Yes, of course.'

'Anyway, Pat said it was common in adoption cases – when parents are married – for the pregnancy to be the result of an affair or something . . .'

Since January, Helen had witnessed Sam swinging back and forth between elation and world-ending misery, depending on how things were going. Quite like her old self, Tom had commented, remembering the lifeless, hopeless girl she had become after Anna's death. Helen couldn't quite work out where Peter fitted into the picture – not a boyfriend, apparently – but she suspected that he had made a huge difference. She smiled and looked over at her eager daughter, perched on the edge of the seat, bouncing one leg across the other and fiddling with her hair.

Helen was concerned, though, that Sam was treating her hunt for her natural mother as a huge game. Not once had she seen evidence that Sam had considered the possible consequences of her detective work. That the truth might be unpleasant, worse still, uncontrollable, did not appear to have entered her head.

Outsiders had always judged Sam the more outgoing twin, the more extrovert. Ever since they were little girls, Sam had craved the limelight as much as Anna'd liked to get on with things in her own quiet way. Like Tom and me, I suppose, reflected Helen. But for all her noise and thunder, Sam's confidence had always been easily dented. She needed approval, an audience. Despite her pessimism, Anna was emotionally more robust than her sister. More independent, certainly. And although being a twin was fundamental to them both, Helen had always suspected that Sam had built her identity on that single fact whereas Anna saw it as one characteristic among many that made her who she was.

After the accident, Helen had watched Sam becoming obsessed with blood-lines. The idea that it was physical origins and genes and biology that mattered most. More than love or shared history or behaviour. Eighteen years is a long time, thought Helen fiercely. What if she finds Gayle, but the woman won't see her? After all she's been through, I couldn't bear it if her life was shattered all over again. She's come so far. We all have.

Mesmerised by the sound of her own voice, Sam was still talking.

'The point is that Pat was right.'

Helen suddenly felt uncomfortable. 'I'm sorry, sweetheart,' she apologised, stalling for time.

'God, Mum,' Sam drawled. 'I was saying that Pat was right.'

'Right about what?'

'Mum! Haven't you been listening to a word I've said? About them divorcing.'

Sam stressed the words, as if she was talking to an idiot. 'They *did* divorce. In December 1967.'

'Was anyone else named on the record, a co-respondent?'

'I don't think so,' answered Sam, not altogether sure what her mother meant. 'So then I went back to St Catherine's House . . .'

'Hold on, hold on,' interrupted Helen. 'Back from where?'

'From Somerset House,' Sam said, as if talking to a half-wit. 'Because it occurred to me that Gayle might have got married again. And if she had, then she would have a different surname – not Faye or Driver – which would explain why I couldn't find her.'

Sam fixed her mother with a determined look. 'So, as I was saying, I went back to the marriage bit and went through the women with surnames beginning with D from January 1968. And, lo and behold, she had married again. In April 1973. To a Colin Saunders.'

'And did that marriage last?' asked Helen.

'I don't know,' answered Sam. 'I only just had time to apply for the full certificate and pay, before they chucked us all out at four-thirty.'

'Hence the Our Price bag?' smiled Helen.

'Hence the Our Price bag,' admitted Sam, tipping her head back and pouring the crumbs of the crisps into her mouth. Having brushed the speckles from her fingers, she then folded the maroon packet into four neat squares and wedged it into the top of her empty coffee cup.

The train rattled out of the Surrey countryside and into Sussex.

They were home by ten. Sam went straight to the phone to update Peter. As she talked, she imagined him carrying the phone from the hall to the crooked claw-footed table in the corner of the living-room, flicking the wire to stop it getting caught under the door.

'Anyway,' she said, finishing up, 'I'll probably have to go back in case she got divorced from husband number two . . .'

Peter suddenly slammed the receiver down on the table. Sam could hear him thumping about at the other end.

'Peter?' she shouted. 'Peter?'

What the fucking hell is he doing, she muttered to herself. No answer. She sighed, jigging around from foot to foot while she waited. One minute passed. Two.

'Yes, I am still here,' she said stroppily when his voice suddenly reappeared in her ear. 'What? Yes, I've got one here. Hold on. 0–8–6–5,' she repeated. '7–8–5–9–9–6. What? Peter!'

Sam stood holding the silent receiver in her hand, pulse racing. Her fingers felt like icicles. The address Gayle had given on her marriage certificate in 1973 had sounded familiar to Peter. He'd checked and there it was, fourteen years later, on his list from the 1981 phone directory. 13 Banbury Drive, Oxford. 0865 785996. Mr S. Faye. Snatching up the receiver, he'd shouted energetically at Sam, 'Ring – now – and call me back. OK?'

Slam.

Sam's heart beat out a tattoo behind her ribs as she looked at the number on the pad. Giant black numbers. The adrenalin pumped at her temples. I can't do this, she panicked, putting the receiver back. I'm going to faint. Resting her elbows on the hall table, she leaned forward on to the cool wood until the dizziness had gone.

She realised she had to pull herself together. Slowly does it. Standing. Clearing her throat. Sam held her hands out flat, palms down, and watched them tremble. Like an amateur pianist anticipating the baton. Sam pressed the button in the middle of the phone, let it go, then heard the dialling tone purr in her ear. It sounded threatening.

CHAPTER 10

When Sam had finally got through on the phone the following morning – after six attempts – a chatty voice had confided that Mr and Mrs Faye were away. I've just popped in to feed the cat, she gossiped. Lovely animal. I'm after their daughter, Gayle, really, hedged Sam, crossing her fingers behind her back. So stupid of me, but I just can't seem to lay my hands on her address. You don't happen to have it, do you? Phone number too? No? Just address then. The woman laughed. Only just moved back this way a month or so ago. But then she's not the type to send change of address cards. No, not at all, Sam agreed. Thank you. Thank you very much. Two minutes later, she'd found herself the proud possessor of the address she'd spent three months trying to get.

Sam looked down at the precious information, written neatly on her headed notepaper. Perhaps she should read it through one last time, just in case she'd missed a spelling mistake or something.

Mrs Gayle Saunders
10 Kingsland Close
Headington
OXFORD
OX3 1AJ

3 April 1981

Dear Gayle

I don't know how to start this letter, so I think the best thing is to just begin. I hope it makes sense and does not come as too much of a shock. I believe that you gave birth to twins at St Saviour's Hospital in Oxford on 12 November 1962. I am one of those twins.

My sister Anna and I had a very happy childhood. Our parents are wonderful and we are a very close family. I love them more than I can say. (PS They know I am writing to you now and have completely supported my decision to trace you. They understand why it's important to me to find out about my background.)

Anna and I were always made to feel special, because we were twins and because we were adopted. But I always wondered about you and what you looked like and hoped one day I would be able to meet you.

I do not know why you decided you could not keep us. I admit I did feel hurt when I was younger, but now I am eighteen I understand that there were good reasons for doing what you did. I appreciate it must have been a difficult time in your life.

I do not want to rake up the past or intrude in any way, but I would very much treasure a photo of you (and Julian) as well as any information you feel able to share, such as your birthday, his birthday, what you do, how you met, etc. etc. I've also always wondered about our birth and family history.

If it is not too painful for you, could we meet? I could tell you a little bit about myself in return. Please write.

She hoped she'd hit the right tone. Warm, friendly, but not too personal. But how to sign off? *Yours sincerely* seemed too formal, and putting all her middle names seemed too pretentious. So she simply wrote *Sam Whittaker* at the bottom of the page, then folded the letter three times. Exact, straight lines. Then two licks, one up and one down the foul gummed strip. There. Sealed.

Suddenly the memory of a game she and Anna used to play when they were twelve or thirteen bounced into her mind. They were two career girls, with boyfriends overseas, who shared a flat, cooked for themselves. It was a make-believe that involved much sprinkling of cheap pink envelopes with Mum's perfume and writing personalised variations of SWALK. on the flip side. SEALED WITH A LOVING KISS. Sam, more often than not, added an 'E' if there was room. A LOVING ESKIMO KISS. The best sort of kiss because it was for everyone. Mothers, fathers, friends, sisters. She smiled to herself. All those childhood bedtimes when she and Anna were little, the ritual of nose rubbing instead of routine peckings at lips or cheeks. The scratch of Dad's beard on her chin, the faint smell of Mum's perfume, nearly worn off by the end of the day. How Anna's nose was always cold. SWALEK. What would Gayle's reaction be to that sort of inscription . . .

Sam allowed the smile to fade from her lips. Back to business. I ought to allow at least a week, she calculated as she swivelled round on her chair to reach the radio on her music centre. Silence. Bryan Ferry cut off in his prime. Time for my letter to get there, time for Gayle to write, time for hers to get to me. About a week. Ten days, to be safe.

April 1981. London. Brixton erupted, a volcano of violence and racial hatred and petrol bombs. The news was full of burning cars, a divided urban battleground of ash and smoke. Everything painted grey, soiled black. Scorched. Belfast on our own doorstep, said Tom, shaking his head, as he and Sam and Helen sat watching the BBC news. A half-dressed mannequin from an old-fashioned men's outfitters stood alone in the street, surrounded by broken glass and looted shops. It cut a poignant figure on its single spindly leg. Its fresh-pressed white shirt was immaculate, an unintended symbol of surrender.

Sam heard nothing from Oxford.

May 1981. London. After three months of trial, a thirty-five-year-old long-distance lorry driver was jailed for life at the Old Bailey for thirteen murders and seven attempted murders. A five-year rule of a modern-day slasher, over. Just before Easter 1979 he had killed a girl called Josephine Whitaker. Whitaker with one 't', not two. Sam remembered how upset Anna had been at the coincidence of the name, at the screaming crassness of the tabloid headlines. 'Yorkshire Ripper 10 – Police O.'

Still no word.

June 1981. London. The Jam released 'Funeral Pyre', ambulance workers threatened to strike, The Specials released 'Ghost Town'. More signs and sounds of the volatile times.

Preparations were under way to revive the nation's sagging spirits. Queens and dukes and heads of state, white gold and sapphires and diamonds and ivory taffeta. Five hundred thousand pounds for one Royal Wedding. Diana said yes quite promptly, boasted the Prince of his nineteen-year-old bride-to-be. Half a million pounds, cheap at twice the price.

In Chichester, Sam broke up for the summer. One week of holiday, two weeks. Peter went away with Annette. Sam ate to pass the time. Ice-cream, chocolate, wine gums. The silence boxed her ears. Peter came back. After three weeks of freedom, she'd had enough. I can't afford to wait any longer, she thought as her itchy fingers dialled Peter's number. It's driving me mad. Please come with me to Oxford, she begged as he answered the phone. Please.

A Monday morning in July, sunny after dawn, about seventy-two degrees Fahrenheit. No wind, becoming humid later. Sam was standing in front of the full-length mirror in the bathroom, pulling a loose thread from her waistband. Her skirt was a little tighter than she remembered.

Sam had spent ages getting ready, nervous and desperate to create the right impression. She'd briefly considered the Tory-blue interview suit her mother had made her buy from Marks & Spencer last autumn. You never know when you might need something smart, Helen had said at the time, ignoring Sam's caustic remarks about politicians' wives. She had worn it once, to her grandma's seventy-fifth birthday party. Despite wanting to be seen to have made a special effort, the second they walked in the door Sam realised that she might as well have come in fancy dress. She would have felt no more out of place in a fairy outfit or pirate patch than in this middle-aged uniform. Adults kept telling her how nice she looked . . .

The weather forecast had predicted another hot day. Given they would be spending several hours on the train, Sam decided comfort was the priority. A clean white T-shirt, her calf-length pink and grey patterned fifties skirt and new black cotton espadrilles. Bare legs, quite brown. She thought she did herself justice. Interesting, chic but not formal, confident in a relaxed sort of a way. A smattering of burgundy lipstick, the slightest hint of eye-liner, and she was ready.

As she turned to go downstairs, she caught sight of the heap of rejected clothes on her bed. I'll tidy them up later, she lied to herself, knowing full well that Helen would get there first.

The clock above the kitchen door tapped out the time. Tick. Tick. Nearly half past eight. Tom folded his paper in on itself, then flapped it down on the table. *The Times. Monday July 27 1981. No 60,990.*

'Morning, Dad,' said Sam, kissing the top of her father's head before going over to kiss her mother at the window. Comforting early morning rituals.

'Sleep well?' enquired Helen, as always.

'Not bad,' Sam replied, as always. 'Any coffee left in the pot?'

'I'll bring you a mug.'

Tom looked up from his crossword.

'What time's your train?'

'Twenty to ten,' Sam replied, helping herself to a piece of cold toast despite the butterflies in her stomach. 'But I'm meeting Peter at the station at half-nine.'

'Do you want a lift?'

'No, thanks. I've got loads of time. Might as well walk.'

She put her hands up to feel the back of her head. Her hair was now just about long enough to go up in a bun. This morning it felt a bit lopsided and a few stray wisps were already escaping from the leather holder skewered to her skull. Sam adjusted the stubby wooden stick.

'Right-oh,' said Tom.

Sam looked at her reflection in the shop windows, bag swinging against her side, as she walked down through the pedestrian precinct towards the station. Up North Street, past the Cross, down South Street. Her fingers played with her locket as she anticipated the day ahead.

Sam hadn't altogether decided what she was going to do once they got to Oxford. Maybe she'd just go to the house, to see if she could get a glimpse of her natural mother. Maybe she would ring the bell, pretend to be selling something. Make out she was lost. She'd put together a package of photos, just in case. A *This Is Your Life* of the Whittaker twins. At the last moment, she'd added the picture of Anna playing her violin at a music competition in July 1979. It was the most up-to-date photo of her sister that she had.

Everyone thought she was making a mistake. Even Peter. But Sam had made excuses for Gayle for nearly four months. She must be ill, she must be on holiday, the letter must have got lost in the post. To make sure, Sam sent a second copy. Recorded delivery this time. No response.

Just before college had finished, Sam had become convinced that a phone had been installed since she'd spoken to Mr and Mrs Faye's neighbour three months ago. Perhaps she could ring Gayle? The operator informed her that there was no number listed for a Mrs Gayle Saunders in Kingsland Close, ex-directory or otherwise.

I've done everything I possibly can, Sam defended herself, as she waited at the pedestrian crossing. The only logical thing left is to go there in person. I don't have to identify myself if I don't want to. The anonymous flashing green man started bleeping. Sam crossed the road and went into the station car park.

It was nearly lunchtime when she and Peter arrived in Oxford. The sun was beating down on the pavements, sending up a shimmering haze above the tarmac surface of the road. Rows of black, white and green cars were baking in the car park below. Triangular pennants drooped in the still air, bunting for Wednesday's wedding. Doesn't look very royal, Sam thought. And I don't remember there being so many yellow bicycles when we came before. Why yellow?

Peter was studying the tourist map of the city pinned outside the main entrance to the station, shading his eyes from the glare.

'We need to take a bus. Headington's way out there,' he said, tapping the right-hand edge of the glass. 'And we're here, west of the city.'

Sam looked down towards the main road with its steady stream of cars. She felt sick with apprehension, now they were here.

'Let's start walking,' he suggested, 'then see if we can't pick up a ride in the centre. OK?'

Sam nodded, happy to have the decisions taken out of her hands.

The two friends linked arms and walked. Big Wizard of Oz steps took them over a little river, past a bus and coach station and up a road bulging with artistic cafés, an Army surplus shop. At the top, they hit a junction. It looked like university to their left and straight ahead, broad grey-stoned streets with colleges and monuments. To their right was the shopping bit. The autumnal colours of W. H. Smith, the turquoise of Barclays Bank, friendly and familiar high street names. Peter was sure he remembered this street from their trip to the County Records Office in January, just from the other end. There are a whole bunch of bus stops up at the top in any case, he said. Going the wrong way, surely, Sam murmured, but she followed him anyway.

Everything smelt festive, a town itching to celebrate. Pastry and beer, strawberries, the odd waft of pizza. Herds of tourists scuttled up and down the red, white and blue pavements clutching guidebooks in Italian and German and Japanese. Resolute standard-bearers held umbrellas aloft in an attempt to prevent their flocks from straying.

'*Allons-y* . . .'

Sam drank in the atmosphere, all five senses heightened by anticipation and purpose.

They kept walking, looking back over their shoulders every other step for a bus with HEADINGTON stamped across its forehead. They were on a road with proper traffic now. Mini-cabs, estate cars and refrigerated lorries thundered by. Open-topped air-conditioned tour buses crawled, instructing the hungry eyes of their passengers to lurch from side to side like spectators at a tennis match.

'To your right, you will see the Examination Halls, to your left The Queen's College. Ladies and gentlemen, we are now approaching Magdalen Bridge where we will stop for an opportunity to take photographs. Magdalen Bridge is the traditional site of May Morning celebrations and in 1873 . . .'

What did happen in 1873, wondered Sam, as the double-decker moved out of earshot.

Sam and Peter always seemed to be between stops, as bus after bus shot past. Nearly an hour later, they had sweated their way up a sharp hill – where they stopped while Peter rolled them both a cigarette – trudged on past what looked like a college and into a suburban parade of shops. The straps of Sam's espadrilles were starting to rub.

Headington was anonymous, like most outskirts. Characterless babies in pushchairs, harassed mothers, the occasional father bribing his child with sweets. There was an impatient line outside a newsagent-cum-post office, queuing for the moment when CLOSED would be turned to OPEN. Ready, steady, go. The crowd surged forward, desperate to cash giros, buy tax discs and stamps.

'They're sure to know Kingsland Close,' said Peter. 'You wait here.'

Sam stood in the heat, letting her eyes wander. She'd imagined Gayle in a beautiful place, a far cry from these ordinary daytime scenes. There were fewer bikes up here. Lots of sunhats, mint and apricot sleeveless vests, unflattering white shorts, denim skirts, occasional students in old-fashioned summer frocks or flannels. Any of these women in their late thirties could be Gayle.

'Right,' said Peter in her ear.

Sam jumped, aching with nerves.

'Sorry,' he apologised, handing her an open can of Coke. 'OK. We keep on this street for a couple of blocks, cross over by the gas station, then take a right. Go left at the bottom of that street, take the next right and we're there. About fifteen minutes. You up for that?'

A quarter of an hour to blast-off, thought Sam. *Mierda*. She counted down the minutes as they followed the directions. Fourteen minutes to go. Thirteen minutes to go. Twelve. Eleven. Ten. Safely over the road, exhaust fumes hanging in the polluted hot air. Nine minutes. The throb of the pumps on the garage forecourt, the gallons ticking away. All the way down Princes Drive. Four minutes. Left into Queens Avenue. Just sixty seconds to go. And we're here. Sam found herself next to an elegantly engraved sign, black letters on white.

Kingsland Close was a pebble-dashed cul-de-sac, come down in the world since its glory days of the 1950s. About a dozen semi-detached houses faced one another impassively across concrete driveways and rusted iron gates. Homes the colour of sand, fit for heroes. Despite the defiant bunting hanging from the streetlamps, ready for Wednesday, there was an air of defeat about the place.

Peter squinted at the nearest blue front door, identical to its neighbour except for the number. Odd numbers on their side, even numbers opposite.

They crossed over. Nobody was about, although occasional sounds escaped into the mid-afternoon silence. A radio, someone calling, a lawn-mower. The heat gobbled the noises up, leaving no trace. The people in Number 6 had hung a Union Jack from one of their first-floor windows, CONGRATULATIONS CHARLES AND DIANA sewn across it in tidy black letters.

Sam felt as if every house was watching, sizing them up as they passed. Her thoughts of simply observing from a safe distance seemed absurd now. She felt she was moving at half-speed.

Towards her own happy-ever-after? Now here they were, at the end of the row. No more numbers left. Sam looked straight ahead at the scuffed playing-fields. A few kids were kicking a ball about. They sounded happy. In that suspended moment, all Sam wanted to do was to run across the grass and join them. To be a child again with her head full of nothing but fun and summer holidays and the promise of swimming-pools.

'This is it,' said Peter, pushing his fingers through his floppy black fringe. 'Ready?'

'No,' she muttered, squeezing his left hand tightly.

This was it. She took a deep breath, then pushed open the gate. Peacock blue, she registered. Anna's favourite colour. A good omen? There was no car in the drive.

The sound of the gate grating on the concrete announced their arrival.

CHAPTER 11

As she waited for the door to be answered, Sam fiddled with her hair. Amazing that it had stayed up.

'Knock harder,' suggested Peter.

She felt sick with apprehension. Deep breaths. In, out, in, out. Fussing with the pink and grey material of her skirt, Sam rapped again. The glass stung her knuckles. Inside, nothing stirred. Peter cupped his hands over his eyes, trying to peer into the dark hall.

'*Nada*,' he said, straightening up.

All that was visible through the front window which overlooked the unkempt lawn was white curtain lining. Probably the lounge, commented Peter. Unlikely to be drapes in the kitchen. He disappeared round the corner of the house, just in case Gayle was at the back and hadn't heard them. The blue paint of the six-foot-high side gate was blistered and peeling round the edges. Not used much, he figured. He stretched his right hand over the wood to see if there was a bolt, then paddled around, picking up tiny red flakes of rust. Short of climbing over and forcing it from the other side . . .

'No luck?' Sam asked, as he came back into view.

He shook his head.

'I knocked again.'

'I guess she's not here,' he said, putting his wrists on Sam's disconsolate shoulders and resting them there. She felt punctured, as though all the energy had oozed out of her.

'Got some paper,' he added, 'so we can leave a note?'

Sam's wicker basket was still leaning against the frosted glass of the front door. Bending down, she started to scramble around for a pen that worked. Immediately, she became aware of a noise in the house. A person's feet, bare feet, were coming towards her. She stood up, rigid, heart thumping, and automatically took a step back

114

into thin air, off the concrete step. As she struggled to regain her balance, the door was opened, no more than a couple of inches.

'Yes?'

The voice was aggressive, shooting suspiciously through the narrow gap. Sam was paralysed. Her shocked legs had turned to jelly. Cold jelly knees, cold jelly arms, cold jelly tongue. If she attempted to open her mouth, she knew that nothing but squeaky cartoon babble would pour out.

Nobody moved, nobody spoke. Then Sam felt Peter shift at her elbow as the woman repeated her question. Combative, serrated. It sounded like a threat.

'Hi. We're looking for Mrs Gayle Saunders,' Peter said into the space between the sharp edge of the door and the frame.

'What of it?'

'We've come about Sam and Anna. Sam Whittaker?'

Peter's words hung in the air, the suburban silence of the afternoon crackling around the three of them. Then, without warning, the woman unslotted the guard-chain and let the door fall open.

Sam felt as if she'd been punched in the chest. Anna. The woman was painfully thin, like someone who no longer had any need of food, and her face was ravaged and worn. But the raw material was the same. The same British blonde hair, fine and cut in a long bob, the same eyes, the same nose, the same chin. Only the forehead was wrong. Where Anna's birthmark should have been, crimson under her fringe, was white, white skin.

'You'd better come in,' said Gayle.

Peter and Sam made an awkward crocodile as they followed Gayle down the gloomy hall, then into a room to their left. The room smelled sour, of stale cigarette smoke and dirty cups and recycled breath. Gayle made her way over to the window and drew one of the heavy velvet curtains. A little surprised daylight filtered in, illuminating the specks of dust floating in the air. Sweeping a pile of newspapers on to the floor, Gayle motioned for them to sit on the sofa. She pulled her dressing-gown tightly across her emaciated chest, tucked her feet up and flopped into the armchair opposite. Immediately, she bobbed forward again to get the lighter and packet of Camels lying on the coffee table between them.

'Please excuse the mess,' she said, waving an arm to take in

the room and herself in one wide gesture. 'I was asleep, when
you . . .'

She stretched over to offer Peter a cigarette and a light, then fell
back in the chair to light her own. She noticed his eyes stray to
the green bottle and empty tumbler on the table.

'Medicinal purposes only,' she said in a baby-doll voice. 'I've
not been well.'

Barely looking at Sam, she caught Peter's gaze. 'Will you
join me?'

Peter sensed Sam squirm beside him, felt the heat of her
disapproval. Shaking his head in answer to Gayle's question, he
watched her pour a generous measure of gin, with a please-yourself
shrug. He recognised the signs. Until his father died, he'd lived
with that sort of medicine all of his life.

Sam sat appalled. By the house, by the squalor, but most of all
by Gayle herself. The mother of her dreams – Anna's mother –
surely not a woman like this? If only she could turn the clock
back. Ten minutes, that's all she needed. No grand reunion, just
her and Peter walking slowly back down Kingsland Close. The
camera would pick out their disappointed faces. Disappointed,
but not disillusioned. The scene would finish on a close-up of
the note they'd left, a clean white rectangle sticking out of the
silver letter-box. And . . . fade the lights. And . . . cut. Well done,
everyone, the director would gush, wonderful. If that doesn't get
them crying into their hankies, nothing will.

Sam's brain was overheating, throwing up images like confetti
in the vain hope of obscuring the truth. Tiny pieces of paper, pale
pink, pale blue, pale yellow, fluttering down over the big, black,
real Monday afternoon. She knew it was too late. She'd knocked
at her mother's door and the door had been answered. Too late.

'So you're Sam,' flirted Gayle. 'Not quite what I expected.'

'Excuse me?'

'And you are? Who? Not Anna?'

'No . . .' said Sam.

'I think there's some sort of mix-up here,' interrupted Peter.
'I'm Peter Newman, a friend of Sam's.'

She could feel the protective pressure of his hand on her back
through her T-shirt, felt grateful for it.

'This is Sam. She wrote you. You got the letter?'

Gayle lit a second cigarette from the burning stub of her first, narrowed her eyes. The temperature in the room dropped several degrees.

'What do you mean?' Gayle said slowly, her voice alert and wary once more. 'What's going on?'

Sam and Peter jumped in, misinterpreting her confusion. Words all jumbled up together in a competitive duet.

'You are Gayle?' said Peter. 'Gayle Saunders?'

'I came on my own,' said Sam simultaneously. 'Without Anna, because . . .'

But suddenly Gayle was shrieking, on her feet, yelling for them to get out. Her words rained down on them like blows, mindless and wild and threatening. Sam scrambled to her feet, terrified. She saw Peter go over to Gayle, ducking the flailing arms, the frenzied mouth, saw him link his arms firmly around Gayle's thin body. 'It's all right,' he was whispering. 'It's all right.'

As if from a distance, Sam watched Gayle sag as her panic subsided. She heard the sobs, but felt nothing but revulsion. No pity, no curiosity even. Just revulsion. She's your mother, your *mother*, Sam repeated over and over to herself. Gayle looked like a rag doll, a pathetic rag doll as Peter lowered her gently into the armchair. Sam felt her legs shaking, clutched the back of the sofa with her hands so as not to fall over.

'Watch her,' Peter whispered to Sam as he left the room in search of coffee.

'Don't leave me,' she pleaded, but he'd already gone. One minute. Two minutes. No sound in the fetid room but the rising and falling of breath, the occasional cry from the chair. Somewhere, Sam could hear the splash of water, as if Peter was washing up, the chink of a spoon against china, cupboards opening and shutting, then the comforting squeak of his trainers coming back.

'No milk, but major sugar to make up for it,' he said, giving Sam one of the two mugs. He stroked her damp cheek with the back of his free hand. 'Careful. It's hot.'

'What's going on?' she wailed under her breath. 'Why did she go mad? Who does she think we are?'

'I don't know,' Peter replied. He sounded determined. 'But we'll find out. Be patient for a while.'

He smiled at Sam, reassuring.

She nodded, wiping away the tears from her eyes with the back of her hand.

'I'm gonna try sober her up. You sit. Try to drink some coffee.'

Nearly four o'clock. Sam got up and ambled stiffly over to the window. It was humid now, the sun hidden behind muggy clouds. For once, the weather forecast was right, she thought, turning round again. Every corner of Gayle's living-room was branded on her mind. The imitation coal fire. The tiled mantelpiece, completely bare except for a blue glass ashtray. The florid red and pink carpet, wet where the gin had gone over.

Sam felt utterly drained, as if the tide had gone out. All afternoon Gayle had talked and Peter had listened, patient in the face of the long sentences punctuated by booze and cigarettes and tears. Round and round and round, until a disjointed tale had begun to emerge. There was a man. Colin Saunders? Her husband? No, he was long gone. A boyfriend, perhaps? Yes, once upon a time. Quick with his fists, though not at first. Not true that she owed him money. Gayle thought he'd found out about her babies, that he was using the knowledge and them to trick his way into her home. Terrified he'd hunted her down like before. Paranoia or justified fear, it was impossible to tell. In a way, it didn't matter.

Sam was convinced it was all a pack of lies to get Peter's sympathy. As Gayle talked and Peter listened, Sam appointed herself prosecutor, started to conduct her own mental interrogation. May I address the defendant? So, Mrs Saunders, when Mr Newman said they had come about Anna and Sam, why did you let them into your home? If you thought they had been sent to intimidate you by this aforementioned – may I suggest imaginary – man? Do you really expect us to believe you were in fear for your physical safety? And once Mr Newman and Ms Whittaker were inside, why your sudden change of heart? I can think of no adequate explanation.

It was a vicious voice and Sam knew it. Forcing herself to look at Gayle, she struggled to feel compassion. But her anger was too powerful. I HATE you, screamed the voice. Sam felt disgusted at the idea that she was related to this woman, contaminated. You make me SICK, screamed the voice. The fact that Gayle looked so like Anna made it even more unbearable. An obscene, mutated copy of her perfect Anna. I want to KILL you, screamed the voice.

Don't think about it, Sam said to herself, at once ashamed

and exhilarated by the violence of her thoughts. Rocking-horse emotions, to and fro, to and fro. Don't think about her. Don't think about what she is to you. Listen to Peter. Concentrate on Peter. Sam looked at him crouching in front of Gayle's chair, hands resting on each of the arms. She felt guilty about letting him do all the work, while she did nothing. Her dirty work. But she couldn't move.

'Gayle?' Peter was saying encouragingly, as if he was talking to a child. 'You did get a letter? Yes?'

Gayle nodded, head bowed.

'OK, good. Now, why did it upset you when I said Sam wrote the letter?'

'Because you were lying.'

'Lying about what?'

'You said you were . . .' she trailed off, not able to remember his name.

'Peter,' he slipped in.

'Peter,' she repeated, hollowly. 'Yes, Peter. That's right. You said you'd come about the twins.'

'Sam and Anna,' said Peter.

'I thought you were my Sam. But you said you were Peter.'

'For God's sake,' Sam snapped, irritated by the crippled exchange. '*I'm* Sam.'

Gayle slowly turned to look at her, blinking as if she'd forgotten she was there.

'But you can't be.'

Peter quickly glanced at Sam, pressing his index finger strongly against his lips, then carried on talking to Gayle in the same, low voice.

'Why can't she be Sam, Gayle?'

'Because,' she replied, 'my Sam was a boy. Two babies. A little girl and a little boy.'

Sam was sitting cross-legged in the middle of an over-priced double bed in the centre of Oxford. A last-minute cancellation, the landlady had said. Lucky to get anywhere at this time of year. The tourists have all gone up to London for the wedding. Peter was sitting in the window rolling himself a cigarette, looking out over the narrow street into the rooms of the imposing grey-stone college opposite.

She had no idea how Peter had got her out of the house in Headington. Sam remembered sitting on the wall outside, on her own, and hearing the goodbye and the front door slamming shut. And she remembered stripping her clothes off as soon as they got up to their room, as if a shower would wash away all traces of Kingsland Close. But everything in between was a blank. The free sachet of shampoo and tiny tablet of odourless soap hadn't been up to the task. My hair's nearly dry now, she thought, fingering the frizzy ends.

Peter's voice cut into her thoughts. 'Let's go grab something to eat. OK?'

The idea of putting food into her mouth was disgusting. But she thought she might as well do something, so she shuffled to the edge of the candlewick bedspread, then bent over to wrap the long black ribbons of her espadrilles round her ankles.

'Do you know where you're going?' Sam asked flatly, when they got out into the early evening air.

'No,' Peter replied. 'But we'll find something.'

They turned right and walked up the old street, overlooked by stone and timber and lascivious gargoyles. Sam could hear the silent snuffle of her sandals on the pavement. Amazing that her legs seemed to work. They felt as if they were nothing to do with her. Left, right, left, right. Spirals of laughter, chinking glasses, summer sounds scampered up a tiny alleyway into their path. Happy people having fun.

Peter had stopped at the top of the road. Smelled like a pub.

'The King's Arms?' he read.

Sam shook her head. Too chaotic. They crossed at the corner and carried straight on up a wide, wide street which got narrower the further they went. She heard herself babbling as they walked, enunciating the names of bookshops, pubs, streets, like a chant. Broad Street, Blackwells, The White Horse, Parkers, Trinity College, Balliol College. Her own private Oxford tour, with commentary. She was talking to drown out thinking. Anything, to stop herself from thinking. Peter just walked silently beside her, holding her hand tight.

Another junction, this time one they recognised. Ahead was the street that led back to the station, to their left the friendly shopping street they'd gone up earlier.

'We've walked in an enormous circle,' muttered Sam. 'Back to where we started.'

Her voice sounded dead, no character to it. As the irony of what she'd said hit her full in the face, she started to laugh. Sharp, bitter barks of laughter, like slaps on skin.

Peter watched her, eyes fixed on nothing, as the hysteria faded.

'What did you say to Mum and Dad?' she asked suddenly.

He was used to Sam's *non sequitur*s now, the way her mind kangaroo-hopped. And her habit of talking to herself out loud. Usually he'd've teased her. Not today.

'I said we'd found the address, no problem, but there was no one home. That we'd stay in Oxford and try again tomorrow.'

Sam didn't look at him.

'I thought it better to be cute with the truth,' he continued, 'until you'd worked out how you're gonna tell them.'

'*What* I'm going to tell them,' she said, starting to move on.

'OK, OK,' said Peter. '*What* you're gonna tell them.'

He glanced up at the street sign as he followed her. The Cornmarket. His head was reeling at how the conversation with Helen and Tom might go. I'm really sorry, Mr and Mrs Whittaker, but it turns out those kids you adopted are not twins after all. Anna, yes. But Sam? Sadly, we don't know where she came from right now. We're not sure what happened to the boy baby. The other Sam. Jesus, he thought, pushing his fringe away from his face.

They walked for a couple more minutes, until Peter noticed a jazzy sandwich board on the street promising pizza at reasonable prices. He looked at the squirling chalk letters, the hand-sketched pictures of wine glasses and balloons.

'How about this?'

Sam poked her head in the doorway and peered up the steep flight of stairs. The walls were covered with bright graffiti, black, purple and scarlet slashes of paint. Upstairs she could hear the muffled thump of music. Spiky pop. *More Songs About Buildings and Food.*

'Looks fine,' she answered.

A few hours later, they heard the bell of the college opposite their little B&B strike eleven.

Sam and Peter were lying in bed in T-shirts and underwear, his arm under her neck, two left hands tangled together. It was hard to tell where Peter's fingers finished and Sam's began. She could feel his breath, warm, barely there, brushing the top of her head.

It might have been awkward. They might have found themselves stranded unannounced in that grey physical no man's land between close friendship and intimacy, terrain almost impossible to negotiate. But the experiences of the day had thrown all normal patterns into shadow. At first Sam had thought Gayle was lying. But why would she lie, Peter'd said. She's got no reason to lie. Sam could see he was right. As the implications of what had happened in Kingsland Close sank in, her shoddily-built defences had crumbled. In the restaurant, in the road outside, up the stairs to their room. Drip by drip by drip, like blood seeping through a bandage.

Sam was trying to remember what she'd expected to feel on this red-letter day. A sense of achievement, for one thing, at having seen it through. Yes. Pride and self-respect at a painful task fulfilled, the telling of Anna's death. She had anticipated nerves, curiosity satisfied. And if she was honest, she had wanted to feel a sense of connection. A primary, instinctive blood-bond.

More than anything, Sam had expected to feel that it was over. Today should have been a full stop, before the start of a fresh chapter for them all. 'To make an end is to make a beginning.' Who wrote that? Can't remember, she muttered to herself. Finding Gayle should have been the final piece in a jigsaw, a one-thousand-piece deluxe puzzle. There. Done. A beautiful colour picture of a dignified woman with a sad face, smiling now. Just like on the lid.

Instead, Sam felt as if she had been buried alive. Because if Gayle was telling the truth, eighteen years of emotions and history and experience had been stolen from under her nose. If Gayle was telling the truth – and why should she lie? – Sam had lived her life in borrowed shoes, wearing somebody else's clothes. A boy's clothes. The trouser role, like a pantomime.

From the darkest corners of Sam's mind swam terrifying amaranthine Christian images of retribution and punishment and come-uppance, symbols so much stronger than those of redemption or love or hope. She had been arrogant, unworthy. Now she feared she had also been blind. Someone was holding up a looking-glass, hissing in her ear. Here, look through this. Truth is like the dark. It can't hurt you. Truth is good.

But it was too bright. It did hurt. The whiteness was scalding her eyes. You have to look, said the voices, insistent and rasping. Knowledge is power. You can't turn away now. Numbers danced in Sam's mind. Eighteen years. Eighteen years. I have nothing to put in their place, she sobbed. Please don't make me give them back.

As the New College clock across the road struck the quarter, grief began to trickle from Sam's shut eyelids. Slowly at first, then faster and faster until her cheeks were saturated. Peter held her safe in his arms until the nightmares loosened their grip. One o'clock, two o'clock, three o'clock, four.

As the pale dawn light started to leak round the edges of the thin floral curtains, Sam's breathing finally became regular and deep and steady. No more tears. Peter carefully extricated himself from under Sam's body. He creaked to his feet, stretching one arm, then the other, then shook the night out of his shoulders and crushed elbows. His bones felt rusty. Jesus, he was thirsty. And desperate for a cigarette. Ransacking his pockets for his papers and tobacco, he wished he had a jumper to take the chill off the early morning.

On impulse, Peter turned back to the sleeping bed. He braced himself against the wobbly headboard, then lowered himself towards Sam until their noses were almost touching. Gently, gently. His long black hair swung down like a veil, lapped against her eyelashes.

Sam did not feel the kiss. She was not conscious of him tenderly parting her warm mouth with his tongue, licking, tracing the soft line of her lips with his fingers. But in her sleep, she stirred.

CHAPTER 12

Sam counted the chimes of the bell – eight – nine – ten. Opening her eyes slowly, she rolled peacefully on to her back, listening to the reverberations dying away in the air outside.

There was no sign of Peter. She felt woolly from dozing, sticky everywhere. Perhaps she should summon the energy to get up and go to the loo? Perhaps. Shifting position, Sam stretched her legs and pointed her toes, like a ballerina. The bathroom was too far away, she decided. She was starving too and her mouth felt dry, all furry. I wonder where he is, she whispered to herself, relaxed and comfortable under the covers.

About five minutes later, Sam heard the sound of fumbling in the corridor outside. She turned her head towards the noise, half-propping herself up on an elbow, and watched as Peter bumped open the door and backed into the room. His hands were full.

'Hi, you,' he smiled, seeing she was awake. 'Room service.'

He seemed just the same as usual as he unloaded his picnic. Sam sat up, feeling a little self-conscious. First, he put two styrofoam cups on the bedside table, sending steam puffing out of the little holes in their plastic lids. Then he deposited a packet of chocolate digestive biscuits and a carton of orange juice on to the bed. Sam moved her legs to make room for him as he plonked down on the edge of the bed. Hands free, he slid a greasy package from where it was being squeezed under his right arm. Sam noticed it had left a sweaty mark on his T-shirt. His grey T-shirt. She blushed.

'The finale,' he said. 'One toasted cheese and tomato sandwich to go.'

'Tom-ay-toe,' mimicked Sam, still a little awkward. 'The perfect breakfast from the perfect waiter . . .'

Peter eased the lid off one of the coffees and took a sip, before starting to wrestle with the biscuits.

'I picked these up in this neat place at the top of the street. Big, black windows and an old-fashioned wooden sign above the door. ARTHUR WHITE. CONFECTIONER.'

Finally, he succeeded in prising out a biscuit. It looked devastated. Peter shook the packet, sending shards of plain chocolate and crumbs over the ridges of the bedspread.

'Shit!'

Sam laughed, then started choking when she inhaled a piece of cheese.

'Serves you right,' he teased, leaning forward and stealing her last bit of sandwich with his teeth. She felt the tip of his tongue dart against her fingers, like a serpent.

Peter slapped his hands down on his knees.

'Right, I'm outta here. I'll see you later outside that big bookstore just past the lights. OK?'

In the restaurant last night, they'd decided it'd be better if Peter went back to Headington alone. To talk to Gayle, to ask questions. Perhaps to tell her about Anna's death. He'd play that by ear.

'You remember where it is?' he added. 'The first block after the lights, on the right?'

While she was still sleeping earlier, Peter had taken a photo from Sam's stash in the brown A4 envelope tucked in her basket. She'd brought five or six from the family album, thinking she might show them to her new-found mother if things went well. He hated sneaking stuff behind Sam's back. But, after yesterday, he was sure she'd refuse to let him show Gayle a photo of Anna, and it'd be crazy to go without one. Just in case. Peter figured that Gayle had too many troubles of her own to care about anybody else's. He doubted if she'd even thought about them between then and now. She seemed swamped by her own life.

He knew it was gonna be hard to get Gayle to trust him in any case. He realised there was no immediate way of proving her story, but gut reaction told him she was speaking the truth. Or at least, what she thought was the truth. Peter twisted his hair back into a pony-tail, then let it fall loose. *Mierda*. Just the word of a freaked-out alcoholic. The whole thing was crazy.

'What time?' asked Sam.

'Three? A quarter after?'

Sam watched him drain his cup, then lob it into the rubbish bin by the door.

'You gonna be OK?'

'I'll be OK,' she replied, smiling up at him. 'Blackwells bookshop at fifteen hundred hours it is. And Peter . . .'

Her voice tailed off, suddenly embarrassed.

'Thanks. You know. For going.'

'No problem,' he said softly, kissing the top of her head, then went.

Sam drained the last of her sweet, milky coffee and snuggled back down. We don't have to be out of the room until one o'clock, so I've got nearly three hours. No hurry. Plenty of time. Drawing her knees up slightly, she took hold of a handful of fat at the top of her thighs and wobbled it. Definitely more than an inch . . .

'Disgusting,' she announced to the empty room. 'Tomorrow, I diet.'

She paused, weighing things up in her mind, then took another biscuit. One more wouldn't hurt. And she really was hungry this morning.

'Eighty-eight calories,' she read from the side of the packet. I don't have to eat anything for the rest of the day, she added in her head. Then, taking a defiant bite, chocolate side down, Sam let her mind free-fall back two hours. To every word, every smell, every movement.

At eight o'clock, she'd also been woken by the bells and by a prickling sensation that she was being watched. She'd opened her eyelids a fraction to see Peter sitting at the open window. Such a typical Peter position, she remembered thinking. Left leg dangling down, right leg drawn up, chin resting on his knee, right hand holding his fringe back off his face, burning homemade cigarette pinched between his thumb and finger. Statue of Peter Newman. A study in marble. Circa 1981.

He smiled at her sleepy face. For no reason, she shivered. A delicious cold ripple from her spine to the back of her neck.

'OK?' he said softly. She nodded as he flicked the soggy end of his roll-up out of the window and swung his legs down off the sill. Sam felt something shift in the pit of her stomach as Peter padded over towards the bed.

'You are lovely this morning,' he said, meaning it. The mattress wobbled as he sat himself down in the middle and crossed his long bare legs.

Sam blushed, the banter fizzling out on her lips.

'So are you,' she replied, meaning it too.

He was beautiful, in fact. Shit. This is Peter, she thought . . . Embarrassed, she looked at her scrunched white top, the visible marks of her troubled night.

'I feel a bit crumpled actually.'

Her voice sounded so croaky in her ears. Different.

'Why not take it off . . . ?'

In one fluid movement, Peter had folded his arms diagonally across his chest and pulled his long grey T-shirt up over the back of his head.

'You can have mine.'

Sam was astounded to find herself doing as she was told, without question. Awkwardly easing out first one arm, then the other, she inched her T-shirt up her face, trapping her nose and the chain of her locket, up over her forehead. She shook her hair free and tossed the ball of white material on to the floor, with a casualness she did not feel. She was aroused at the idea of being on display, she realised, as she dropped her eyes to Peter's grey top. Lying on the bed between them. She did feel modest, but still didn't reach for it.

Peter leaned over and touched the bridge of Sam's nose with the backs of his nails. Her eyes slipped shut and she sat very straight, very still, giddy at his fingers tracing a line down her nose. Now they were bumping softly over her lips, now over her chin, now doubling back to follow the line of her jaw.

'This OK?' he whispered. So close, she could feel his breath tickling her face as she nodded. Yes, this is OK.

Sam sucked in her ribs as the sheet slithered off her naked legs. She and Peter looked like an echo of one another. Crossed legs, brown arms, white bodies, one plump and one slim. Instinctively, Sam folded her hands across her lap, self-conscious about her soft, round stomach. She started when Peter rested a nonchalant hand on the inner side of her knee, firm and possessive. Its heat chilled her. Sam was sure the pounding of her heart would tear her chest apart. So loud, so exaggerated. The pulse of blood, in her ears, in her chest, between her legs, seemed to fill the corners of the room.

Her eyes flew open as Peter's subtle fingers trickled down between her breasts. He caught her gaze. He was naked now, somehow. Just the leather bracelet on his right wrist, earring in his left ear. As always. His black mane of hair was off his face, grazing the backs of his shoulders. Unconsciously, Sam tucked her hair back behind her ear. I never realised how solid Peter was, she marvelled, lapping the sight of him in. His tall body, his luminous skin, the slight ruffles of hair round his nipples and in the hollow of his chest. Wiry, strong arms. No waist.

Sam's pupils flared as her eyes slid lower. She'd never known a man so sensual, so easy, arms resting patiently by his side. His penis was erect. Pale and thin and long, it belonged exactly with his body. She could feel his never-ending gaze on her, but she couldn't look him in the face.

Relaxed, Peter leaned over and gathered up all four pillows. The mattress tipped. Sam felt herself being pressed back into the soft pile. Now she was half-sitting, half-lying. Her legs came uncrossed at the ankles, shifted slightly apart. He unfolded her protective arms, positioned them carefully alongside her body.

'Don't move,' she heard him whisper.

Still she did as she was told. He kissed her eyelashes, then the tip of her nose. Sam waited to feel his lips on her mouth, but instead tasted a finger sliding up and over the tops of her teeth. Then felt his hair nuzzling under her chin, just seconds before his tongue licked the underside of her nipples. One, then the other. Her head felt too heavy for her neck. Prickles of heat shot through her body.

Suddenly, she felt the bed rock as Peter shifted on to his front.

'Keep your eyes closed,' he breathed.

His hands were kneading the hidden skin of her thighs. His hair, like a sheet of water, was falling over her body. She was only half-aware of the scratchy material of her knickers as Peter eased them down, expertly unfolding her legs and straightening them out.

He lay still, cheek against her stomach, as if listening for the heartbeat of a baby. It was too intimate a gesture. Tears came to Sam's eyes as she stroked his head, loving him. She felt the long strands of hair slide away through her fingers. Now he was kneeling on the floor. Anchoring his hands under her, he pulled her body down the bed towards him. He draped first one leg, then the other, over his shoulders, left and right, crooked at the knees.

Sam heard herself whimper as the tip of his tongue swam over her, darting like a fish. Teasing, pricking her clitoris with tiny sucks, butterfly kisses, never staying in one place for an instant.

Sam felt as if she was blindfolded, being spun round and round by dozens of multiplying hands. Helter-skeltering until active desire at last found its voice.

Harder, harder, shouted Sam in her head. More. And Peter's fingers responded, as if they could hear, plunging without warning inside her. Thousands of wet and craving fingers, pushing, sliding, lashing, colliding, penetrating, slipping, satiating.

Five minutes later, Sam was cocooned safe between Peter's legs. Lovers between the sheets. Resting on his chest, Sam could hear the rhythm of his heart. The world looked the same as when she'd left it, everything back in focus, as if nothing had happened.

'What about you?' she whispered shyly up at Peter's chin. He smiled.

'You,' he said, 'are very lovely. Now go to sleep.'

Ten – eleven – twelve.

Fucking bells, thought Sam automatically, amazed to realise she had aroused herself simply by thinking about what had happened. '"The poor man's only music,"' she muttered. Off-hand, she couldn't remember where the phrase came from. It was in her little book, though, its pages crammed with lines copied from poems, novels and songs. Alphabetically by author, Armatrading and Costello, Dickinson, Eliot and Milton, Thomas and Shakespeare. The quotable wisdom of hundreds of years pressed inside its square, fabric covers. I can look it up when I get home. Honest.

It was the first time Sam had made love for two years. Not since that one and only join-the-dots time with Andrew. She remembered the smell of the rubber, the sense of experiment and purpose with which they'd set about things. His parents' kitchen afterwards, their wedding banquet of Coke and toast and fags. It seemed so adolescent, looking back on it. So innocent.

Shit, nearly two years ago. Wednesday, 8 August. 1979. The day before Anna had been killed. The very day before. And the two things had become linked inextricably in her mind, a tangled mess of limbs and blood and semen and guts. Until this morning, Sam had never thought she would wriggle out from under the cliché that sex equalled death. That they were one and the same thing.

'And now Peter . . .'

Sam linked her fingers above her head, wondering if the desire had always been in her, just hidden. Him too? Her joints cracked.

'I'd better get up,' she sighed, kicking the covers back. The three remaining biscuits fell on the floor. In a rare tidying mood, Sam scooped them up and put them on the bedside table. Crumbs and paper and rubbish to the bin, the unopened box of orange to her bag for later. Picking up her scrumpled T-shirt from the floor, she then retrieved her knickers from under the bed and started looking for a comb.

Without warning, Sam's spirits were suddenly punctured by an image of Peter in Gayle's airless sitting-room. Heavily, she sat herself down on the end of the bed and let the world come rushing in. All morning, she'd successfully declared Kingsland Close off mental limits. Sex had acted as an anaesthetic. The scene-of-crime barriers had stayed up, the cameras had kept away. Now, Sam felt her throat constrict as everything came back to her, vulgar and bright.

She shut her eyes as questions started swarming all over her again, wrapping the bedspread round her like a cloak. Questions like wasps, stinging in her ears and her nose. The thing was, she had to force herself to remember. Because she had to work out what she wanted, before Peter came back, before she got home to her parents.

So. What did she think? At the instant Gayle had denied her yesterday, Sam had been engulfed by white rage. Erotic and obsessive. She'd felt overwhelmed with the need to destroy, to torture, to smash bones against a wall until the bricks ran red. She'd felt exhilarated, bloated by violence. As if nothing less absolute would do. If Peter hadn't got her out of the house, she would have attacked Gayle.

Next had come the shock. No thought, no feeling, as she babbled through the streets of Oxford at Peter's side like a zombie. She'd watched him eat, watched him swallow, as if these were alien acts. Beyond her comprehension.

Back in their room, the horror of it all. The sense of desolation when she accepted that Gayle was telling the truth. Sam realised she didn't care that she'd been cheated of her blood-mother. The bereavement was the loss of Anna, as it sank in that they could not be twins. Not sisters, even. Anna was not hers any more. Lessons in Grief, Part Two.

Unintelligible irridescent dreams, hour after hour. She was standing at a crossroads, a fairground hurdy-gurdy grinding in her ears.

This way, ladies and gentlemen, for fixed fate. An easy path to follow to the harsh Old Testament world of your nightmares. Roll up, roll up. You know what to expect. You choose. The other path, ladies and gentlemen? Free choice. An uphill struggle, ladies and gentlemen, a question of mind over matter. Much better to choose the way you know . . . She couldn't remember everything, only that Peter had been there. Holding her like a child.

And now? Sam remembered the next stage from before, from after the accident. The point when she would have to accept the knife sticking into her heart was hurting, when feeling returned. When pain began to seep remorselessly outwards in widening circles. A dull ache, infecting everything, from the tip of the blade, its serrated sides.

Except that wasn't where she was at. Not this time. Sam pulled the cover tighter around her shoulders. She did feel angry and curious, but somehow strangely level-headed. It was as if her brain had been having a dialogue with itself behind her back. Ancient playground rhymes for modern-day predicaments. Victim, quarry, fighter, swimmer. Choose. Monday's child, Thursday's child. Choose. Which do you want to be?

What was it Peter had said? She hadn't been able to hear what he was saying yesterday. Now she could. It's love that matters, he'd whispered. You love Anna just the same. Nobody can take that from you, unless you let them.

Sam found herself standing again. Her whole world had been turned upside-down, but somewhere along the line she had chosen to fight. It would be hard, but if she held her nerve, nothing fundamental had to change. She would not go under again.

'It's only blood,' she repeated under her breath as she started to get dressed. Her voice sounded strong. Mum would love her the same. Dad would love her the same. And what she and Anna had meant to one another was the same. She wouldn't hand over their history without a battle.

Just gone eight o'clock. Sam hung out of the train window, sniffing the humid Sussex air. It wasn't dark yet, wouldn't be for an hour or so. The sky presented the same undistinguished horizon it had been all day.

Behind her she could hear Peter getting their few belongings together as the wheels juddered to a halt. Watching the platform jogging beside them, Sam reached her hand down, turned the mucky handle and let the door fall open. Slower and slower and slower and stop.

'We seem to spend our entire lives on trains,' she said to Peter, ducking her head back in.

'We do,' he smiled, kissing the nape of her neck.

Hands passing tickets to the collector, feet walking over the level crossing, mouths silent. Everything had already been said.

As they walked up through the deserted town, both were imagining the conversation to come. They hardly noticed the sleeping hardware stores and tobacconists and boutiques, the colours of their awnings bleached away by the thickening dusk. Only the occasional restaurant or twinkling pub broke the purple silence of the city centre.

Past the old Market Cross they strolled and along North Street. The door of the fish and chip shop that sold homemade pickled onions the size of golf balls was standing open.

Nearly home, Sam thought to herself. I'm nearly home.

CHAPTER 13

'I can't believe it,' Tom kept saying, over and over again. 'I just can't believe it.'

After the hugs and the welcome home, Peter had given Mr and Mrs Whittaker the unemotional bare bones of the story in three or four sentences. Sam stood holding his hand in silence, watching their faces for signs of distress. Their only immediate concern had been for Sam. Tom had thrown his arms around her. Are you all right, sweetheart? Helen had asked. Not really, Sam had replied gruffly, brushing the tears from her eyes roughly. But I'll live. What about you? Mum? Dad? Peter had waited, unobtrusive, on the sidelines as they had comforted and reassured one another.

Tick. Tick. Twenty past nine. Tom, Peter, Helen and Sam were now sitting round the kitchen table, bolstered by the usual paraphernalia. For the second time that day, Peter began his résumé of his afternoon's conversation with Gayle. His gentle American voice spilled out into the room, yellow from the overhead neon.

'I know it seems crazy,' Peter started, 'to believe Gayle. On the basis of nothing. The whole thing is crazy.'

Mouth closed, Sam nodded her agreement. On the train, Peter had agreed to break the news to her parents only on the strict understanding that she would not interrupt the whole time.

'Gayle is not a happy lady,' he continued. 'She drinks, has had a rough time. She's clearly caught up in some pretty weird stuff.'

'Such as?' enquired Tom.

'OK. For a start, she believes somebody's out to get her. Partly she freaked yesterday because she figured we were using her past – Anna and Sam – as a way of getting into her home.'

Tom offered round his cigarettes, then half-stood, long legs pressing into the table, to circle the light. Peter, Helen, Sam, himself. All four, from one match. Lucky.

'But you think she got the letter Sam sent?' asked Tom.

'Yeah, she did. She admitted it today. But she'd got no energy to think about it. She has a sorta siege mentality. Like she's been moving around from place to place, a few months here, a few months there, to avoid this guy who says she owes him money.'

'The second husband, do you mean?' asked Helen. 'Colin Saunders?'

'No, he's out of the frame,' replied Peter. 'This is some other guy.'

'Most natural mothers do think about the children they gave up, wonder how they are, where they are,' Sam interrupted, ignoring the warning look in Peter's eyes. 'Gayle is the exception that proves the rule.'

Helen pulled the ashtray towards her. MUM. MUM. MUM. MUM. She tapped her cigarette precisely on the rim.

'Yeah, thank you, Sam . . .' grimaced Peter, miming zipping her lips shut. Sam smiled as he took a drag of his cigarette and blew the smoke down his nostrils like a dragon.

'First out, Gayle says they never made it to the hospital until after the twins were born.'

'Hold on,' Tom interrupted. 'Who is *they*?'

Peter marked the cast off on his fingers. 'Pamela Greene, whose place it was. Gayle's husband, Julian. And Julian's sister, Lauren, who it turns out was living with them at Raphael House. Or at least, Gayle thinks Lauren was around. She can't recall actually seeing her until much later.'

'Lauren!' repeated Tom, raising his eyebrows.

'I think it's a nice name,' said Sam. 'Very romantic.'

Ignoring the pair of them, Peter carried on.

'The other guy who lived there in the house, David Rogers – known as Dylan apparently – was out someplace.'

'We haven't heard mention of Lauren before, have we?' said Helen.

'She was too young to be listed on the Electoral Register,' Sam answered. 'Only about seventeen or eighteen. Something like that.'

'Sam . . .' warned Peter.

She winced. 'Sorry, sorry.'

Helen and Tom exchanged glances. They had never been quite sure of the nature of Peter's relationship with their daughter. Platonic friendship, as Sam defined it. Bit unlikely at their age, Tom had laughed afterwards. Anyway, whatever it was, Helen thought to herself, it's changed. Something happened in Oxford.

'I tried to find out about her from Gayle,' Peter continued, 'but I got a definite feeling that she didn't much like Lauren. Anyhow, getting back to Gayle. She says the babies were premature – about three weeks early – and that she was ill at the time.'

'Ill?' questioned Tom. 'What sort of ill? Drunk?'

'From what she said – and didn't say – I'd guess at something a bit heavier.'

'Such as?'

'Well,' said Peter, trying to decide how honest to be, 'I'd guess at drugs of some sort, from what she was saying. And Mescal maybe?'

He suddenly shuddered, at the thought of Gayle in labour, hallucinating.

'Anyhow, Gayle says that she had a fall, late morning . . .'

'Sorry,' said Tom, interrupting again, 'but this is when? The twelfth?'

'Monday, November twelve,' answered Peter. 'Yeah. Gayle has a fall about midday. She's out of it, she's obviously scared and she claims they're ignoring her. She says she called and called and it was a real long time before anybody came.'

'Pamela Greene was a nurse,' threw in Sam, a propos of nothing.

'I'm getting to that,' said Peter. 'Pamela tried to get Gayle to go to hospital, just to be checked over. But Gayle refused point-blank, said she was fine, that she just wanted to rest.

'This is when her memory gets a little fuzzy. She says she lay there in bed for a while – she remembers noticing it was dark outside – then, suddenly, she says she was being torn apart by this pain in her back. She's screaming and Julian and Pamela are there and Pamela is saying it's too late to move her and shouting at Julian to get hot water and newspapers.'

'Why didn't they ring for an ambulance?' demanded Tom.

'Can you believe there was no phone?' replied Peter. 'And Gayle says that Raphael House is right out in the middle of nowhere. When I asked why they didn't send Lauren for help, she looked at me like it had never occurred.'

Tom lit another cigarette. The air seemed tightly stretched, vibrating with suspense. It went through Helen's mind that she had never heard Peter talk so much before. Hard for him to get a word in edgeways, usually. He looked as if he was concentrating hard, so as not to forget anything of substance.

'Gayle says she thought she was dying. Then she gets this incredible urge to push, like her whole body was puking – that's the word she used – and this feeling again that she's being ripped apart.

'The next thing is the sound of a baby crying. Somebody is saying it's a girl and shoves it – again, her word, not mine – in her face. She said it looked repulsive and that she yelled at Julian to get it out of her sight.'

'Repulsive?' questioned Tom.

'I guess she meant the birthmark,' replied Peter carefully.

What Gayle had actually said was that the brat was deformed, an obscene red mess covering half its face, like it was unfinished. He'd not repeated that to Sam on the train and couldn't see any reason to distress Mr and Mrs Whittaker now. He twisted the ring in his ear.

'Right. Then she was being told to be brave and push some more. But she didn't have anything left. She remembers hearing Pamela whisper to Julian that the baby was coming the wrong way.'

'Bottom first,' elaborated Sam.

'Hold on,' added Tom. 'What's happening to the first baby – Anna, we assume – while all this is going on?'

'Tom!' reproved Helen.

'Sorry,' he excused himself quickly.

'I asked that,' replied Peter. 'She didn't know. Anyhow, then Pamela starts shouting at her in this real loud voice. Saying that the next baby is a little boy and she must try hard to push out her son. She remembers the word son. She was totally clear about that.

'Suddenly Pamela is punching her in the belly. Gayle felt something else slithering out. She says it's the noise she most remembers. A sucking noise.'

Tom looked alarmed.

'Placenta,' said Sam.

Helen shifted position in her chair.

'Gayle thought she was bleeding to death. She says there was blood everywhere. Then she remembers rain on her face, suddenly feeling cold and being in a car. It must have been Julian driving. She couldn't recall. Lauren was there at that point, because Gayle remembers she had one of the babies. The car was full of the sound of crying. She's hungry. Gayle remembers Pamela saying that, but that's about all. She doesn't really recall much about the journey, except screaming for someone to shut the noise up.'

Helen and Sam and Tom and Peter sat in silence in the cool summer kitchen, each imagining the darkness and the November rain and the sheer horror of it all.

Tick. Tick.

Tom scratched his beard. 'So . . .'

The fridge hummed.

'So,' said Peter, suddenly exhausted, 'that's it. Gayle doesn't have any idea what happened at the hospital. The twins were spirited off someplace. At least, she says she never saw them again. She does remember doctors and nurses telling her over and over she was lucky to be alive. And she remembers a needle being stuck in her arm and rushing down a corridor on her back, lights shining down in her eyes. She thinks Julian was with her, but again wasn't sure.'

'But what about afterwards?' asked Helen. 'The next day?'

'Well,' muttered Peter, digging around for his tobacco in his pocket. 'I'm guessing now, because she got evasive at this point. But I reckon she did a vanishing act.'

He smoothed a tissue-thin paper out on the table. Helen was mesmerised by his fingers, expert, deft, automatic. Sam looked at his hands and blushed scarlet.

'The drug would be wearing off by now, so she'd be feeling bad. Real disoriented and paranoid. She lets them fix her up, has no choice about that, but as soon as she can, she disappears.'

Peter sprinkled tobacco lightly along the Rizla, rolled it evenly into place.

'I don't know,' he shrugged. 'But Gayle says she can't remember anything else and I believe that.'

One perfect lick along the edge, a tap and into the mouth. Tom passed him the matches.

'So where did the names come from? Who chose the names Sam and Anna?'

Peter pulled a face. 'I didn't ask. Sorry.'

Tom sat quiet for a moment, as if he were putting mental

weights on a set of scales. Motive. Opportunity. Plausibility. Evidence.

'It is possible she did a vanishing act at that point,' he said slowly. 'We had to wait a long time for the adoption order, much longer than usual, because they couldn't find her to sign the final release papers. Remember?'

Helen nodded. It was only thanks to Tom's persistence, and willingness to make a nuisance of himself, that they had been told what the problem was. Without the mother's signature on the final release papers, the twins could not be handed over. Stalemate. The deadlock had been broken by the Adoption Society swearing an affidavit to the effect that – in their professional opinion – it was Mrs Driver, rather than her husband, who was the prime mover in the adoption process. Because Gayle had signed all the papers earlier, before the birth – and because she had made no attempt to see the twins or contact Mr Driver in the intervening period – the court ruled that in this one exceptional situation, the father's signature alone would be sufficient.

'I mean, the hospital would hardly have got it wrong,' Tom was saying in his classroom voice. 'The Adoption Society gave us the pink hospital bracelets, one for Anna, one for Sam. Birth weights, date, everything. Both pink.'

Tom was bouncing the box of matches against his blue and white Rothmans packet on the table. Heel, toe, heel, toe. Like a tap dancer.

'It's not that I'm questioning your analysis, Peter,' he said, 'and I'm sure the unfortunate woman thinks she is telling the truth. But, on her own admission, she was in a poor mental and physical condition. Given she didn't ever get a proper look at the second baby, isn't the most likely explanation that she simply misheard what Pamela Greene said? That this is all something out of nothing? Gayle thought Pamela said son, so simply jumped to the wrong conclusion that the baby was a boy.'

'It is possible Gayle misheard. Sure,' responded Peter. 'And I don't think the hospital made a mistake either.'

Sam listened to him, seduced by his American way of saying either. Ee-ther, she mimicked in her head. Address. Ad-dress. That was fantastic too. Pree-mature.

'Two girls arrived at St Saviour's,' he agreed. 'Whatever

happened, happened before. It's like some sort of weird conspiracy theory. But already we do have one thing that doesn't add up.'

Tom looked at him.

'I don't know how these things work over here,' Peter said slowly, as if thinking out loud. 'Who's supposed to register the birth of a child and stuff like that?'

'I think it's a question of where the child is delivered,' answered Helen. 'It's their responsibility, the hospital or midwife, to inform the Register Office, who then wait for the parents to come and register the baby's name. I think it has to be done within about six weeks.'

'Is that right?' nodded Peter. 'My point is that the birth certificates say Anna and Sam were born at the hospital. Right? But Gayle says they were born at Raphael House and were taken to St Saviour's a few hours later. They can't both be right.'

His words hung in the air between them. Tom frowned, rubbed his beard as he thought. The women sat like spectators at a tennis match. Sam heard the distinctive fizzle of Peter's spindly cigarette, pinched between his thumb and forefinger.

'It's a fair point,' conceded Tom, 'fair point. But *if* Gayle is not simply mistaken – and it's a big if – then for some reason that I cannot begin to fathom, Julian Driver and Pamela Greene substituted one baby for another somewhere along the line. That's the only explanation and it's preposterous.'

He looked over at his wife for support. She didn't react, just sat still, waiting for things to play themselves out.

'It also leaves us with three major questions,' he added. 'One. Why? Two. What happened to the little boy? Three . . .'

Sam finished the sentence for her father. Her expression was fierce, skin taut across her face. And her voice sounded determined. In control.

'Three. Who am I?'

They'd talked round in circles for another hour or so before Peter had finally gone home at about half past eleven. Helen and Tom had turned in shortly after.

Convinced she wouldn't be able to sleep, Sam had gone upstairs reluctantly. She was on a high of caffeine, nicotine, adrenalin and sex. Lying on her narrow single bed, she squinted round at her room, redecorated from top to bottom last year. All those tell-tale drawing-pin marks, testament to years of glossy pop-stars crucified on her wall, hidden by new paint. A new colour scheme, new furniture. Her black Habitat bedside lamp, her matching floor cushions, her books, her records, her make-up on her dressing-table. Her this, her that. It should have been a boy's room, she'd murmured as she slid into a deep sleep.

Sam woke up feeling good. She'd worried things might seem impossible in the morning. But they didn't. In fact, she thought, I feel ten feet tall. Like I can take on the world. She hurried out of bed, proud of herself, and went into the bathroom. What was most odd was realising that roots and blood connections felt less important than at any other time in her life. She still wanted to know who her mother was, of course she did. But it was an intellectual rather than an emotional need now. It was the sheer black and white, give-it-to-me-straight story that she wanted. What, exactly, had gone on in Raphael House when Anna was being born? When the Sam who was not her was being born?

'Who the fuck are you, girl?' she said in her Aretha Franklin accent. The reflection in the mirror grinned back. Sam bent over to splash cold water on her skin and started to wonder when her real birthday was. The Saturday? The Sunday? Maybe the twelfth itself, although perhaps that was too much to believe. She dragged a towel across her face, then charged out and downstairs for breakfast.

Sun was streaming into the kitchen, the percolator was belching on the side, the smell of toast and melted butter filtering out of the kitchen window. All the usual things, in their usual place.

'Morning, Dad,' said Sam, kissing the top of her father's head as she sat down with him at the table.

'Sleep well, sweetheart?' enquired Helen, as always.

'Not bad,' Sam replied, as always. 'Any coffee in the pot?'

'I'll bring you a mug.'

She could feel them both looking at her, trying to assess how she felt.

'I'm fine. Honestly. I really feel fine.'

'Good,' said Helen, resting her hand on Sam's shoulder as she put the mug down in front of her.

Sam disdainfully picked up the innards of the paper, a special Wedding Day magazine unwanted by Tom.

'What time's kick-off?'

'Oh, you've missed that,' replied her father, without looking up. 'ITV was up and running at half past seven, BBC1 trailing behind fifteen minutes later. BBC2 has left itself a lot to do, not joining the game until nine forty-five.'

'Tut-tut,' said Sam, rolling her eyes.

'There's no score,' Tom added, grinning.

'He leaves the Palace at ten-thirty, she leaves Clarence House in a glass coach at ten thirty-five,' detailed Helen from the kitchen window, ignoring the sniggers. 'The marriage service itself is at eleven o'clock. And I don't care what any of you think, *I'm* going to watch it.'

'We're all going to watch it,' said Tom. 'Aren't we, Sam?'

Sam was letting her mind drift as the good-natured banter flowed backwards and forwards.

'I absolutely can't wait,' she replied, on automatic pilot.

Her next steps were obvious. First, she needed to talk to Pamela Greene. If necessary, she would go and camp out at Raphael House. Second, Julian Driver would have to be tracked down. Anna's father. They both knew what had happened that day. Somehow, she would make them tell her the truth.

Feeling like a warrior going into battle, Sam sealed her campaign plan with a final gulp of coffee. Then she rose to her feet, straightened her dress, and offered her sleeveless arm to her father.

'Lead me to this wedding,' she said. 'Maybe a bit of this Happy Ever After stuff will rub off on me.'

CHAPTER 14

Sam had ripped open the cellophane of her M&S salmon and cucumber sandwich before she'd even got out of the side door and into the narrow road. Starving, as usual. She'd been lucky. It was the last one left and it was the only thing she really fancied.

As she ambled, Sam eyed up the boys, awarding them marks out of ten. Body, teeth, face, skin. All-round fanciability. The town was full of tourists, most of them in shorts and T-shirts and tans. He's out of my league, bite. That one's got potential, chew. God, not him, no way. Definitely in the 'Not If He Was the Last Man Left On Earth' category . . .

Sam was wallowing in her newly acquired knowledge that desire, just like grief, had the power to refashion a life. Sexual obsession left no room for anything else, no befores or afters. She looked smug the entire time, pitying those deprived mortals who were not sleeping with Peter. All the people, in all the towns, in all the countries, in all the worlds, in all the planets, in all the galaxies . . . She grinned and bit into her second sandwich, chucking the wrapping into the August rubbish bin. Only lunchtime and already it was vomiting its ice-cream wrappers and lolly sticks out on to the pavement.

Since Oxford, Sam had been in a permanent state of lust. She couldn't help it. Phallic images, shapes, transparent material stretched tight, all the mundane things had taken on sensual new colours. It was like living in some sort of porn movie, a universe with a fixed come-hither expression. When she stood back, she did feel embarrassed. Like she had a shameful secret in a brown paper bag. But it still didn't stop her peering at girls in the street, wondering if sex was what was on their minds too.

The only downside to this new, exciting world, was that she had become tormented by her weight. Sam was never without her naked body. Every minute it was there, wobbling, flabbing about, reproaching her. Inside her jeans, under her T-shirts, in the bath, watching television. She had thought she'd grown out of adolescent miseries over clothes size and not looking like Debbie Harry, along with blue eye-shadow and being a vegetarian. All those things that had seemed so fashionable in 1978 and 1979, all the normal things, the belonging-to-a-club things, she used to do. Before the accident.

'Shit, don't start,' Sam muttered to herself, alarming a white-haired woman with an elderly Highland terrier. Sam smiled an apology. Mistress and dog looked suspiciously at her, then crossed over to the opposite pavement.

The irony was, Peter could not have cared less about one inch more of skin here or there. Until now, Sam had not recognised how idiosyncratic a physical world Peter inhabited, how untouched he was by other people's values. Lovers don't like bones, he'd said to her a couple of days ago. It's softness that matters. He found Sam's new-remembered hobby a little weird, a waste of energy and time. It reminded him of the Barbie-doll girls he'd grown up with.

He thinks exactly how Anna used to think, Sam rumbled to herself as she licked a stray bit of cucumber from her palm. God, those endless one-way conversations with Anna on the subject of beauty. Sam pushed her untamed hair back behind her ear, as she composed a stilted stage dialogue in her head.

The Two Sisters. Act I, Scene IV. Lights up on two girls. The second, although plumper, is more confident and attractive.

First twin (who looks bewildered): 'Explain why appearance is so important to you.'

Second twin (looking committed): 'It matters because it is immediate. (*Pause.*) It makes the first impression. (*Pause.*) You might be clever or funny or brilliant, but people have to find that out. Beauty is there, unmissable. (*Pause.*) If you are beautiful, you stand out without having to do anything. (*Exit stage left.*)

Sam's language had become more persuasive over time, but she'd never convinced Anna. Sam shrugged her shoulders at the memory. She looked up and realised that her theatrical self-absorption had taken her to Priory Park, halfway to Peter's house. There's a homing instinct for you, she giggled. The park was brown round the edges, a summer's worth of cricket and country fayres taking their toll.

Deciding it would be just as quick to walk as wait for a bus, she set off across the stubbled grass. Sam felt time snapping at her

143

heels. It was August already. She had to try to find Pamela Greene and Julian before college started again in just under a month. As much as anything, this made practical sense. Sam knew she'd fucked around rather a lot last year, allowing Gayle and letter-writing and trips to Oxford and London to take priority over Anne Boleyn and Shakespeare.

Her parents had been surprisingly good about it, more concerned with her spiritual than her academic well-being. But Sam knew they weren't going to be happy if she continued to divert all her energies away from her set texts and homework and teachers. Come September, they would expect her to knuckle down. It didn't leave long.

She'd repeated this brainwashing over and over again, pretending she really did care about qualifications. But, in a funny way, it was guilt that made her want to resolve things quickly. For a couple of days now, Sam realised she'd dragged Anna into a limbo, Anna who'd never wanted to trace their biological parents, not really. But because of Sam's curiosity, Anna's history and her own history were all up in the air. A Pandora's Box, lid wide open. For her own peace of mind, Sam wanted to achieve something at least before 9 August. It was Monday today. The anniversary of Anna's death was six days away. It didn't leave long.

'What would you have thought about all of this, PB?' she muttered to the blue sky.

Sam was sweating now, walking faster as she thought about last year's anniversary. Awful. The worst thing had not been the bloodiness of her own memories nor the pain she had felt. But her father's grief. At the end of the day itself, when everybody had already gone to bed, Sam had been disturbed by coarse screaming. At first, she'd thought it was coming from the road outside. But gradually the sound had come into focus and she'd realised it was closer to home. Pulling the duvet up over her head, she'd tried to drown out the raw sound of a grown man crying. Completely powerless to help. Her father, crying.

Sam shivered. Will it be like this forever, she wondered, every year distancing ourselves further and further away? Five years after the accident, ten, fifteen? She tried to shrug the thought away.

Here she was suddenly, at Peter's dappled front door. One of the first things Annette had painted when they'd arrived, its green, orange and yellow swirls dominated the whole street. Laurel, amber and marigold actually, Peter clarified, when Sam had asked. It's Annette's celebration of England and the fall.

She knocked, waited. The door opened.

'Hi, you,' said Peter in his languid way. Like a purr. Her stomach flipped at her first sight of him for an eternal twenty-four hours. She felt suddenly shy.

'Come on in.'

He stroked her flushed cheek with his fingers before slipping them under her hair, cupping the back of her neck and pulling her mouth towards him. One sensual, possessing movement. Sam just stood there in the cool hall, eyes closed, tasting the kiss.

Thump. The distinctive sound of the heavy front door falling shut and Peter releasing her.

'You look like you could do with a drink.'

'I walked from town,' she admitted.

Annette was sitting at the raggedy claw-footed table in the corner, phone in front of her. She waved a greeting and carried on talking as Sam stepped over the wire. Waiting in the middle of the room, Sam realised she felt soggy between the legs. Uncomfortable. She pulled at her knickers, discreetly, as Peter yanked open the fridge and rested his long, tanned arm along the top of the door.

'OJ? Coke?'

'Got any Diet Coke?' Sam asked.

He buried his head inside and poked around.

'Sorry. Just regular.'

'Fine,' she answered. 'It doesn't matter.'

He pulled out two cans, holding them both in one hand, then flipped the fridge shut with his bare foot. At the table, Annette slammed the receiver down, leaped up, gathered up the phone and its lead, and made for the door.

'Hi, Sam. 'Bye, Sam. I've got to rush.'

From the corridor, they heard the sound of her swapping the phone for her keys and shouting what time she'd be back. The information was swallowed up by the slamming of the door.

'Don't ask,' he grinned, carrying their drinks over to the table. 'Something to do with saving whales.'

He pressed the cold can into Sam's hand, looking her straight in the eye.

'As in the fish, not the country.'

'They're mammals actually,' said Sam in her know-it-all voice, holding his gaze.

'Are they now . . . ?' said Peter, putting down his Coke on the sideboard.

Lazily, he strolled round behind her. Sam's pulse quickened. Suddenly, he struck. Hands all over her, tickling her sides and ribs and stomach.

'No, no,' she squealed, sinking to the floor.

Peter didn't let up, following her down to the ground, tickling her under her arms, behind her ears, as she squirmed and writhed on the rug. Now he had trapped her under his chest, pinioning her elbows to her sides with his knees.

'Get off,' she shrieked, half-flirting, half-outraged to have been so thoroughly caught. 'Let me go, you big bully.'

He grabbed her impotent hands behind his back, clamping his bare feet and knees into the sides of her legs.

'You,' he laughed, 'are such a pain in the ass . . .'

'And you,' she simpered in her best Southern belle accent, 'are so st-rong.'

Sam felt the weight of his body shift as he tipped forward, at the last moment slapping their four hands down on the floor either side of her head. The crush of the kiss stole her breath.

Too soon, Peter sprang off.

'Later,' he said decisively. 'We've got stuff to do.'

Sam felt all dressed-up with no place to go. She stayed lying flat on the ground for a couple of seconds, willing him back. She watched him adjust the belt of his black jeans, push his hair back from his face and twist his bracelet back to its right position. Then he held out his hand and she accepted it was over.

'I saw the doctor today,' she said, pulling an extra chair up to the table. 'I have to take them for two weeks before we can do anything. I mean, without using something else as well.'

'That's great, Sam,' he said, clinking his can of Coke against hers. 'Here's to two weeks!'

'You're so fucking responsible,' she grimaced, spitting out the word like an insult.

Peter raised his eyebrows. 'Temper, temper . . .'

Sam poked her tongue out.

'I've been thinking,' he said, 'about Pamela Greene. She still owns Raphael House, as of last fall. And now we know that she hasn't seen Gayle since the day the twins were born in November '62.'

'She might not be there,' challenged Sam.

'Scenario number one supposes she *is* there,' insisted Peter. 'What would you do if a letter arrived, addressed to somebody who used to live in your house eighteen years ago?'

'Open it,' replied Sam, without hesitation.

'Right. Because Gayle's not just anybody. Pamela went through something awful with this woman. And she's implicated in what happened that night. Maybe even something criminal. Think about it. We don't just have you alive and kicking to explain, but a missing baby boy.'

Suddenly, it all seemed serious. Not a game. Sam shivered as Peter's comments flipped over one another in her mind. A missing baby. A dead baby? For the first time, a trickle of cold fear seeped through her veins.

'Don't,' she murmured under her breath.

'Hey,' he said quickly, putting an arm around her. It was a perfect fit, as if designed to hug those very shoulders. Fluffing her hair with his fingers, like the teeth of a huge comb, he waited until she waved him on with his idea.

'Right, I'm still on scenario one here. Pamela gets the letter, she opens the letter. Now, she can do one of three things. First, return it to you at the address at the top of the page. We know she didn't do that. Second, she can ignore it, not wanting to get involved. That's a possibility. Third, she can do something about it.'

'But why—'

'No way!' said Peter immediately. 'You are forbidden to say anything until I'm done. Not one single word.'

He dropped the tip of his finger lightly on to her mouth, stroked it along her bottom lip. Sam bit it. Hard.

'Shit!'

Sam smiled innocently as Peter shook his injured finger.

'Scenario number two,' he continued, 'has no Pamela Greene at Raphael House, but some other guy instead. A lodger, a friend staying for a while. Who knows, maybe she has grown-up kids?'

Sam banged her elbows down on the table, then elaborately plonked her chin into her curved hands. Peter grinned.

'These guys see the letter. They've not heard of Gayle Driver, so they either throw it away or ignore it or—'

'Or ask Pamela about it,' interrupted Sam, unable to stop herself.

Peter ignored her.

'Scenario number three,' he said loudly, 'has nobody at Raphael House. Your letter gets delivered and has been lying there unloved ever since.'

'Poor letter,' cooed Sam.

'And *cuatro* – my last and final shot – is the letter getting lost in the mail. Never made it to Oxford at all.'

'Can I speak now?' asked Sam coquettishly.

'Go right ahead.'

'Thank you so much. I have one or two criticisms of your theory, Mr Newman.'

Peter wolf-whistled at the courtesy.

'My first point – well, my main point really – is that this all sounds like something out of a film or something. Letters don't just go astray in the post in real life.'

Real life. Sam was suddenly winded by childhood memories of trying to reassure Anna that nothing ever happened to ordinary people in real life. She'd believed it back then. Peter watched the sadness slip around her, wrapping her in its brown arms.

'Thinking about Anna?'

She nodded. He pushed his chair back, and went over to get them both a cigarette. Real cigarettes, from the packet of ten in Sam's bag.

'It's funny how they sneak up on you,' he said quietly, sitting back down. 'After my dad died, the trailer didn't smell the same any more. Later – a year, eighteen months, I can't recall – there I was, in a bar hundreds of miles from home. And some guy next to me ordered a bourbon. And – bam! – it was like my dad was right there with me again.'

He struck the match, the flame leaping red between them.

'They're friendly ghosts, though,' he added tenderly, 'yours and mine.'

'I know,' Sam mumbled softly. 'It's just that, every once in a while, it strikes home that she'll never be there again.'

They sat in silence for a moment, all four of them. The quick and their dead, still in the afternoon light.

'Well,' sighed Sam finally.

She dropped her cigarette butt into her empty Coke can, heard the sour hiss.

'This won't get us anywhere. There's no point trying to speculate about what Pamela Greene might or might not have done. I think we should go there, to Raphael House itself. At least we'll see if the place looks lived in.'

'I'm not against that,' responded Peter. 'But I think you should write first. Tell her you've met up with Gayle and there are one or two things you'd like to check out.'

'One or two things,' snorted Sam. 'That's one way of putting it . . .'

Peter laughed.

'Let's do it right now,' he said. 'Annette's typewriter's around here someplace.'

They found it after five minutes, shrouded under an Indian shawl and a pile of Greenpeace newsletters. Sam pulled the gossamer, gold-shot material through her fingers as Peter lugged the machine to the table and plugged it in. Ready to go, he pulled up a chair that didn't wobble and plonked himself on it.

'I'll type. You talk.'

He fiddled around, looking for the ON/OFF switch, checking the cable was pushed firmly in, reacquainting himself with the positions of the keys. The machine hummed with electric life.

'OK,' said Peter, feeding in the paper. 'What's the date today?'

CHAPTER 15

The luminous roman numerals of Tom's bedside travel clock glowed green. He half-flipped his glasses on to read the time. Only needed for reading and things close up, not bad for a man of fifty. God. Only half past six. No wonder he felt tired.

Tom flopped back against the headboard. He and Helen had talked late last night, keeping their voices low so as not to disturb Sam through the thin bedroom walls. He twisted his head to look at his wife, her sleeping face towards the window, short grey curly hair on the peach pillow-case. Not bad for an old lady of fifty either, he thought with affection.

Adjusting his pillows carefully, not wanting to disturb Helen, Tom put his hands behind his head and let their conversation rewind.

All through this whole business with Sam, he and Helen had been enthusiastic and supportive. At least, he hoped that was what Sam felt. In secret, they'd congratulated themselves on how she had shared everything with them. Well, at least, *he* had congratulated them. Everything played by the book. Sam hadn't shut them out, like he'd read some adopted children did in these circumstances. Through guilt or embarrassment or fear of hurting their parents. That was a relief.

Then the abrupt change of direction, into waters uncharted by the counselling leaflets. The script was thrown up in the air, lines jumbled up, with the shock of discovering that Gayle was not Sam's mother after all. The fact that Sam was not Anna's twin made not a jot of difference to either Helen or Tom. Genuinely. And when they'd stood in the kitchen back in July, listening to Peter's account, their concern had been only for their daughter. How did Sam feel about the loss of her sister? Could she cope with theft of the roots that had always been so important to her? Later,

150

Tom had felt outraged on Sam's behalf, then a little intrigued. He felt ashamed at that, so hadn't owned up to his curiosity. You can't recapture innocence, was all he said.

Helen had been very anxious. Like him, she did accept that Sam couldn't pretend nothing had happened. She understood that Sam would have to see things through to the end. But privately, she felt they were all under a cloud, couldn't banish thoughts streaked through with black pessimism.

Uppermost in both their minds was Sam's mental health. She seemed fine, a normal eighteen-year-old girl with an appetite for life. Her laugh was back, her volatile emotions, her enthusiasm. But who could tell? What about the future? How would she react if the truth was even worse than their worst suspicions? Over the past eight months or so they had sat in the kitchen and post-mortemed each new development in Sam's search. We were deluding ourselves, Helen had said to him last night. Or at least, I was. All the time, pretending to be so calm about it all.

Tom looked at the clock again. For the first time, Helen had admitted to him the terror the nights held for her. Fingers of the past stretching out for her neck, that's how she had put it. The missing baby was haunting her and it seemed that every paper and news bulletin was full of stories about kidnapped, mutilated and abused children. Something has changed inside me, she'd whispered. I feel like a woman whose life history is carved in stone, days marked by the birthing and dying of babies. There's been a sensation loitering at the edges of my mind. Like it was shy. At first, I couldn't recognise it. Tom had been surprised by the descriptive language, had put his hand on her bony shoulder for support. And what is it? he asked. Three children, she answered. I feel we have three children, not two. Sam and Anna and Anna's twin brother. The other Sam.

Tom turned to look at his wife's long, sleeping body. She looked so young. Hip to hip, their bodies thin and straight, we look like a knight and his lady on a cathedral tomb, he thought to himself, rather pleased with the simile.

But it was ironic that the tragedies that had hit their family should have helped him and Helen fall back in love with one another again. Anna's death and Sam's consequent breakdown had somehow freed them to talk and feel in ways that had become buried years ago. Theirs had always been a contented partnership. Married twenty-eight years last February. They'd had their fair share of ups and downs, but you'd expect that. As they'd got older, they had slid into the usual pattern of living on the surface of things. Tom, the husband and father, Helen, the wife and mother. Mr and Mrs Whittaker. Middle age and responsibility seemed to have little need of a lover or a confidante. Their conversations were about practical, everyday matters, not emotions. Arrangements scribbled in the diary, routines, finances.

Then the accident. Suddenly Tom found he could understand Helen's shadows. He remained, by nature, an optimist, although more cautious. But no longer did her dark moods take her out of his reach. For the first time, he saw the world as she had always seen it. An uneasy place, where disaster might be hiding behind any tree, holding its arms in tight like a child playing hide-and-seek. Always there, if not always visible.

Only once had Tom slipped into the pit. On the first anniversary of Anna's death. He had never told a soul what he'd seen that night in the police station. For the following eight days, all he could see was Anna's tortured body. Everywhere he looked. A plate of spaghetti, the spirograph pattern on a lampshade, the crazy paving in the back garden. Everything seemed the shape and colour and texture of his daughter's livid lacerations.

Two days after the funeral, he had withdrawn into himself. He'd cried a little in private, not wanting to burden Helen, then he'd wiped away his tears, dusted himself down and banished Anna's broken face from his world. The months passed until August came round again. All three of them had nearly made it through the day of Anna's death. But at eleven o'clock, her exiled bloodied face had sneaked back into his mind. Without warning, Tom had been ambushed by the sights and smells of the emetic morgue, infecting his nose and throat and mouth. Helen rocked him close in her arms all night, like a child, until they were rescued by the light.

'Brrrrrrr . . .'

Tom lashed out and smacked the top of the clock, to stop the 6.45 alarm disturbing his wife.

'Sam,' shouted Tom up the stairs. 'Phone!'

'I'm in the bath,' yelled a steamy voice. 'Can you take the number and I'll call whoever it is back?'

Tom carefully put the receiver down and tiptoed up the stairs, as if the person on the end could see what he was doing. He knocked a couple of times, then hissed at his daughter through the flimsy plywood door.

'Sam. I think you'll want to come now. It's Pamela Greene.'

'Shit,' said the door. 'I'll be right down.'

Sam pulled herself out of the water, stepped on to the mat, wrapped the biggest towel she could find around her wet skin, then yanked the door open. She could see Tom hovering nosily in the downstairs hall.

'I told her you were on your way,' he whispered as she got to the last-but-one step.

Sam shooed him away with her hand and pulled the kitchen door shut after him. Then, wiping her damp hands down the side of the towel, she picked up the phone.

'Hello?'

Tick. Tick. Half past ten.

Twenty minutes later, Sam put the phone down and went upstairs to get dressed. She wanted to reflect before she replayed the entire conversation for her parents.

I'm still in the dark, she thought, idly shuffling clothes on their hangers for something to wear. Odd that I don't feel like killing someone. The sound of 'Girls on Film' crackled from her radio. Sam sucked in her cheeks, accepting that the Chrissie Hynde look was well out of reach. So, she hadn't got her answers. Not yet. But at least the answers were there for the asking. Soon she would know who she was. She really believed that. If not today from Pamela, then tomorrow or next week or the week after that. She felt as if there was an ocean of patience inside her.

Sam pulled out her new fifties suit from the wardrobe, thinking about Julian. In the past, she had always painted him as the villain. Black moustache, black cloak, a Dickensian seducer. Crude images. Condemned for the crime of being a man, Peter teased. That's usually reason enough, she'd snapped back. After her trip to Somerset House at the beginning of April, there was hard evidence. *He* divorced *her*, she reminded Peter whenever the subject came up. Hardly the act of a Mr Nice Guy. Case proven.

Then she'd met Gayle. Everything seemed less clear. And now Pamela. Sam was finally prepared to accept that she had got Julian all wrong. Ten years and more of prejudice demolished in a matter of weeks. The danger was that she would start idolising him, see him as some sort of hero.

Sam zipped up her skirt, feeling confident and magnanimous. Anna's father will tell me everything, she said to herself as she smoothed the material down over her hips. The man who should have been my father. Flicking the radio off, she headed into the bathroom to search for a tampon before going back downstairs to update her parents.

From the kitchen, Helen and Tom were aware of Sam's feet coming out on to the upstairs landing. They looked at each other, curiosity unsatisfied. Tom got up to open the door and peeked his head round.

'In the bathroom, I think,' he said.

Another couple of minutes passed, then the sound of feet coming back down. They both panicked, as if they were about to be caught out snooping. Helen dredged around in the sink. Tom scrambled for his glasses and pretended to be having a second go at the crossword. Sam grinned as she appeared in the kitchen, not fooled by them for a moment. She looked very summery.

'Well?' Tom had shot out, before Sam had even sat down. 'What did she have to say?'

'Dad, you are worse than me . . .'

'Coffee, sweetheart?' said Helen, moving towards the percolator.

'Lovely. Thank you.' There was a pause.

'New outfit?' Helen asked, putting one mug down in front of Sam, another in front of her husband.

'Jumble sale in the Scout Hut on Saturday,' admitted Sam, looking down at the blue and white seersucker. 'A real bargain.'

'Never mind the fashion discussion,' interrupted Tom. 'What did she say?'

'Oh, nothing you'd be interested in,' replied Sam, teasing him. She dropped two Sweetex into her coffee.

'They're very bad for you,' Helen commented.

'Yeah, yeah.'

'What did Pamela Greene say?' repeated Tom, voice now impatient and booming.

'Patience is a virtue,' said Sam, enjoying herself. 'Isn't it, Mum?'

Helen sat down at the table.

'It is indeed. Not that you would know anything about being patient . . .'

Sam pulled a face. Right. Time to put her father out of his misery.

'We–ll,' she dragged the word out. 'Pamela was very friendly. Very apologetic at not having got back to me before now.'

'Why hadn't she?'

'Be quiet, Tom,' said Helen sharply. 'Have a cigarette or something and let Sam tell the story in her own time.'

'Oops,' he said sheepishly. 'Sam?'

Smiling, Sam took the offered cigarette, leaned towards him for a light, then rested her smoking wrist on the table.

'Pamela's a VSO nurse, so is out of the country for months at a time. She's been in India since December last year and only came back to England a few weeks ago. To get things sorted out for her new tenants. She's off again next week.'

'How old is she?' said Tom.

'I didn't ask,' replied Sam. 'Early- maybe mid-forties, I should think. Why?'

'No reason. Just wondered.'

'Anyway. Both the letters were waiting for her at Raphael House, the one I sent last week and the one from January. She admitted it was a shock to see Gayle's name staring up at her.

'She isn't in touch with Gayle, which we knew already, so she decided to open the letter, just in case it was important. After she'd finished reading, she went straight back to the rest of her post . . .'

She felt Tom building up for another question, so jumped in quickly.

'Because she'd noticed another envelope and postmark with the same handwriting and stuff in the pile.'

'Right-oh,' he muttered.

'So . . . yes. There was the letter I sent last week, explaining that I'd now spoken to Gayle and hoped she – Pamela – might be able to throw light on one or two things . . .'

'Remind me,' said Tom. 'How much detail did you put in the letter?'

'I was quite vague, given everything. I simply said that Gayle's

memory was confused in places and that what she'd told me –
about the second baby being a boy – had come as a huge shock
to me. Obviously. That's all, really.'

'You didn't tell her about Anna?' asked Helen.

'Not in the letter, no. But I did just now on the phone. Explained
things.'

Tom stubbed out his cigarette. 'How did she react?'

'Very nice. Very sympathetic. Said she appreciated how this
must be a difficult time of year for us. For your family, is what
she actually said. She seemed to understand how Gayle's news
must have been doubly painful for me.'

'But did she *tell* you anything?'

Sam got up and wandered over to the coffee for a refill, holding
up the jug questioningly to her parents. Both Helen and Tom shook
their heads.

'I have no doubt that she knows as much as anyone,' said Sam
thoughtfully, coming back to the table. 'But she gave nothing away.
She was very nice about it, said she wanted to help, but kept saying
that they were not her secrets to share.'

'That's ridiculous,' exploded Tom.

'Did you get the impression that she knew who your natural mother was?' Helen asked, trying to sound as detached as
possible.

'Definitely,' replied Sam. 'I couldn't get a scrap of information
about my background out of her. So then I tried to get her to
talk about Anna's birth instead, hoping she'd let something slip.
But she'd clearly thought long and hard about how much she
was going to say before she rang. She was very apologetic, kept
saying how awful it must be for me, but still she wouldn't be
budged.'

'Oh, for God's sake,' said Tom. 'What are you supposed to
do now?'

Sam leaned over and patted his arm.

'It's all right. Really. We did agree two things. Well, she
suggested two things. She thinks that I should talk to Julian. He
is Anna's natural father, after all, even if he turns out not to have
been mine. He and Pamela are still in touch, although she's only
seen him twice in the past thirteen years or so. Before you ask,
Dad, partly because she's abroad so much and partly because he
now lives in America.'

Tom grinned, scratching his beard. 'What a telepathic daughter I've got.'

Sam pulled a face at him.

'Anyway, Pamela was certain he'd want to talk to me – be delighted, was what she said – so wanted my permission to forward my letters to him. As a first step.'

Helen lit herself a second cigarette. 'Which you gave?'

'Absolutely.'

'Where in America does Julian live?' asked Tom. 'Did she say?'

'Washington. His sister does too. He has a second-hand bookshop, specialising in first editions and stuff like that. The second step – which will probably be the first step in terms of action – is for her to send me a few photographs of them all, as they were then. Julian, her, Gayle, everyone who was living at Raphael House in 1962. She promised to do that straight away.'

'There's guilt for you,' humphed Tom. 'Leaving aside the obvious, did she tell you anything you didn't know already?'

'One or two things,' nodded Sam. 'Like she'd been left Raphael House by an aunt and that it's enormous. Most interesting was the stuff about the mysterious Lauren. Her arrival in 1961 was a last-minute thing, something to do with someone dying and Julian being her only relative and them not knowing each other at all. It was all rather complicated, so I didn't get the ins and outs of it. She was under age or something . . .'

'Perhaps she was his ward,' suggested Helen.

'How very Victorian of you, Mama,' giggled Sam in a melodramatic voice. 'Pamela clearly liked Lauren a lot. She said she was charming, full of life.'

Sam tucked her hair back behind her ears, mentally running through her telephone conversation to make sure she didn't leave anything out.

'What else? Ah, yes, that Dylan Rogers was a resting actor, working in an art gallery in Oxford, and that Rebecca Lawson was a nurse like her. Actually, she said that – in Dylan's case – rather more resting was involved than acting.'

Tom and Helen smiled at this daub of colour.

'But mostly,' continued Sam, 'she confirmed our suspicions. Mine and Peter's, that is. Pamela was careful not to be too critical of Gayle, given she was Anna's natural mother. But Gayle

157

was obviously a total nightmare to live with. Spoilt, demanding, always ill. And when I asked her point-blank if she was an alcoholic even then, she sounded relieved that I'd worked that out for myself.'

Tom fiddled with his beard, as his thoughts drifted for a moment. He tried to picture the bohemian cast of characters, living in a way as far removed from his own personal experience as he could imagine. Yet here they all were, nearly twenty years later, lives colliding. Random names and faces, connected to one another without any choice in the matter. He rubbed his eyes, wondering if he should put his glasses back on.

'I got the impression,' Sam was saying to Helen, 'that Pamela believed Gayle had driven Rebecca out. Pamela told me she was away a lot in 1962, from about June to November. When she came home, she found a letter from Rebecca saying she didn't like the atmosphere in the house any more and was sorry not to have the chance to say goodbye in person.'

'You seem to have covered a lot of ground in twenty minutes,' Helen commented. 'Are you going to meet her?'

'She didn't suggest it,' replied Sam. 'And, honestly, I'm not sure there's any point. Not if she isn't prepared to tell me anything more than she already has.'

'You seem surprisingly calm,' said Tom. 'I'd be climbing the walls with frustration.' Then added, in his hold-all cowboy voice, 'So close, and yet so far.'

'I know,' agreed Sam smugly. 'I surprise myself sometimes.'

Helen watched the Cheshire cat smirk fade.

'Seriously, though . . .' she continued. 'I don't know what I expected from Pamela Greene. Perhaps not even to find her, I'm not sure. But she sounded, well, normal. Not frightening or sinister. It made me feel like I'm in the home straight. I know it's only one conversation, but I felt I could trust her.

'So,' she said resolutely, 'all I can do now is to wait. For Pamela to send the photographs and for Julian to make contact.'

She stopped, suddenly worn out by the morning's emotion.

'I know he will,' she added in a quiet voice. 'I can feel it in my bones.'

Tom leaned over and kissed the top of her head.

'I'm sure he will,' he said warmly. 'And Sam?'

She looked at him.

'We're very proud of you, you know, and the way you are handling all of this.'

Sam smiled.

'I know you are,' she said softly. 'Thank you.'

part three

Love is most nearly itself
When here and now cease to matter.

T. S. Eliot, 'East Coker', *Four Quartets*

Scarlet is the colour of loving. What else . . . ?

Imagine. A father sucking away the crimson seam of blood on the end of his child's cut finger. The homesick hearts of lovers separated. The pomegranate inside of a woman's mouth. Kissing. The red of for ever and ever.

The man stood motionless in the empty shop. He looked dependable, reliable. An adult. Mellow, four o'clock sun was filtering through the plate glass of his windows, stroking the spines of the books stacked floor to ceiling all around him. Blue leather, olive-green and maroon, the colours of learning. On each flyleaf, a price lovingly written in pencil. The man was thinking about another afternoon, not this one. An afternoon a long time ago, in a country that used to be his.

In his mind's eye, it was all still so clear. Him, alone, young, in that misty English garden, coat pulled up to his ears. The space all around, the prickly evergreen of the holly bush in the grove at the back of the house. The brown earth alive with winter insects. The damp smell of November in his throat.

At his feet was a grave, just wide enough to hold the shrouded body of a baby. So very small. No bigger than his man's hand. There'd been no time for ritual, no one to mumble empty last rites for the child. Just a battered shoebox and a few lines from a favourite poem scribbled as an epitaph: 'There's such a thing as keeping a remembrance in one's heart.'

He remembered how he'd suddenly turned back to the house for comfort then. It had looked almost black in the murky lunchtime dusk, no light warming the windows. How, without warning, he'd been swept by a feeling of fierce and protective love. He'd wanted to run back across the wet lawn and fold her safe in his arms. Time had not diminished the memory of that emotion.

The man slowly shook his head, remembering the feel of the cold handle of the spade in his hand as he'd softly scraped the soil over the white lid of his son's coffin. Hearing again the dull patter of the mud on the cardboard, the prickling of his wet eyes, rimmed red in the chill afternoon air. As he pressed the earth down, he had grieved for the feet that would never go to that secret grave, the flowers that would never be laid.

Suddenly, he had an overwhelming need to read the lines again. In the here and now. There had to be a copy of the poem somewhere, surely? He swung round to the bookcase immediately behind him and feverishly started to run his finger along the alphabetical spines.

'Brontë, Brontë, Brontë,' he muttered under his breath. 'Charlotte.'

He pulled out a dusty black volume from the shelf and sent his eyes down the small print of the index. The book smelled of churches, as if it had lived untouched for years. Smoothing the page down, he began to read. One by one, the verses floated through his head.

'And where none shall dare restrain us, we can meet again, in thought.'

There was nobody there to witness the expression in the man's eyes as he pressed the covers shut and looked up into the lengthening shadows of the afternoon.

'And now?' he murmured to himself. 'What about now?'

CHAPTER 16

Perhaps Julian stood here, thought Sam, reciting their names in her head. Julian Driver. Sam Whittaker. And now here she was, thirteen years later, tracing his footsteps from east to west. Following the flight of the sun. It would have been different in January 1968. Cold outside, everyone clutching coats and gloves and scarves. September 1981 and the world was lush behind the hermetic glass windows, burnished round the edges, the colour of a wet summer on the verge of autumn.

Sam squeezed her bag, reassuring herself that everything was still there. Passport, boarding card, dollars, Julian's letter. All around were the shimmering yellows and whites of the airport shops, the pillarbox red and royal blue uniforms of the air hostesses, just off duty. She stepped back, tilting her head up so that she could read the flickering television screen. It never stayed the same for more than an instant. Names, words, numbers, like the football results on Saturday's *Grandstand*. Tokyo, New York, Paris, Munich. We could fly anywhere in the world, Sam muttered to herself. Anywhere at all.

'Would all passengers travelling on British Airways flight 742 to Washington now please make their way to Gate 29, where your plane is now boarding. This is a call for passengers travelling to Washington on British Airways flight 742. Thank you.'

'Ready?' said Peter, appearing out of nowhere.

Sam nodded, hitching up the strap of her wicker basket to stop it from slipping. Peter helped wedge in the pack of two hundred duty-frees so that it didn't drop out as she walked, then bear-hugged her jittery shoulders.

'Don't be nervous.'

Sam's stomach was somersaulting. She was frightened as well as incredibly excited. Never mind Washington, never mind Julian.

She'd only ever flown twice before, both times as a child and with her parents. It was a cliché, but how was it possible that hundreds of tons of metal could stay up in the sky? She'd actually spent the last half-hour furtively hexing fat people in the departure lounge just in case they were on their flight. The lighter the passengers, the less likely the plane was to plummet out of the air. It stood to reason. She had not shared her theory with Peter.

'Would Mr Wilson and Mr Sadawi, travelling on Air Egypt flight 431 to Cairo, please make their way to Gate 76 immediately. This flight is now ready to leave. This is a call for the two remaining passengers travelling to Cairo on Air Egypt flight 431, Mr Wilson and Mr Sadawi.'

Sam's jitters were soothed by the confident, everyday voice of the tannoy. Peter took her hand and they started walking, perfectly in step. Sam felt the carpet change to tile under her feet, but didn't look down. She was imagining a film crew tracking her from behind. Two legs in fishnet tights, vibrant tartan mini-skirt, baggy donkey jacket, red beret, halo of hair silhouetted against the milky glass walls.

'We won't crash, will we?'

Peter gently squeezed her fingers. 'Everything's gonna be fine.'

Sam breathed in, long and hard. The rubber smell of the airport flooded her nose. Sparkling advertisements for Beefeater and Chanel and Dunhill dazzled her eyes.

'This is it,' she breathed. 'No turning back.'

The hours were passing. Four down, nearly four to go. Four hours and she'd be in Washington. At first Sam had talked a lot, drowning out the sound of her fear with endless babble about this and that. Overhead lockers, seat-belt, shush, I'm listening to the emergency landing procedures. White wine, please. Peter? Can I have your pudding if you don't want it . . . ?

After a while, Sam had worn herself out. Peter was dozing, head curled up against the porthole window and his suede jacket drawn up under his chin. Sam fished around her feet, wading through crumbs, bits of plastic wrapping, the battered covers of her new P. D. James, her kicked-off yellow ankle-boots. Finally, she found the panda eye-patch thing she was looking for and positioned it over her eyes.

Immediately, her other senses started to compensate for the loss of sight. Now Sam could hear every clink, every scrap of conversation from the seats in front. Now she could smell the stewards scraping away the unwanted dinners, was distracted by the aftertaste of coffee in her mouth. The oblong armrest was imprinting its metal self into her kidneys. Peeling off the mask, she sat up again and sighed loudly. Every other passenger seemed to be asleep in the timeless blue gloom of the plane.

'Can't you sit still . . . ?' muttered Peter, eyes still closed.

'I'm bored.'

'Read that book you got at the airport.'

'I can't. Did you see what it was about?'

'Mmm . . .' He did not want to be woken up by a restless Sam.

'It's about a girl who's adopted who goes looking for her natural father. And finds out he's a murderer. I can't read that, can I?'

Peter smiled, amused despite himself. 'Didn't you look *before* buying it?'

'No, I didn't,' she hissed stroppily at him.

'Jesus,' he grunted, bowing to the inevitable.

He pushed his fingers through his fringe, then twisted upright. His jacket slipped down his body on to his knees. Peter looked at Sam, sitting hunched up next to him. Dark blonde hair tucked behind her ears, scowling blue eyes, legs criss-crossed, tucked under her skirt.

'Come here,' he murmured indulgently. Sam slithered over towards him, half-snuggling, half-lying across the two seats. Threading his left arm behind her neck, he made a tent over them with their jackets. Then, discreetly, he slid his other hand under Sam's jumper. She felt his adroit fingers undoing her bra, then settling themselves lightly over her right breast. Spread out like a spider's web. The leather of his bracelet was cold on her skin.

'Now go to sleep,' he ordered.

Sam woke after only an hour, with a cricked neck and cramp in her hip. Inching her way along up the hushed aisle, she stumbled through the concertinaed door of the loo, then fumbled with the bolt inside. There. Shut. The cubicle was flooded with unwelcome light.

'Fucking disastrous,' she muttered at her dishevelled reflection, squinting through slit eyes. She felt all desiccated, as though her skin had shrunk while she was asleep. The cold water helped her face, but her hair was irretrievable, sticking out like a huge static puffball. A touch of lipstick would help. She pouted into the mirror. There. White face, red mouth, red eyes.

Sam popped her arms out of her jumper, then spun her bra round so that the clasp was at the front and she could do it up again. Three hooks – one, two, three – done. Then she swivelled the elastic back, pulled the bra up her body, threaded her arms through the straps and wriggled into her sleeves. A bloody tedious sequence of events, but she had never worked out how other women managed to do their bras up *in situ*. All that reaching behind their backs at such an awkward angle.

While she sat on the loo, failing to remember all the lyrics of 'Tainted Love', Sam read the official notices stuck on the walls. Threats about smoking, flushing away the wrong sorts of things.

Peter was still sleeping when Sam got back to her seat. She pulled her bag up on to her lap and got out Julian's letter. The pale blue airmail envelope was stained with strawberry milkshake from the cafeteria. Next, her cache of photographs, a new selection from the Whittaker family album – taken with Helen's knowledge this time – together with the few that Pamela Greene had sent.

Pamela's package had arrived three days after their phone conversation. Virtually every bit of post she got seemed to come from Oxford. Sam half-expected the postman to comment on it. He didn't, of course, not noticing one postmark among thousands. Just over a week after that, she had received the letter from Julian. Polite, warm, it had suggested that – if it was not too impractical a suggestion – she should come to Washington.

Tom had blown up, thinking the suggestion ridiculous. Why couldn't Julian come to her? Helen had voiced worry at the idea of Sam travelling halfway across the world, on her own, to meet a man she didn't even know. That man in particular. No, it's out of the question . . .

Sam had chipped away at their resistance rather than flying into a temper. Her parents couldn't forbid her to go, but they all knew that she couldn't afford to buy herself a ticket. In any case, Sam wanted their blessing. After a couple of days, Tom's curiosity had got the better of him – as his wife and daughter had known it would. It's only America after all, he'd started to say, not Libya.

Helen knew then the battle was lost, that it was only a matter of time before he surrendered.

We will pay for you to go, Sam, Tom had said twenty-four hours later, on four-non-negotiable-conditions: one, that you stay in a hotel – not with Julian himself; two, that you are back before term starts; three, that someone goes with you; and, four, that you ring us every day.

Ecstatic at their volte-face, Sam had suggested that perhaps Peter could go with her. He's half-American, after all, she'd reminded them in as persuasive a voice as she could muster. It would make everything so much easier. The only problem is, Dad, that neither he nor Annette has any money . . .

It doesn't seem much of a compromise to me, Helen had commented with resignation as Sam skipped out of the kitchen to ring Peter. Two return fares, two hotel rooms for four nights and spending money. Tom pretended to be apologetic, but she knew that really he was thrilled with himself and his unaffordable plan.

Or at least, thought Sam, pulling her tartan skirt down over her cold knees, that was what Peter figured. Your dad knows you'll figure out a way to see Julian, he'd said. And he knows you'll bug the hell outta everybody until you do. So, the sooner you meet with Julian, the sooner you'll get on with your life. I bet he persuaded your mom that it might as well be on their terms, if not their ground. It makes sense. And they're great parents, he'd added, you know that . . .

Sam fidgeted in her seat. Shit, all this in nine days, she marvelled. And just five days to fit everything in. She knew she'd been rather selfish as she'd planned and booked and bustled and packed for America. Absorbed by her own emotions, she'd barely given her mother and father a second thought. In a way, it was superstition. A sneaky sense that her good luck would evaporate if she analysed it too closely. But she knew she should have taken more care to be sensitive. I'll ring Mum and Dad the minute we've landed, she vowed, and tell them how much I love them.

Feeling better, Sam looked down at the pile of black and white photos on the flip-down table. Five smiling faces looked innocently up at her, arms and legs bare in the sunny garden. A big gabled house was just visible behind the group, solid and friendly. There was a caption on the back: *Raphael House, September 1961. (L to R) me, Dylan, Gayle, Julian, Rebecca.*

Pamela looked as she sounded on the telephone. Sensible, organised, slightly older than the others. Dylan was sitting in a yoga position at the front in embarrassingly thick glasses. Sam peered at what looked like a joint. In 1961? Surely not.

When she'd first got the photos, Sam'd found her heart racing as much as it had in that doorway in Headington. Genuinely curious about the faceless people who were so much a part of their lives, her parents had asked to see. Without thinking, Sam had passed the group shot over, realising that it was going to upset her mother. Helen stared wordlessly at it, then passed it fractionally too late to Tom. He did comment on Gayle's physical likeness to Anna, but under his breath. Nothing more was said.

Gayle was stunning, though, marvelled Sam, staring again at the photo. Before the drink and drugs and unhappiness. Hair piled up on top of her head, china-doll face, wispy arms in a fitted black and white sleeveless summer dress, dreamy expression on her face. Nothing was out of place, the sort of woman whom men describe as a creature. A glamorous creature, a fey creature, a beautiful creature.

Sam's eyes skipped over Julian. She wanted to save him for last. Instead, she sized up Rebecca. It had half-entered Sam's mind that Rebecca Lawson might be her mother. She and Peter had agreed that her mother had to have been living in or close to Raphael House, otherwise where had Sam come from? There just wasn't enough time. But then Pamela's information that Rebecca had moved out in the summer of '62 had pretty much ruled her out, and the photograph confirmed it. Assumptions being what they are, it had never occurred to Sam and Peter that she might not be white. Her name sounded so English. According to Pamela, however, Rebecca was now something very high up in the Ministry of Health in her native Ghana. They still exchanged cards at Christmas. Shame, sighed Sam. She liked the idea of an international high-flying mother.

So what about Julian? Did he look like a man whose life was turning out right? Who could say? Fair Cliff Richard hair, side parting, clipped and neat. The style suited him better than it did Dylan, but Sam still cringed. Handsome features, in a leading-man sort of way. Average sort of height, so far as she could tell as he knelt beside his wife-to-be with an arm round her shoulder. Slightly wooden. Sam had stared and stared, but failed to read anything in his face.

There were also a couple of photos of Julian and Gayle on their wedding day, outside the Register Office in Oxford. The happy couple alone, the happy couple with friends, Gayle with her parents. When Sam had first opened the package and seen that one, she'd been struck by the bizarre thought that she was looking at Anna's grandparents. Here they all were, the family Anna might have had.

Sam peered at the pursed lips and judgemental eyes of Mr Faye, the whippet-like wife standing at his side. It all seemed so haphazard. That one decision, taken over eighteen years ago, could dictate the course of a person's entire life. That it was luck that she and Anna had ended up with Mum and Dad, rather than some Jehovah's Witnesses or something. Sam smoothed her hand over the photo, wondering what Anna might have been like as part of this family. A little different? Unrecognisable? She shook her head, remembering the hours spent wrestling with all those blood-is-thicker-than-water ideas that she'd once thought all-important. Biology up against life.

Finally, she shuffled out the last photo from the bottom of the pile, flipping it over to remind herself of the date. *Lauren, December 1961*. Sam had pictured a timid, skinny girl, stuck in adolescent clothes too young for her age. But this Lauren was plump, with a full, smiling mouth and wavy hair pulled away from her face with a big bow on top of her head. Very pretty. She looked quite like Julian in some ways, just more unreserved and relaxed. In the photo she was standing in front of a decorated Christmas tree, wearing a checked shirt and a pair of workmen's dungarees, the sort that all the men wear on farms in Hollywood musicals. Christmas 1961. She'd be younger than I am now, calculated Sam, hoping she'd get the chance to meet Lauren too while she was in Washington.

Sam banged the higgledy-piggledy photographs into some sort of order. All edges neat, like a new pack of cards. As she leaned under the table to put them back in her bag, her fingers touched her passport, then the moth-eared material covers of her quotation book. Essential travel reading. She worked it free from the mass of snagging corners and slapped it on to the plastic table. Like an angler landing a fish.

Sam bent the spine back and started to flick through. Every now and again, her eyes were caught by a word or a phrase that hit home.

'You gain strength, courage and confidence by every experience in which you must stop and look fear in the face. You must do the thing you think you cannot do.'

She remembered copying that from a magazine, at the time meaning to look up Eleanor Roosevelt. Another thing on her meant-to-do-but-never-quite-got-round-to-it list. What about that quotation from St Matthew that had struck a chord with Anna? Where was that? Sam skimmed the pages until she found it.

'So do not be anxious about tomorrow: tomorrow will look after itself: each day has troubles enough of its own.'

She let the lines seep in, thinking of her sister and their altered relationship. On paper, that is. The museum-like hush of the plane was getting to her. Throwing up ideas from a childhood spent together. Most adopted people had brothers and sisters to whom they were not linked by blood. That was the norm. For eighteen years, she had believed that they were unusual. But they turned out to be no different, the same as everyone else in their position. Would Anna have minded so very much? Sam didn't think so.

Leaning back in her chair, she pressed the square covers of her book shut. All those public things through which she'd defined herself. All those external signposts she'd thought mattered so much. Dates, times, days, part of a common folklore. When she was fifteen, she'd even gone through a Chinese astrology phase and worked out the exact horoscope for the moment of her birth. She'd spent hours transcribing her revelations into an oriental-looking chart, willowy letters, bamboo, Chinese white, using thin felt tips. 'My Destiny by S. M. C. Whittaker'.

But you don't know the exact time you were born, Anna had pointed out. We only know that I came first. I made an inspired guess, Sam had retorted, ploughing on in the face of Anna's scepticism. We were born in the year of the Tiger, which means that our element is wood, our colour is green, our symbol is the compass. Actually, we're Tigers Rising through the Forest. She'd been pissed off when Anna'd started laughing.

Now she looked back on it, she could remember being a little dishonest – selective was a nicer way of putting it – and only copied down the character traits she'd liked the look of. Leadership, loyalty, passion, being stimulated by a challenge, had all been included. Being ruled by anger or being over-keen on the sound of their own voices, had not.

Anna had never understood Sam's willingness to put her faith in a system based on the fact that where, and when, you were born defined who you were. Astrology. Numerology. Horoscopes. How can we possibly have near-identical charts, she'd demanded, given we're unalike in so many ways? How can you possibly believe that the twenty minutes or so between my birth and yours could account for so much? It's stupid.

Sam smiled. She'd always accused Anna of being cynical. With hindsight, she could admit that 'less impressionable' would have been a more just description. But how intense everything was at fifteen, how crucial every second, every passion! Shit, thought Sam. Would she look back on her eighteen-year-old self with the same sense of disbelief and embarrassment?

Suddenly, the overhead lights were turned on and the plane started to come to life. Everywhere was the sound of joints cracking, seats flipping upright again. Sam was aware of Peter stirring next to her, wobbling his head from side to side to iron out the stiffness.

'Been awake long?' he asked, locking his fingers and stretching his arms above his head.

Sam nodded. 'I've been looking at photos and stuff. Thinking.'

'Had any great thoughts?'

'Not really. I'm dying for a drink, though.'

'I'm sure they'll give us something,' he yawned.

Sam could see the soft red inside of his mouth.

'Anyhow, what's the time?'

Sam tipped her wrist towards him so that he could see her watch.

'Less than two hours to go,' she said.

173

CHAPTER 17

Although exhausted, Sam was exhilarated beyond her wildest dreams by the smells and tastes and sounds of America. In her imagination, it had always been a country of heat, endless desert highways and cops with guns, backed up by the squashed guitar chords of The Eagles or Janis Ian or Simon and Garfunkel. But Washington was an adrenalin-spiked city, vibrating and speeding. Not the high skyline of Dallas or New York or Chicago, but urban America none the less.

To Sam, the paradox was that somewhere so unpredictable could be so neat and so precise. The grid of horizontal streets working their way up through the alphabet, south to north. The numbered roads lining up east to west. Not like England, where you were lost without a map or prior knowledge. Here, you could work it out. So logical.

Sam and Peter emerged from the subway into the copper September light, their bodyclocks trying to cope with their second afternoon of the day. Peter's mother didn't know the city, so hadn't been able to suggest anywhere particular to stay, and Sam's parents had never been to America at all. In the end, her father had bought a guide to Washington in W. H. Smith and come up with a reasonably priced hotel not too close to Julian's apartment in Adams-Morgan. Walking distance. Before leaving for the airport, Tom had pressed a piece of paper into Sam's hand with directions printed on it in big block capitals. In the car, he'd tried to run through them several times, until Sam had threatened to scream.

'Get off at Dupont Circle,' she said, squinting around to find her bearings. 'We've done that. Now we go up 19th Street – or Connecticut Avenue, although 19th is better – as far as the junction with R Street. Then turn right and the hotel should be just there. They told Dad that we couldn't miss it.'

'OK,' said Peter, linking her arm through his. 'What are we waiting for?'

Twenty minutes later they were lying on Sam's huge double bed. Tom had booked two rooms, lip service to etiquette rather than a naive belief that both would be used. Sam's room was bigger and two floors higher, so they'd decided to base themselves there.

Sam was staring dumbly at the chunky cream telephone. So distinct, so American, like all those other objects and attitudes subconsciously assimilated from imported mini-series and soaps. Sam couldn't believe that she'd never actually touched a phone like this before. She wound her fingers round the receiver, just to try. It was much heavier than she'd expected. Tentatively she put it to her ear, heard the alien dialling tone. That, too, American through and through. The whole experiment made her feel as if she was in a film.

'Are you sure you wanna call right now, rather than wait till after we've eaten?'

'I'll be asleep by then.'

'No way,' said Peter, shaking his head. 'You gotta think in US time, otherwise you'll never get straight.'

Sam ignored him, just carried on whizzing her locket up and down its chain. Peter left her to it and wandered over to the window, amazed that it opened. Most hotel windows were welded shut, to prevent the air-conditioned air escaping into the pollution outside.

He leaned out. It was the first time he had been home in nearly two years. Not that Washington was home. But it felt good to be back. Perching himself on the sill, left leg dangling down, he rolled himself a cigarette as the noise of the traffic on New Hampshire Avenue filtered up into the room. He rested his chin on his knee, his black pony-tail trailed like a ribbon down his back. Thin reeds of smoke twisted gracefully out into the autumn afternoon.

After a couple of minutes, Sam made her decision. She tried it out loud, to see what it sounded like when put into words.

'The thing is,' she said, 'I think I have to ring now. First, because Julian will be wondering if we've arrived safely. But second, and more important, I know I won't be able to relax until I've fixed something up. Until I know what I'm doing.'

Peter flicked his wet butt out of the window, then came back to the bed.

'OK,' he said, kissing the top of her head. 'I'll just take a shower while you call.'

Sam watched him hunt out his shampoo and disappear into the bathroom. The click of the door, then the rattle of the fan starting up. She'd already nosed around in there, touched the thick white towels for size and checked out the sealed soaps and shower gels and sewing kit. It was the second thing she did in a hotel, a habit she and Anna had stumbled into as a result of summer after summer of hit-and-miss Cornish holidays. The first thing was reading the room service menu. Anna could never believe that food ranked higher in Sam's list of priorities than the emergency escape instructions on the back of the hotel door.

She realised that her heart was pumping furiously. Her body was waiting for her to pick up the phone, even if her mind had wandered off. Leaning over, she slid Julian's letter off the squat bedside table and flattened it out so that she could read the number. Muttering it to herself, she wedged the receiver between her chin and shoulder and punched the digits out. She heard the connection, heard the flat, shrill ring. What if there's no answer? What if a machine answers? What if . . . ?

Sam was taken by surprise by a living person repeating the number back to her. A woman's voice, saying hello. Before she could stop herself, Sam had slammed the phone down. One deep breath. Two. She tried to take her emotions in hand, feeling pathetic to have panicked. Nine. Ten. She put her hands firmly down on her thighs, then picked up the receiver and dialled again.

This time she concentrated hard on the numbers to make sure that there was no mistake. The same pleasant, low voice answered. This time, Sam managed to ask for Julian.

When Peter came out of the shower ten minutes later, Sam was in exactly the same position at the edge of the bed as when he'd left. Hitching his towel round his waist, he walked over and sat himself down beside her, leaving a trail of wet footprints on the carpet.

'D'you get through?'

Sam nodded.

'And?'

'And . . . he sounded nice.'

'Nice?' quizzed Peter. 'What's nice?'

'Oh. I don't know. Friendly. Efficient. Quite casual.' Sam flapped her hands hopelessly. 'You know. Nice.'

'Right,' he said. 'Nice it is.'

Sam pulled a face. 'A woman actually answered.'

'Did Julian say who she was?'

'No,' she yawned.

'You can't crash out yet.'

'Yeah, yeah. Anyway, I didn't have to insist on a neutral meeting place, like Mum and Dad wanted me to, which was brilliant. I could see that being a really embarrassing start.'

Peter got up to get a couple of proper cigarettes from Sam's duty-free stash, then headed for the dressing-table which had the courtesy matches arranged in a pyramid shape in the glass ashtray. Out of the corner of her eye, Sam saw the flare of four red tips, two real, two reflected.

'So what did you fix up?' he said, plonking the ashtray on the bed between them and putting one of the cigarettes in her mouth.

'There's a little triangular-shaped park close to where he lives, between 19th Street, Columbia Road and Kalorama Road. We just carry on walking up 19th Street and we can't miss it, fingers crossed.'

'What time?'

'Ten o'clock tomorrow morning.'

He ran his hand along the line of her leg, over the red and yellow checks of her tartan skirt. Despite her exhaustion and nerves, the pressure of his fingers made her feel warm and forgetful.

'Aren't you cold in just a towel?' she murmured.

Her body was feeling so heavy. All she wanted was to lie back on this bed forever, be a sleeping beauty. Let the briars grow around her.

Peter moved the ashtray to the floor. Sam felt him take the cigarette from between her fingers, heard the hiss as he stubbed them both out.

'I'm fine,' he answered quietly. 'Aren't you hot in all those clothes . . . ?'

Kneeling behind her on the giant bed, he started to rub her temples. Slow, circular massage. Sam's eyelids gently closed as she leaned back into him.

Sam was wide awake at five o'clock. Too apprehensive to go back

to sleep, she finally slid out of bed, showered, and pulled on jeans
and a jumper. Four hours to kill between now and Julian. The more
she thought about it, the more sick she felt. This time this evening,
everything would be different. She had to do something, something
physical, otherwise her brain would explode. Tracking down a few
famous sights might be the only way to divert her mind from the
day to come.

From the *Welcome to the Plaza* folder on the dressing-table, Sam
dug out the free colourful street map and a piece of headed paper.
Scrawling that she'd be back by eight, she propped it against the
base of the bedside light so that Peter couldn't miss it. Then she
folded the map into four, slipped a handful of dollars into one of
the voluminous pockets of her donkey jacket and sneaked out of
the room.

There was no one at the front desk as she let herself out on to
the quiet Washington streets. It was slightly misty, the buildings
and trees romantic in the early morning light. To be a tourist,
Sam worked out she needed to head south. Clutching the map
in her hand, she made herself walk calmly. It was supposed to
be a gentle stroll to shake the sleep out of her arms and legs, not
a race. She didn't have to shriek along.

Dupont Circle already felt a familiar landmark. From there, Sam
went down Massachusetts Avenue to Scott Circle, right on to 16th
Street. Heat from the few trains already running huffed up through
the subway grilles. Sam practised speaking American as she went,
substituting sidewalk for pavement, trash can for rubbish bin. It
made her feel sophisticated, despite her butterfly stomach.

On H Street, she found herself unable to go any further.
Zig-zagging, she found herself taking in elegant buildings with
European pillars and arches, rather than needle-thin modern blocks.
Now, she was on Constitution Avenue. It was all so green. So
beautiful. So not what she'd expected. Parties of tourists were
already swarming towards the Washington Monument, hungry for
culture. Anxious to distance herself from them, Sam turned back
to the White House. It looked freshly scrubbed, much smaller in
the flesh than the television news suggested. Her heart swelled at
the sight of it all. She felt like an angel surveying her kingdom.

Out of habit, she glanced at her watch and was shocked to
discover it was late. She'd have to rush if she was to get back
to the hotel by the time she'd promised on her note. She needed

another shower too. Sam set off again, nearly jogging, dreaming of coffee and bagels and cream cheese.

'Your black denims?' suggested Peter. 'They're pretty neutral.'

For forty minutes, Sam had been dithering about what to wear. Nothing felt right and there was now a heap of clothes discarded on the unmade bed.

'We'll look like twins,' replied Sam, looking at his black legs. 'Too coordinated.'

Her expression sagged when she realised what she'd just said. She turned back to the wardrobe. Peter came up behind her and put his arms round her shoulders. They swayed close for a moment, then he briskly rubbed her bare arms with his hands. As if trying to warm her up.

'How about your blue denims, then, and the black turtle-neck, since we're gonna be outside?'

'I think we're only meeting at the park, before finding a café or something nearby.'

'OK,' said Peter, managing to stay calm. 'Then wear your grey turtle-neck . . .'

He rummaged through the clothes on the bed to find the jumper, then tossed it over. Sam half-caught it as she struggled with her jeans, lying flat on the floor to pull the zip up. The effort made the tops of her fingers sore.

'They've obviously shrunk,' she muttered as she walked stiffly over to the stool at the dressing-table.

Crouching at her feet, Peter eased her boots on for her, then turned her round to face the mirror and started to brush her hair. Erotic, methodical, hypnotising strokes.

'Right,' she heard him say too soon. 'You're done.'

Sam looked at herself, wondering what Julian would see. Someone confident? Someone he liked the look of? She plucked a couple of stray hairs from her jumper, then pursed her mouth to put on her lipstick. Ruby.

'We should get going,' said Peter.

Sam pushed back the stool, kissed a tissue to take the shine off her lips, scrumpled it into the ashtray, then jigged impatiently from foot to foot. As she settled her coat over her arm, Sam caught sight of her red beret. That might look good.

'What about this?'

Peter pulled a let-me-see face. 'I'd skip the beret.'

'Ber-ray,' she imitated, and chucked it back on to the bed.

The sun was rising as they walked. Over S Street, T and U Streets, California Street, Wyoming Avenue, past coffee bars, drug stores, offices.

'Columbia Road,' Sam read from the sign standing to attention on the corner. 'That must be it over there.'

'Where precisely in the park are you meeting?' asked Peter.

Sam gestured to the green space opposite as they waited at the lights.

'Right there, at the tip. I can't see anyone waiting, though . . .'

A chill sweat crashed over her. Perhaps he wasn't coming. He had cold feet. He wasn't coming. Her throat suddenly seemed to be blocked, as if she had swallowed cotton wool. Her tongue felt glued to the roof of her mouth.

'Hey, we're early,' said Peter, squeezing her hand. 'Let's walk round the block for ten minutes. OK?'

They crossed over and followed the boundary of the park along 19th Street. Strolling hand-in-hand, they looked like any other couple out enjoying the Washington morning. No rush, just a pleasant meander round the neighbourhood.

A young headphoned guy on skates flashed past. Up ahead, Sam could see a little girl on her father's shoulders and a man and a woman, arms linked, talking and talking. The woman's curly hair was gathered into a loose pony-tail at the nape of her neck, swaying against a brightly coloured shawl. Annette would like that shawl, murmured Sam, as she watched the couple turn into the park.

Turning right at the corner, their faces were flooded by sunlight as they stepped out of the shadows. They were overtaken by a man and his muzzled boxer, by a fluorescent purple jogger clutching a Walkman in her right hand, then by an elderly couple, both in hats. Right again, back on to Columbia Road. The third side of the triangle. More people here, a sense of purpose, hurry. Sam watched her shiny yellow feet clipping along the pavement, counting each step.

'One minute to blast-off,' she said as they arrived back where they'd started.

She and Peter stood in silence, backs to the park, still holding hands. Waiting.

'Sam?'

Startled, Sam spun round in the direction of the sound.

'I'm sorry. I didn't mean to alarm you,' said the man. 'You are Sam?'

'Julian?'

Her voice sounded squeaky to her, barely audible above the noise of the traffic surging forward on the green light.

Julian held out his hand, first to Sam, then to Peter. Julian Driver, Peter Newman. Introductions over, the three of them found themselves standing awkwardly. Nobody knew how to begin. Small-talk was too trivial. Anything else, too big.

Julian cleared his throat.

'You found it without any difficulty?'

'Yes,' Sam leaped in, but then was unable to think of anything else to follow it up. 'Thank you.'

She couldn't stop staring at this real man standing here in front of her, with his real hair, real eyes, real teeth.

'You sound quite American,' she heard herself blurt out. 'Sorry. That sounded really pathetic.'

'I think we're all a little nervous,' he smiled. 'Why don't we walk for a while?'

He stood back to let Peter and Sam go into the park ahead of him. As they made their way along the winding path, Julian talked to Peter. Safe questions, about where Peter came from, what he thought of England. The usual. Sam listened to the differences between them. Peter spoke American, whereas Julian spoke English. Public school English, with a hint of an American accent. It was odd, but she hadn't expected him to talk so much. In Sam's mind, handsome men equalled quiet men. Always had. Handsome, as opposed to good-looking or sexy.

She watched Julian out of the corner of her eye, concentrating on her first impressions so as not to forget. It was amazing how familiar he was. Taller than Peter – although nowhere near as tall as Dad – blond hair, blue eyes, chiselled jaw. Early forties. Quite like that actor in *Colditz*, what was his name? Recognisably the man in the photos Pamela Greene had sent. If anything, twenty years had made him more handsome.

Suddenly it came to her. 'David McCallum . . .'

Peter grinned, guessing at Sam's train of thought.

'I'm sorry?' said Julian, turning towards her.

Sam could only smile, too embarrassed to say anything. She'd not intended the comment for public consumption. They strolled in silence for a few seconds.

'I thought we might go for a coffee a little later,' Julian said, stopping by an empty bench. 'But what about sitting and talking here for a while first?'

'That's fine with me,' replied Sam.

She parked herself down on the wooden seat, clutching her jacket tightly against her chest like a shield and trying to force herself to relax. She didn't want Julian to see quite how terrified she was.

'I think I'll take a walk,' said Peter. 'Give you guys a chance to talk.'

He bent and kissed Sam on the mouth, caressing the back of her neck with his hand. Sam smiled weakly up at him, trying not to panic.

'I'll be back in fifteen minutes. OK?'

Sam watched him go as Julian sat down beside her. The smaller Peter got, the more vulnerable Sam felt. Now she couldn't see him any more. She was on her own.

'It's very hard to know where to start,' she said, glancing sideways at Julian.

'It is,' he replied.

Silence again. Sam felt grateful that he was not rushing straight into things. If only she could think of what to say.

'You know about Anna?'

Shit, that sounded harsh. Sam hoped she hadn't sounded too blunt. She hadn't meant to sound blunt.

'Pamela told me in her letter,' said Julian quietly.

Sam realised the atmosphere between them was changing. Just for an instant, it was as if Anna was sitting on the bench between them. His daughter Anna, her sister Anna. Lost to them both.

'You must miss her very much,' he added in a soft voice.

Sam could only nod, the familiar lump in her throat stealing her words. All the unknown years stretched between them in the busy silence of the park. No tears, Sam said to herself, brushing her eyes roughly with the sleeve. Please, no tears. The cuff of her jumper was wet, transformed from light grey to dark.

'That's why it was so awful,' she started to explain, 'when I found Gayle. When she told me . . .'

'There's no rush,' said Julian quickly. 'We have plenty of time for all this.'

Sam watched him rubbing his palms along the top of his jeans, as if he was trying to come to a decision. He's nervous, she realised. He seems composed and adult and in control, but he's nervous too. The thought made her feel less ill at ease. As if they were in it together.

Julian cleared his throat, surprising Sam. The sound seemed to ricochet off the trunks of the trees.

'Sam. Before we go any further, there's someone I want you to meet. Would you mind waiting here for a minute or two?'

Sam felt her heart start to beat furiously as Julian stood up. Bang. Bang. Red blood crashing through her veins. She jumped up too. She didn't know why, she just felt stupid sitting on the bench on her own. As she watched him striding away, she had to force herself not to run after him. A small side path, then he was out of sight. Hidden by the burgundy leaves of the bushes.

Sam felt like a victim waiting to be mugged, lost without a clue what was going on. Time stretched like elastic. Every second seemed twice the span of a minute, every minute twice as long as an hour. Was that him? Sam narrowed her eyes into the light. Yes, the right cream jumper, the right pressed blue jeans. He was walking back towards her, getting closer and closer. A woman was with him. Sam recognised her from earlier. That distinctive rainbow shawl and wavy blonde hair tied back from her face.

Now here they were, standing right in front of her.

'I'd like to introduce you to my sister, Laurie,' said Julian. He sounded very formal. 'Sam Whittaker, Lauren Driver.'

Automatically, Sam held out her hand. She was in a trance, holding her breath as she looked into the woman's eyes. Extra-ordinary chestnut eyes, the colour of autumn. Sam was aware of every smell around them, every noise. The impatient cars hooting on Columbia Road, the leaves swishing high above them, the fast rattle of parents negotiating with their children, friends exchanging news. English, Spanish, languages she'd never heard before.

The two women stood, their clasped hands making a bridge between them. The tension burned red as they looked into each other's face. Two pairs of eyes, one brown, one blue.

Sam felt the world fall into place.

'You know,' said Lauren. 'Don't you?'

It was a low voice, floating from far, far away. Echoing and light, in half-time.

'I think so,' whispered Sam, suddenly shy. 'You're my mother. Aren't you?'

CHAPTER 18

Their waiter Dwayne was hovering again, pad and pen at the ready.

'Hi. Would you ladies like a refill? Something to eat?'

Sam glanced at her watch. Amazing. Nearly twelve o'clock already, slap, bang, wallop in the middle of brunch. Suppertime at home. She and Lauren had been sitting at this same quiet table for over an hour and a half, talking and listening. Getting to know one another.

After the first exhilarating moment, it had been awkward. Floating slowly back down to earth, trying to work out where to go from there. Luckily Peter had reappeared almost immediately. Sam had introduced him to Lauren and the four of them had taken refuge in the usual social subjects as they'd walked out of the park. The weather, flights, the exchange rate. Then Peter had tactfully headed back to the Plaza and Julian had tactfully remembered some work he had to finish back at the apartment. Mother and daughter had found themselves alone outside Mezzo's Diner.

A table for two, please. Sam had felt physically clumsy, as much as anything, as she and Lauren had followed the chatty Dwayne round tables for single diners, family tables for four to eight. But they were natural born talkers, both of them, and caffeine had loosened their tongues. As the sun clambered higher in the sky, eighteen years' worth of stories had tumbled out, a patchwork of the separate lives they'd led. Like new lovers out on a date. Childhood, school, ambitions.

Sam explained she wasn't sure what she wanted to do when she left college. Not yet. Television, maybe? Journalism? She knew all the really interesting things were hard to get into. More importantly, she'd shown Lauren photos of her parents and talked and talked about Anna. Their Paddington Bear birthdays, their differences and similarities. Her death and all that came after it.

In return, Lauren told Sam about her job at the Theater School round the corner, about Julian's antiquarian book business, about being an American in England and the countries she'd visited. All over the world. Quickfire questions and answers, each hungry for basic facts and statistics. They self-censored anything too close to the bone. It was too soon to pry, they both knew it. Anything before the winter of 1962 was out of bounds, as was anything that had happened in the past six weeks. When the tapestry had started to come unstitched.

'Ladies?' repeated Dwayne.

Lauren looked to Sam for an answer. Sam was torn. It was probably inappropriate to be thinking of food at a time like this, but she was ravenous.

'I could manage something,' she admitted.

Lauren laughed out loud at the boggle-eyed expression on Sam's face when Dwayne produced two gigantic menus out of nowhere. Hash browns, eggs sunny side up, muffins, maple syrup, waffles. Full, half and no-fat non-dairy creamers. Blueberries. Muffins. So many things she'd never had before.

As Lauren ordered for both of them, Sam watched her surreptitiously. She wasn't beautiful, not like Gayle, but she had a sort of candid sensuality that drew the gaze to her face. Her extraordinary chestnut eyes, her wide mouth and milky skin, improved by a few thirty-something lines round the eyes. She also had the sort of fabulous long messy curls Sam had always aspired to. And descriptive hands, never still, movement accompanying every word she said.

Dwayne was already rearranging the cutlery on the table to make way for their food. Checking the salt and pepper were full, bringing Sam another knife to replace the one she'd elbowed on to the floor, killing the conversation. Sam felt as if she was in an interview. She desperately wanted to impress Lauren, to be thought attractive and witty and intelligent. Sparkle, sparkle, sparkle. She hadn't even smoked. Although she would never have admitted, a part of it was wanting to make Lauren regret the choice she had made eighteen years ago.

When they'd first sat down, Sam had dreaded the conversation veering into more intimate territory. The thought of honest talking had made her squirm. But as her confidence had grown, she'd become less inhibited, felt a little bolder. She didn't want to over-step the mark, not when everything was going so well, but she was finding it harder to keep the intimate questions from jumping out of her mouth. For the past ten minutes, one question above all others.

Sam prodded random bits of fruit around her plate in the maple syrup. Trying to pluck up the courage to ask.

'I hope this is not too personal . . .'

Lauren looked at her. 'Go ahead, Sam.'

'Do I . . . ?'

At the last moment, she chickened out. Heard the wrong words coming out instead.

'Did you ever get married?'

Shit, thought Sam. I'm being pathetic. She wriggled on her chair in her uncomfortable jeans, wishing the waistband wasn't so tight.

Lauren put her fork down and looked across the table, as if she'd realised that Sam had intended something else.

'No,' she answered slowly, smiling lightly. 'I never did. Had a couple of offers though . . .'

Sam barely heard, too caught up in her cowardice. Be confident, she was saying to herself. Fucking well get on with it . . .

'Sorry. What I'm trying to ask is . . . well, do you have any other children?'

Lauren shook her head. Understanding.

No. The denial hit Sam between the eyes. That was it, then. No sisters or brothers. What did she feel? Disappointed? Relieved? She supposed it was good that there were no other significant complications to deal with, but it didn't feel good. Without thinking, Sam put her hand up to her locket.

'It's very special to you, isn't it?'

'I'm sorry?' said Sam, confused.

'Your locket,' explained Lauren.

Sam looked down to find her fingers instinctively twizzling the silver oval up and down. Like a pendulum. She smiled.

'Most of the time, I don't know I'm doing it,' she confessed. 'Anna gave it to me when we were thirteen. By complete coincidence, I gave her a cross. A little gold cross on a chain. We always swapped presents the night before our birthday.'

Sam felt the shadow fall over her. She carefully laid her fork down, hearing the subtle chink of the metal against china. She did not want to cry, not here in front of Lauren. She wanted to seem someone who had her emotions under control, someone who'd coped with the tragedies in her life. She forced herself to keep talking.

'Anna never took hers off either. It was buried with her when she died . . .'

Lauren looked at the girl sitting across the table with her piercing eyes, swimming-pool blue. Her frizzy dark blonde hair she kept tucking back behind her ears. For over eighteen years, this girl had been a lodger in her head. Never leaving. And now? Now, after all the wondering and all the missing, here she was in the flesh. Not the tiny baby of her memory, not a child even, but a confident young Englishwoman.

She felt swollen with a lifetime of wasted love. She caught her breath. All she wanted to do was to wrap Sam in her arms and rock her until the pain went away. But knew she could not. Too much, too soon, might scare her daughter off. Reconciliation had to come before love.

Tentatively, she reached out her hand. Palm down. She felt Sam take it, hold it tight. Lauren slammed her eyes shut, with relief.

'You were born on the same day as Anna,' she whispered. 'That much was true.'

As their linked arms hovered in the air above the debris of the meal, tears began to roll down Sam's cheek. Healing, not of grief. She didn't know why she was crying, just that she was.

'I think we should go now,' Lauren was saying softly. She sounded calm. 'It's time you knew what happened.'

It was no more than five minutes to the apartment Lauren shared with Julian. When she'd been offered the job at the Theater School two years ago, they'd decided to sell their two tiny apartments in different parts of town and go for something a little more spacious. All the promises Sam had made to her parents were forgotten, assurances of staying on neutral territory and of never going anywhere without Peter. Through the lobby and into the elevator. Sam stared blindly at her shell-shocked expression in the mirrored walls, barely recognising herself.

Julian showed her to the phone, so she could let Peter know

where she was and that she was fine. Sam realised that she didn't want Peter with her. It wasn't just that she no longer felt in need of moral support. It was a private affair now, between her and Lauren and Julian. No one else. She was relieved when he didn't answer.

Leaving a message with the front desk, Sam hung up, unsure of what to do next. Perching uncomfortably on the sharp edge of a carved chair next to the phone, rigid like an Egyptian cat, she hoped they'd come back soon. Normally, when left alone in a strange place, Sam's favourite game was rifling through the record collection and bookshelves, searching out clues to their owner. But in this apartment, everything was loaded with meaning. Open to misinterpretation. The usual rules did not apply to this bold room with its beads and its folk art and its stacks of musty books on the wooden floor. Somewhere, a clock chimed one. Sam jigged her legs, and waited.

At last, Lauren appeared in the doorway, holding a small round brass tray with an open bottle of red wine and three colourful glasses on it.

'Come and sit someplace more comfortable,' she said warmly, heading towards the windows. Black mohair jumper stretching down to her knees, wide magenta trousers shimmering as she moved. Sam noticed that she had taken her shoes off and her feet were now bare.

A book lay open on the long coffee table, face down. Lauren inched it out of the way with the rim of the tray.

'I thought we could all do with this,' she smiled. 'There.'

Hands free, she then fished a heavy ashtray from her pocket and put it down next to the tray.

'I noticed you had cigarettes in your purse,' she said. 'Go ahead and smoke if you want to. Really.'

Sam blushed, embarrassed to have been caught out. Not that she'd lied. She just hadn't owned up. After a second's hesitation, she went round and sat in the chair with its back to the daylight.

'Thank you.'

'Did you get through to Peter?' asked Lauren, squeezing in between the edge of the table and the chair next to Sam.

'He wasn't there, so I left this number with reception. I hope that was all right?'

'Sure.'

She's so calm, marvelled Sam. So totally calm and open. She was dying for a cigarette now, but was afraid her jittering hands would expose how nervous she felt if she tried to use them. Instead, she preoccupied herself easing off her boots with her toes. One gentle thud, two. That was better. Immediately more relaxed, Sam tucked her feet up underneath her and snuggled into the fat arm of her chair.

Lauren bent over to pour the wine. One glass for Sam, one on the tray for Julian, one for herself. Holding hers carefully, she then sat down cross-legged in her chair.

'They're beautiful,' said Sam, admiring the speckled glass in the light.

'Yes, aren't they?' Lauren answered. 'Julian brought them back from Italy last year.'

She gestured towards Sam's cigarettes, now lying between them on the table. 'May I?'

'I'm sorry, I didn't realise.'

'I don't often . . .'

Relieved to have something to do, Sam quickly flipped the packet open. Next, a light. As both women leaned towards the flame, they were aware that their heads were nearly touching.

The atmosphere changed when Julian came in, his maleness somehow altering the balance of things. What had been a comfortable silence became an expectant one. Sam felt as if she was at a first night at the theatre. That any minute the auditorium lights would dim and the curtain would rise, to reveal the set and the characters. The mother, the uncle and the daughter, sitting with their props and rehearsed lines ready. Her mouth felt dry.

Julian took his glass from the tray and sat down opposite Sam. Down to business. At last, they were down to business.

'I think the most sensible thing is probably for us to start at the beginning,' he said.

'But cut in if there's anything you don't understand,' Lauren added.

The suspense was painful. Sam felt like an athlete waiting for the gun after two false starts, as if every muscle in her body was wired and about to snap. She gulped at her wine to steady her nerves. Its red sourness stung her tongue.

Julian cleared his throat.

'You've been to Raphael House, I presume?'

'No,' she gabbled back, voice too loud. 'No, I haven't. But Pamela did send me a picture of all of you in the garden.'

Sam dug her shivering fingers into her bag for her tatty A4 envelope. Finding the photograph she wanted, she passed it across the table to Julian. He glanced at it, then handed it to his sister. Five smiling faces, hers not among them, twenty years out of date. Sam watched Lauren flip the souvenir over to read the date, before carefully laying it on the arm of her chair.

'You don't get a sense of the place from that,' said Julian. 'But it really was beautiful. Huge. Surrounded by sweeping lawns with a slope down to an evergreen grove at the back of the house. It had been left to Pamela by an aunt in the late fifties.

'Anyway, Pamela was a nurse, as I think you know. She was away more and more, so she'd taken the decision to have lodgers rather than let the house stand empty for six months out of every twelve. I knew Pamela through a friend of a friend, so when she offered me a room it seemed an ideal arrangement.'

'When was this?' asked Sam.

'The summer of 1960,' Julian replied. 'I'd just finished my degree and hadn't a clue what I wanted to do with my life. The only thing I had decided was that I would stay in Oxford. For the short-term at least.'

He glanced sideways at the black and white photo resting on Lauren's chair.

'Dylan was a fellow student from Magdalen. He moved in at the same time as me, August 1960. Rebecca was already there.'

'And Gayle? When did she arrive?'

Lauren suddenly bounced up, the unexpected moment shocking Sam. Drops of wine splashed out of her glass, over her wrist and on to the table.

'Oh God, I'm sorry,' she apologised.

'No, it's my fault for startling you,' replied Lauren. 'I was only going to the bathroom.'

'I thought I'd said something wrong,' Sam said, still looking worried.

Lauren smiled at her. 'Really, the wine doesn't matter. Julian will get a cloth. Won't you, Julian?'

'It makes a change for you to be doing the mopping up rather than the spilling, Laurie,' said Julian as he got up.

Sam watched them walk across the room together, and felt

pricked by jealousy. Their comfortable intimacy made her feel like an outsider, a guest instead of a friend.

Julian reappeared first, carrying a tea-towel and another open bottle of wine. He wiped the table, topped up Sam's glass, then tossed the stained cloth to the end of the table. Mum would never be able to leave it there like that, thought Sam, then smiled in astonishment that such a thought had even entered her head.

The sound of the loo flushing filtered into the room. A couple of seconds more, then Lauren came back too.

'Now. Where were we?' she said, flopping back into her chair.

The interval was over. The mother, the uncle and the daughter were back in their pool of spotlight, waiting. Ladies and gentlemen, please take your seats. The second act is about to begin.

'I was about to tell Sam about how I met Gayle,' answered Julian. 'We were introduced by a mutual acquaintance at a party in April 1961. Gayle had just come back to Oxford to live with her parents, having left college the previous Christmas.'

'Sorry,' interrupted Sam, 'but where did she go? To college, I mean.'

Julian looked at her with surprise. 'The London College of Music. Why do you ask?'

'It was the only thing that Anna wanted to know,' Sam said quietly.

Memory wrapped her warm coils around the room. Lauren watched Sam struggling with her feelings. Earlier, in the Diner, Sam had talked about this part of her life with no problem. Different now. She turned to her brother.

'Sam and Anna felt differently about tracing,' she said. 'About tracing us, I guess I mean.'

Lauren paused for a moment, took a sip of her wine. 'Anyhow, the girls knew Gayle had been at music college, from the notes Tom – Mr Whittaker – had been given by the Adoption Society. Anna was a gifted violinist, Julian. She wanted to be a professional musician.'

She broke off again, looking to Sam for confirmation that she'd got her facts straight. 'Not long before Anna died, she told Sam that she felt weird not knowing if she was applying to the same college as their natural mother.'

'She wanted to go to the Royal Academy,' Sam muttered.

For a moment, Julian didn't respond, just sat looking into his glass.

'The violin was Gayle's instrument,' he said finally. 'But, you know, I never once heard her play.'

Another silence.

'I didn't mean to put you off,' Sam apologised after a second or two.

'It's just all these things,' replied Julian. 'Things I've not remembered for years.'

Sam nodded, skating her eyes over the beautiful room while he just sat for a moment. She didn't want to seem impatient.

'Anyway,' he sighed, 'to cut a long story short, I fell head over heels in love with Gayle. She was such a beautiful creature, so graceful. I was attracted by her vulnerability, I suppose. I was muddling along, really, still working in the bookshop and not knuckling down to any sort of serious job. Her dependence made me feel needed, like I was worth something.'

Julian suddenly gave an embarrassed smile. He looks as if he's about to confess something, thought Sam. Sheepish.

'I proposed to her only weeks after we'd met.'

'How old were you?' Sam asked.

'Twenty-four. Old enough to know better . . . By the summer, though, the infatuation was wearing off. Just little things, like the fact that she had not actually completed her music course. It didn't matter to me that she'd been asked to leave. I couldn't have cared less. It was more that she had lied to me about it.

'Suddenly she seemed to be ill all the time, always flying off the handle and unhappy. I didn't understand it, how she could be so lovely one minute, then all tears and tantrums the next. Of course, if Pamela had been around, she would have spotted the problem right away. I was very naive.'

Sam shivered as her mind was thrown back to that claustrophobic house in Headington, the memory of Gayle's rage and lightning loss of control. The taste of fear in her mouth.

'By this time, I was sure that I was making a mistake,' Julian continued. 'But the wedding was only a matter of weeks away and, well, I know it sounds absurd, but I just didn't feel I could let Gayle down. I thought it was all my fault that everything had gone wrong. I didn't feel I had any choice but to go through with it.'

Sam thought of the other photos in her basket. Julian and Gayle on the steps of the Register Office, husband and wife. What if Julian *had* changed his mind and not gone through with it? Married someone else? Anna would never have existed. A decision, borne out of duty rather than love, and a life had been the result. Her fingers crept to her locket as Julian's voice reverberated in the air.

'Gayle moved into Raphael House in the September, and four weeks later, at the end of October, we got married. Do you know, the first time I ever met her parents was at the wedding?'

Julian glanced towards Lauren, then back to Sam.

'Two weeks later, I was contacted by a Washington law firm, to be told that my sixteen-year-old American sister was coming to live with me. Just like that. I didn't even know I had a sister. It would be fair to say that Gayle did not react very positively. Not that I blame her.'

Neither did Dad, thought Sam. Blame Gayle, that is. Funny that they should think the same, these two men. Her father and her uncle. They were so different. Uncle. Immediately she felt ashamed at how easily she was slipping Julian and Lauren into her family. It made her feel disloyal to Mum and Dad, as if she was making decisions behind their back. Stop thinking, Sam, she told herself, and ask questions. She swallowed hard.

'Actually,' she said, turning to Lauren, 'I don't really understand why you were in America in the first place.'

Lauren stretched her arms above her head. Her baggy black sleeves slipped down towards her shoulders, revealing the pale underside of her arms.

'It is confusing,' she admitted. 'It took us a while to figure it out ourselves.'

Julian smiled at her.

'Here we go,' she said, folding her arms in her lap. 'Our mother was an American. In the summer of 1937 she was in Switzerland with her parents, where she met this English gentleman. He was much older than her and very conventional, totally unlike anyone she'd ever met before. Courteous, proper. Anyhow, she was swept off her feet. He proposed, she accepted and went to live in England. For the first year, things were fine. Not great, but OK. She became pregnant and had a son.'

'You?' said Sam, looking at Julian. He nodded.

'Then he said they were going to live in his family house in the country, rather than in London. He didn't ask what she wanted, just told her to pack. Mom was desperately unhappy there. She'd say that he ruled the household with a rod of iron, even when he wasn't there.'

Lauren held her hands out in front of her for a moment, as if she was looking for something written on her skin.

'His attitude dictated everything. He belittled her all the time, humiliating her in front of people, picking fault at her "ignorant" American ways. Always going on about how such and such a thing was appropriate behaviour for an English wife, how such and such was not. First she was too familiar with the servants – his staff, as he called them – then too aloof. He'd even hired a nanny for Julian without consulting her. The woman who'd looked after him when he was a baby.'

'Why didn't she leave?' interrupted Sam.

'Wives didn't in those days,' replied Lauren. 'Not unless they had their own money. In any case, where would she have gone? She was only seventeen.'

Sam tried to imagine being trapped in a life she hated, owned by a man she feared. Owned. She had to shrug the thought away. It hurt too much. This woman was her grandmother, not just a somebody in a story.

'Then the war broke out in Europe. Mom tried to persuade him to come back to America with her. Or, at least, to let her take Julian to safety. After weeks of cat-and-mouse, he informed her that he would allow her to leave, on two conditions. One, that she took nothing but the clothes she stood up in. And, two, that she left his son – *his* son – behind.'

Sam watched Lauren beating a violent tatoo on the arm of the chair with her fingers. Angry, powerless fingers.

'She knew he only wanted Julian to get at her. He knew how much she loved her little boy and wanted to make her suffer. She'd never have left him, he knew that. That was when he handed Julian over to the nanny. Sometimes Mom wasn't even allowed to kiss him goodnight.'

The cruelty of it all rang through Sam's head, boxing her ears. She tried to blink away the wetness in her eyes.

'Mom stuck it out for another five years. He was in London a lot of the time. It was better when he was. She dreaded his return, the sheer physical presence of him. The things he'd want her to do . . .

'When I asked too many questions,' Lauren added in her low,

soft voice, 'she'd simply kiss my hair and say that I was too young to learn about hate.'

Lauren shuddered, her imagination painting vivid the physical details her mother had never told her. Sam lit another cigarette to calm herself. Only four left.

'I can hardly remember anything before the age of about seven,' said Julian. 'The smell of the nursery, Nanny Tanner's bony hands. Being lonely.'

Lauren leaned over and put her hand on his arm. More the gesture of a big, protective sister, than a little one.

'Then Mom discovered she was expecting another baby and that was it. She knew she had to get out.'

Lauren smiled, unexpectedly. 'She was so sure I was going to be another boy. He's not going to steal another son from me, that's what she'd say to herself. That's what gave her the courage to go through with it.

'Anyhow, in the spring of 1944, she sold a few trinkets and personal pieces of jewellery she prayed he wouldn't notice were missing. By May, she had raised enough for her passage home to America. She'd timed her escape to coincide with the VE Day celebrations. All she had to show for seven years of brutish married life was one battered suitcase.'

'And the unborn you,' muttered Julian.

'She left you behind?' Sam blurted at him, shocked to her bones. 'How *could* she?'

'She felt he was lost to her anyway,' Lauren answered quietly. 'You shouldn't blame her. What choice did she have?'

The three of them sat in a painful silence. A story nearly forty years old had brought them face to face with the facts of the present. Like mother, like daughter. Recurring patterns, abandoned and abandoning children in a never-ending hall of mirrors. Like mother, like daughter. Like father, like son.

Sam rubbed her eyelids, then let her head fall back against the soft quilt draped over the back of her chair. For hours, it seemed, feeling the day fading around her. But when she opened her eyes again, the room looked exactly as it had before. The same colours, the same furniture, the same quality of light.

The clock struck two, precisely.

'Mom talked about Julian all the time,' Lauren was saying. 'I grew up with an image of this beautiful boy. She sent letters every Christmas, every birthday. I remember watching her wrap up packages of books, sweaters, a pair of socks once. When I was little, I thought every stranger who knocked at our door was my brother from England come to visit.'

'Do you know,' said Julian, 'he never gave me one single letter from her. Not one. I don't remember him ever mentioning her name again. I didn't know what had happened, only that my mother wasn't there any more. Perhaps I thought she was dead? Three months after she'd gone, he sent me away to boarding school. As he'd always intended. I thought I must be very bad, for nobody to want me.

'The worst thing,' he added bitterly, 'was discovering all of this from Laurie fifteen years later and realising my mother must have thought I didn't care. That I was punishing her by not replying.'

'I'm so sorry,' Sam muttered under her breath. It seemed so inadequate.

'I never lived under the same roof as my father again. School was all right – better than home – and I spent all the holidays with my grandmother in the Lake District. He would visit me there from time to time. He always seemed disappointed, as if I didn't measure up to his idea of what a son should be.'

He drained his wine. 'I don't know. He was probably right. The only emotion I can ever remember feeling towards him was fear.'

'That's dumb, Julian,' said Lauren angrily. 'And you know it.'

He shrugged but said nothing, just put his empty glass back on the tray. Sam watching his face softening, understood that the good memories were pushing out the bad.

'My grandmother was a wonderful, wonderful woman. She disliked my father, I'm sure of that, although she never would have said so. It was Granny who told me that my mother was alive, living somewhere in America. She made me promise I would never let him know she had been the one to tell me.'

Sam took another mouthful of wine. She should stop soon. Her head was beginning to dance.

'When I was eighteen,' continued Julian, 'Granny became very ill. It was as if the years caught up on her, all at once. I nursed her until she died in 1956, much to my father's disgust. He thought I should have pressed on with my studies regardless.'

He looked down. Sam tried to picture the scene. The young man at his grandmother's bedside day after day, watching her die and not being able to do a thing about it. Your father's a good man, PB, she murmured under her breath. You'd be proud of him.

'I loved her very much,' said Julian.

The clock chimed the quarter.

'Is your father still alive?' asked Sam tentatively.

Julian shook his head. 'He died in 1957.'

'So getting back to the main story,' said Lauren, trying to lighten the mood a little, 'when Mom died, there was only Julian left for me. This English boy of my dreams whom I'd never even met.'

She picked up the cigarette packet on the table. 'Do you mind?'

'No. Go ahead,' said Sam, passing her the matches.

'I could have fought harder to stay here,' Lauren continued, tipping her head back and blowing smoke at the ceiling. 'But I didn't want to stay in the same old neighbourhood without Mom. And, I was curious. I know it sounds crazy, but the fact that Julian was the one person in the world who I was connected to – physically, I mean – meant a whole lot to me then.'

Lauren suddenly looked at Sam, realising what she'd said. 'I guess you understand that . . .'

Sam smiled, warmed by the alcohol and the heightened atmosphere.

'All of my life I dreamed of finding you,' she said, then blushed at her honesty.

CHAPTER 19

Between the three of them, they had stumbled to the point of no return. They all knew it.

Sam seemed to be observing herself from a great height, whirring on the ceiling like a bladed fan. She felt she had been one foot on the mountain for days, skewering in the ice pick, pulling her weight up through her arms, the peak never coming any nearer. Climbing and climbing. In a film, the music would give the significance of this scene away, she thought. You'd look at your watch, you'd hear the roll of drums, and you'd know not to make your cup of tea now. That after so many false summits, this – at last – was the real thing.

Sam looked at Lauren. Rogue strands of hair were curling loose round her face now, her hands still talking nineteen to the dozen. They needed to unburden the secret as much as she needed to take it on, Sam realised that now. She prayed she would not feel any differently about Lauren when the once-upon-a-time had come to an end. She wanted to understand, to listen to her story through grown-up ears. Unjudgemental, sympathetic. Not with the selfishness of a rejected little girl wanting someone to blame.

Lauren crossed her legs in her chair, like a buddha.

'Sometimes I look back and think it was all a dream. That it can't have happened how I remember.'

Intense, gravelly words. Not hurried.

'I don't think what we did was right,' said Julian with passion. 'God knows, we've had to live with the knowledge of what happened for eighteen years. But, at the time, I did believe we were acting for the best. For you. And Anna.'

'You were never far from our minds,' Lauren added. 'Particularly on your birthday, special days, stuff like that. I always fantasised about running into you, that wherever in the world we found ourselves, we'd still recognise something in each other. I don't know. All the time, I wondered if you were happy.'

'We were,' said Sam, anxious to reassure her. 'We were always very happy.'

Lauren smiled. 'Things were very different then. You know, people think of the sixties as being this great time, all liberated, freedom. Well, maybe it was for some. For men, maybe. For most of us, though, the rules were just as rigidly in place as they ever had been. Just a little more subtle. If you stepped out of line, had a baby without that ring on your finger . . .'

She flapped her hands, remembering the myths they'd been force-fed. How gullible they'd been.

'I guess what I'm trying to say, Sam, is that I know how hard it must be for you to understand how any woman could give her baby up.'

Sam felt ashamed, as if Lauren had eavesdropped on all the intolerant speeches she'd made in the past, full of the language of retribution and punishment for the woman who had chosen not to be their mother. Ashamed, she looked away.

'Are you OK?' Lauren asked softly.

Sam nodded.

Julian cleared his throat. 'Well . . . shall I go on?'

'Yes, please,' said Sam in a strangled voice.

Brother and sister exchanged glances, concerned about her, but took her at her word.

'From the moment Lauren arrived at Raphael House,' said Julian, 'my relationship with Gayle deteriorated. She hated Laurie on sight. She was jealous and couldn't accept that I wanted to spend a little time getting to know my new sister.

'Gayle's relations with everyone else in the house were already very uncomfortable. Rebecca had given up trying and Dylan . . . well, Dylan just avoided her. Only Pamela made an effort.'

'More out of friendship for you,' interrupted Lauren, 'than any feelings of sisterhood with Gayle.'

'God, that first Christmas was awful,' said Julian. 'Do you remember?'

Lauren shuddered theatrically, waving her hands around her head like a Hawaiian hello. Both Julian and Sam laughed at the show.

'Dylan even went home to his parents, for the first time in living memory. Believe it or not, I was still trying to make a success of my marriage, so we staggered on through January and February. Battles, truces, nothing much changed.'

Abruptly, he broke off. 'Is this of interest to you?'

'Absolutely.'

'Well, stop me if I get boring.'

He pulled at the neck of his jumper, as if he suddenly felt too hot. Uncomfortable.

'Anyway, my birthday is on the twenty-first of March. Gayle had hardly spoken to me for over a week, but that evening she tried really hard. Cooked a nice meal, went to a lot of effort to make things special. Well. One thing led to another and she became pregnant.'

Sam was aware of Lauren winding a thread from the arm of her chair tighter and tighter round her finger.

'At first I thought it was just another scare. Gayle had thought she was pregnant about ten months earlier and it had turned out to be a false alarm. But Pamela encouraged her to go to our local GP.'

'A doctor of the old school,' interrupted Lauren. 'A real shit. A real shut-up-and-get-on-with-it shit.'

'He was awful,' agreed Julian. 'Anyway, when we went back for the results, he told her the test had been positive. Gayle became hysterical. I could hear her from outside the room. One minute she was insisting she couldn't go through with it, the next that we were all lying to her and she wasn't pregnant at all.

'Pamela thought Gayle was rather large for her dates, so the next time we went back we asked the dreadful Dr Shepherd. He listened and then confirmed that there were two heartbeats, not one. Gayle flew into a rage, screaming that he had to give her something to get rid of them. I will never forget the look of disgust on Shepherd's face . . .'

Sam could hear Julian breathing, fast, as if he'd gone fifteen rounds in the ring.

'The thing was, I was confused. When Gayle said she was pregnant the first time, I was delighted. I thought she was too. Naively, I hoped a baby might bring us closer together.'

He stopped again.

'I'm sorry,' he apologised to Sam. 'This is all harder than I was expecting.'

Sam nodded. She knew what he felt, how the words you could cope with in your head could be too painful in your mouth.

'It was the first time that adoption was mentioned, after the incident at the doctor's surgery,' Julian said. 'By this stage, I'm ashamed to admit that I didn't believe Gayle was capable of bringing up one baby, let alone two. And it simply didn't occur to me that I could do it alone. Very sexist of me, I'm sure . . .'

Lauren pulled a face at him.

'I don't think I slept at all that night,' he carried on. 'But by the morning, I had reached a decision. I suggested to Gayle that we should have the babies adopted. She was pathetically grateful.'

'You did what you thought was right,' said Lauren firmly. 'There's no point beating up on yourself.'

'I know. But it was the wrong thing to do.'

Sam watched him, a troubled man surrounded by his private ghosts. Lauren leaned across again and covered his hand with hers. Sam would have done the same, he looked so vulnerable. Julian frowned. The seconds passed.

'The next bit you know, I think. Gayle and I saw the adoption people in May and arranged everything. I felt like a Judas, signing away my children.'

'But it wasn't final . . .' Sam cut in.

'Not officially,' agreed Julian. 'No. But it felt final. It never crossed my mind that Gayle would have a change of heart. Not once.

'Anyway, for the next few weeks Gayle tried her best. But as the babies started moving more and more, she became more and more distressed. She thought she was being eaten alive from the inside. Sometimes, she even thought she was possessed.'

He shook his head, remembering the dark, dark scenes.

'There was nothing I could do to help her. Dr Shepherd was not sympathetic and Pamela was not due back for another four months or so. I felt completely useless.'

'Skip this, Julian,' suggested Lauren firmly. 'Go to November twelve.'

Sam felt hypnotised by the duet of their sing-song voices, first one, then the other. The words that were floating her back to the English winter when she had been born. To a gabled house she'd never seen, marooned deep in the November countryside.

Her heart blue with cold, Sam burrowed deeper into the armchair for comfort.

'We were expecting Pamela on the Sunday evening. Sunday the eleventh of November,' said Julian. 'I can't remember where she had been that trip, only that she'd very sweetly arranged to cut things short and come back three weeks early, just in case the babies arrived before they were due.

'Gayle had had another very bad night, so at about six o'clock or so, she took something to help her get some rest. I waited until she was comfortable, then tiptoed down to the kitchen. It was still dark. I remember how peaceful it felt, sitting there alone, wrapped in a blanket as the light sneaked up on me. No human sound, just the creaking of the sleeping house.

'After a while, I heard the wheels of the paper boy's bicycle scrunching on the drive. I remember thinking he was early. All muffled up, he was. Bright blue gloves, bright blue scarf pulled up over his nose and mouth. As I opened the door to take the paper from him, the cold air rushed in around my legs. Outside were the makings of a beautiful day. The grass all around the house was frosted white, the sparse branches of every tree sparkling as the weak sun touched them. I felt completely still. Later, I remembered that one moment. How I'd believed anything was possible.

'I went back into the kitchen and pottered around, boiled the kettle. It must have been about half past seven by now.

'Then I heard the sound of a key in the front door and there was Pamela. It was so wonderful to see her. She was exhausted from having travelled thirty-six hours non-stop, but she looked fantastic. All strong and tanned. I made some tea – her first proper cup of tea in days, she said – and she told me what she'd been up to in the past five months. Our news seemed so boring in comparison, although I had to give her the letter from Rebecca about moving out. She was upset about that.'

Sam heard the clock strike three, the sound of parallel time passing. Nobody moved.

'By now, it was nearly nine o'clock. Pamela said she was going to have a hot bath and then fall into bed until dinner. I knew Gayle would be asleep for quite a while, so I decided to take Laurie a cup of tea. She was usually the first person up and about, but she had been a little under the weather. I thought I'd just double-check.

'Perhaps I added this afterwards too, but I swear I knew

something was wrong as I went up the stairs. I couldn't put my finger on it. Like when a favourite painting is hanging slightly off-centre. It wasn't that the house was quiet. More, that it was the wrong type of quiet. I remember thinking it odd that all the doors were shut, downstairs and up.

'Laurie slept right at the top of the house. A lovely little attic room it was, right under the eaves. Full of colour. Little pink curtains, rugs everywhere. I knocked, but there was no answer. I turned the knob and gently pushed the door open a fraction.

'Straight away, I could tell she was in trouble. I slopped the tea on to the mantelpiece and rushed to the bed. At first, I thought she'd been poisoned. White face, her body covered in sweat. She was lying there in speechless agony. All she could manage was to tell me that her stomach pain had got worse in the night.'

'I don't understand,' interrupted Sam. 'What pain?'

'I was in labour,' said Lauren. 'I was in fucking labour and I didn't even know it.'

Shock grabbed Sam's throat. How could a woman conceive and carry a baby for nine months in total ignorance? Not possible. Not possible. A wail escaped from her mouth. She could feel her hair tickling the back of her neck as her head turned from left to right, left to right.

'Sam?' said Julian.

'It's impossible,' she exploded. 'How could you not know you were pregnant? It's not possible.'

Lauren uncrossed her legs and turned towards Sam, her hands held wide apart, as if she was playing some sort of invisible game of cat's cradle.

'I know it sounds unbelievable . . .'

'It's impossible.' cried Sam.

'Really, Sam. I had no idea. No nausea, no tenderness. I got my monthly period, the same as always. I had put on a little weight, been a little tired in the evenings, sure. But other than that . . . Really.'

Lauren looked across at Sam, could see the struggle in her blue eyes between scepticism and trust.

'I have a picture of my mom,' she said, getting up, 'taken the day before I was born. She was the same. You'd never know she was about to have a baby. I'll get it.'

Sam wanted to call out no, to say that she didn't need proof. That Lauren's word was good enough.

'Even when I saw Laurie lying on that bed, I didn't realise,' said Julian.

Sam smiled gratefully at him. 'It's not that . . .'

Lauren reappeared, a small framed black and white photograph in her left hand. She handed it to Sam without a word.

Sam looked down at the woman. Fair hair rolled up away from her face. A neat jacket, buttoned up, skirt just below the knees, the look of 1944. Clutching a handbag in front of her, she looked happily up into the camera.

No one seemed to be breathing. The air was totally silent and Sam knew that it was up to her now. She either took a leap of faith and they went on, or she stayed doubting on the shore. Which was it to be? Carefully, she tipped forward and stood the photograph upright on the table between them.

'She was a very beautiful woman, my grandmother,' she said.

Like unexpected sun glinting through Easter clouds, relief flooded the room. For what seemed like forever, Sam bathed in the intimacy. She felt intoxicated, like a novice shown a glimpse of heaven.

'Shall I go on?' Julian finally said.

Once more, the Washington afternoon faded, pushed away by a cold English morning so long ago.

'I don't remember how I got out of the room, just that I was banging on the bathroom door, shouting that Laurie was ill. It seemed like a lifetime before Pamela appeared. She took one look at my face and ran upstairs. Of course, she knew at once. As she tried to make Laurie comfortable, we had one of those Punch and Judy conversations. Pamela kept asking why I hadn't told her and I kept answering that I hadn't known Laurie was ill. I still didn't know, you see, what was actually happening. Even then. Kept muttering about food poisoning, until it dawned on Pamela that neither of us realised that Laurie was in labour.'

'I remember Pamela telling me that I was having a baby,' Lauren said wryly, 'and me trying to argue. Saying over and over that it was Gayle who was pregnant, not me.'

'I thought I was going mad,' Julian admitted. 'That it was some larger-than-life nightmare. I kept thinking I would wake up and everything would be back to normal. Then Pamela was issuing instructions, telling me to hurry.'

'Why didn't you go to the hospital?'

'There wasn't time. Pamela examined me and said she could see the baby's head. Your head, Sam. It all seemed over in an instant. One minute I was swimming in this pain, this amazing pain. The next, I was holding this perfect baby in my arms.'

'Pamela said that she had never attended such a straightforward delivery,' added Julian. 'Not in Africa or India, not anywhere on her travels. I held you too, before Pamela sent me to make us all some tea.'

For no reason she could think of, Sam blushed.

'You were beautiful,' smiled Lauren. 'So cute. I was shocked out of my skin. We all were. But I just sat there besotted, rocking you in my arms. My miracle baby.'

Sam lit one of the last two cigarettes. Lauren had the other. Julian cleared his throat.

'My legs felt like rubber as I walked down the stairs. My knees buckled at one point, I remember that. I don't recall feeling worried or in a panic about what we were going to do. That came later.'

Sam shifted slightly, aware that her jeans felt uncomfortably tight around the crotch. She tried to ignore it.

'What about Gayle?'

'She was still out like a light, thank God. I pressed my ear against her bedroom door, listened to her breathing in and out for a couple of seconds.

'I don't know where the time went. The three of us – four – cocooned up in the little attic room. You, me, Laurie and Pamela. It was so peaceful.'

'The lull before the storm,' Lauren muttered, flicking her ash.

'Then suddenly there was this bang and an awful shouting. I jumped up and ran out on to the top landing. I looked down and there was Gayle, sitting on the bottom step, shouting her head off. My initial reaction was annoyance rather than concern at the intrusion into our world upstairs. Nevertheless, I hurried down the stairs, followed by Pamela. Gayle immediately started shrieking that she had been lying there for hours and that she could have been bleeding to death for all I'd care. It wasn't very pleasant.

'Pamela quickly examined her. She didn't think there was any harm done, but she wanted Gayle to let me run her to the hospital, to be on the safe side. Gayle refused point-blank, saying that all she wanted was to be left alone.'

'Why didn't you at least call the doctor?' asked Sam.

'Well, there was no phone, to start with,' replied Julian, shaking his head.

'Of course, of course,' muttered Sam to herself.

'So it would have meant either me or Pamela leaping into the car to drive to the nearest call-box. But, in any case, Pamela said she wasn't worried. Not worried enough, at any rate, to go against Gayle's express wishes. Then there was Laurie and the baby – you – to think of.

'So I stayed with Gayle. Pamela didn't think she should be left alone. She was in such an odd mood, kept fluttering her hands backwards and forwards in front of her face, like a fan, and giggling. I don't know how long I sat there, watching the light fading through the curtains. Hours. I memorised the exact position of every single ornament in that room, all the bottles and sprays on the dressing-table.

'At long last, Gayle's eyes shut and stayed shut. I waited five minutes, ten maybe, then carefully got up and tiptoed away from the bed. I was stiff all over. As I reached my hand for the door knob – I remember how smooth and chilled the wood felt – there was this almighty roar in the darkness behind me. I froze. It didn't sound human. The hairs on the back of my neck actually stood on end, I'm sure of it.'

'I heard the noise,' said Lauren quietly. 'I've never heard anything like it.'

'I just stood there,' continued Julian, 'rooted to the spot. I could hear feet outside the door, then the click of the light being switched on. I put my hands up to shield my eyes from the glare. Gayle was screaming, something about birds pecking her stomach and scissor hands. For some reason, it reminded me of *Alice in Wonderland*. You remember? All those sharp creatures when Alice is lost in the wood?

'Then Pamela was telling me to go get hot water and newspapers and towels, just like before. This can't be happening again, I was shouting, like a broken record. Not again, not again. Pamela shouted at me to hurry. It was the only time I ever heard Pamela raise her voice. Hurry, Julian.

'There was an odd thing. For much of October and November, the papers had been following this trial in Belgium. A woman had killed her thalidomide baby and her sisters and doctor had all been involved. The news was full of it. Even the Pope had got involved.

207

As I knelt by Gayle's bed, spreading the newspaper out like Pamela was telling me, I saw a headline that the jury had finally acquitted her. It made me cry. Relief? Compassion? Who knows. For a moment, just one moment, I escaped from Raphael House out into the world.'

Nobody spoke as Julian picked up the wine bottle and shook it. Empty. He stood it carefully back on the little brass tray.

'I will never forget the smell in that room. Of vomit and blood and fear. I thought Gayle was going to inflict serious damage on herself. She was thrashing around, ripping at her flesh, as if she was trying to get out of her own skin. She was convinced the babies were coming out of her mouth.

'Pamela had one of her hands on Gayle's stomach to measure the contractions. I was helping keep her legs apart. Good girl, Gayle, good girl, Pamela was saying in this baby voice. Push, push. Nearly there. Just one more.

'Then there was a baby crying. A mewing sound, like a kitten. Pamela scooped it up, wrapped it in Gayle's favourite yellow towel. Ridiculous, but I remember thinking she'd be annoyed if we'd got blood on it. Now Pamela sounded loud and efficient. No nonsense. You have a fine, healthy baby girl, she said. I thought Gayle would be proud. But when I held Anna to her, she screamed that the baby was deformed and to get it out of her sight. I hadn't even noticed her birthmark until then.'

Sam immediately reached her hand into the A4 envelope lying at the foot of her chair, took out a photograph of Anna and stretched over the table to give it to Julian. Sam watched his eyes fill with tears as he looked at the picture. He offered it to Lauren.

'I saw,' she said quietly. 'In the café, earlier. She was very beautiful.'

Julian nodded, pressing the photo against his chest.

'I held Anna,' he started again in his cracked voice. 'Cradled her, but she wouldn't stop crying. Pamela told me to go upstairs and see if Laurie was awake. Told me to give the baby to Laurie, then come straight back. When I came down again, Pamela was telling Gayle she was a brave girl but she had to keep going for just a little bit longer.

'The look on Pamela's tanned face spoke volumes. Frowning, like she was holding something back. Here comes your son, she was saying to Gayle. Good girl, good girl. Pamela sounded so calm and encouraging. But then she whispered to me that the baby was the wrong way up, that we had to get him out as quickly as possible.

'Suddenly we were knee-deep in blood. It was everywhere. Pamela was punching Gayle's stomach and there was this slithering sound, like water being sucked down a half-blocked drain.'

Julian swallowed, willing the horror not to creep up on him.

'I looked down. On the bed there were two slabs of what looked like meat. I couldn't make them out at first. A butcher's shop, they were the words that came into my mind. One lump was a sort of purple-red, like liver. The other . . .'

He stopped again. One second, two. Three seconds. Time whispering on.

'He never breathed, Sam. He was so tiny. These scrawny little arms and legs. He looked like all those pictures you see now of unborn babies, sucking their thumbs in the womb.'

Why was her skin itching? Sam touched her cheek, felt the tears trickling slowly down her face. She tried to wipe them away with the back of her hand, but they kept coming.

'I wrapped his tiny body in a towel. A white towel, this time. White for a shroud. I wanted to hold him, just for a moment. To tell him about how things should have been . . . But Pamela was telling me that Gayle would die unless we could get her to a hospital immediately. No time for love. I laid him on a cushion on the floor in the corner of the room, promising I would say goodbye later. He felt like china, so precious.

'Then somehow I was sitting behind the wheel of Pamela's car. It was freezing cold, sleeting. One of the windscreen wipers didn't work. I turned the heating up as high as it would go. Pamela was in the back with Gayle, holding one of the babies. Gayle was delirious, screaming that she was being knifed. Look at the red, she kept saying, flinging up her hands to ward off the blows. What was so odd was she looked like she was dancing. Happy and dancing. The seat was staining with her blood, I could see it black in the rear-view mirror.

'Laurie was next to me in the front of the car. I remember turning my head and seeing that she was feeding a baby. I didn't know why she was there too, just that they looked beautiful. A flesh and bone madonna and child, made for one another.'

'Me?' whispered Sam under her breath.

Lauren nodded. Her face looked grim.

'Somehow, we got to the hospital. You and Anna were taken away to be checked. Pamela and Laurie went with you. I had to go with Gayle. I wanted to stay with you, but I had to go with Gayle. She was hurried on to a stretcher. Doctors and nurses sticking needles and drips into her as we raced down the corridor.

'Everyone kept saying how lucky she was to be alive, how it had been touch and go. They were all so kind, so reassuring. They didn't realise they were talking to a fraud, a man masquerading as a loving husband. Because, you see, I didn't care that I had nearly lost my wife. All I could think about was that somewhere else in the hospital was Laurie. And that all the babies were being taken away. Anna and you and little Sam.'

CHAPTER 20

The clock was striking again. Sam thought she counted four chimes. It could have been five.

She had that queasy late-night feeling in the pit of her stomach now, hit by the accumulated cocktail of words and wine and sitting in the same place for hours. Her feet and calves were prickling with pins and needles.

'I need to go to the loo.'

Even her voice sounded done in.

Julian didn't move. Only Lauren had any energy left. Uncrossing her legs, she got up stiffly, then held out both hands to help pull Sam up. Arms straight. For a moment, the two women looked as if they were poised to dance the polka, ready to gallop sideways the width of the room and back.

'How're you doing?' Lauren asked.

'Fine. I think.'

'You sure?'

'Sure.'

She looked into her grown-up daughter's tired eyes, trying to work out whether she was telling the truth or not. But how would she tell, after only a few hours' acquaintance? She smiled, a little sad, and gently let Sam's hands drop.

'I'll show you the bathroom.'

Sam watched Lauren press Julian's shoulder as she squeezed her way between the arms of the chairs. She wanted to copy. Wanted to make some sort of physical connection with him too. But nothing seemed appropriate. She blinked, and the chance was gone.

Sam followed Lauren out into the narrow hallway, their shoeless feet making no noise on the wooden floor. Rainbow woven rugs hung from the pale yellow walls and the mirrored sequins sewn into the cloth were catching the passing light from the kitchen window. A space of summer, light and clean.

'It's the first on your right. Call me if you need anything.'

When Sam came back to the sitting-room, there was a cafetière of coffee sitting on the round brass tray. The wine glasses and stained cloth had been cleared away. In their place were three mugs and an earthenware plate of biscuits.

'Homemade pecan cookies,' said Julian. 'Help yourself.'

Sam sat on the edge of her chair, feeling a little better. Julian put a full mug of coffee down in front of her.

'Laurie's just bringing the sugar and milk.'

'Thanks.'

She took a bite of her biscuit, scooping her hand under her chin to catch the crumbs.

'Wow, they're delicious. Did Lauren make them?'

'No, actually,' replied Julian. 'I did.'

Sam blushed, then giggled, then snorted loudly. Her laughter was infectious, starting Julian off too. And once they'd started, neither of them could stop. The relief of tension on the run, like air wheezing out of a balloon. Sam dabbed at the soggy corners of her face with her sleeves. For a second or two, there'd be silence. Then Julian would catch her eye, and they'd both be off again.

'What's up with you guys?' asked Lauren from the doorway.

'It was the biscuits . . .' spluttered Sam, shoulders shaking. Julian cracked up again. There was nothing Lauren could do but sit it out, an indulgent and exaggerated smile on her lips.

'Hal-le-lu-jah,' she said, waving her hands in the air. 'The blissful sound of silence.'

Sam heaped sugar into her mug, added a little milk from the carton, paused, then added a second spoonful. In for a penny, in for a pound. Then she dunked what was left of her pecan cookie in her coffee, without even thinking about it. Just as if she was at home. Her diet lay shattered around her.

'Do you feel up to carrying on?' asked Lauren. 'Or should we take a break? Talk again tomorrow, maybe?'

'God, no,' replied Sam quickly. 'Please keep going. That is, of course, if you're not too tired . . .'

The very thought of leaving things hanging was excruciating. A bizarre sort of game of endurance.

'No problem for me,' said Lauren. 'Julian?'

'That's fine.'

Straight away, the cosy atmosphere dissolved. Here we go again, thought Sam. Go, stop, go, stop. It was like watching a television serial. Digestible, bite-size episodes, recapped each week for the benefit of those viewers who'd come in in the middle.

Except, of course, life wasn't like that. No tidy or linear plot-lines, no expertly tied loose ends. Real things didn't necessarily happen for a reason or come good in the end. Sam felt the weight of it all slamming down on her again, and frowned.

'What was happening to me and Anna all this time?' she asked seriously. 'In the hospital?'

Lauren raised her mug of coffee to her lips, drank, then set it back on the table again. Dutch courage.

'Before the hospital – you know, at Raphael House – the world might've stopped spinning and I wouldn't have known it. You were quite the most perfect human being I had ever, ever seen. The smell of you, all new and untouched. Tiny eyelashes, nails no bigger than pearls.

'All afternoon, Pamela kept coming in and out to check we were doing all right, giving me clean towels and stuff. There were hundreds of questions she wanted to ask, I could see it in her eyes, but she was trying to respect our intimacy. She didn't want to intrude until she absolutely had to. Do you know who the father is? That was the only thing she asked. I couldn't answer, couldn't even look up. All I wanted to think about was you, Sam.

'I felt more at peace during those few hours in my tiny attic room than I have ever felt. Before or since. The thing was, I knew it couldn't last.'

'Why?'

The word whipped into the room and split the air. Sam was shocked to hear the pain in her voice. She sounded so raw.

'I'm sorry,' she murmured. 'I didn't mean it to come out like that.'

'I don't blame you,' said Lauren softly. 'I think I'd feel the same. In the past, when I dreamed about us being reunited, you know I never could figure out how I would explain.'

She was talking fast now, animated, trying to bridge the gulf of the experience yawning between them. Her hands were like sparklers, tracing words in the fading light of the room.

'You inhabit so different a world from mine then. Sex is out in the open now, you talk about it and read about it. Girls can learn about pregnancy and stuff in every magazine and book, if not from their parents or friends. How can I expect you to understand what it was like to be barely seventeen years old, thousands of miles from home, and to be so totally tricked by your own body? I knew nothing, Sam. Nothing. Until I held you in my arms, I had never even seen a newborn baby.'

'Julian would have looked after us,' Sam muttered miserably.

'But can't you see, Julian was my guardian. He was responsible for my welfare, yet there I was with a baby. It sounds dumb, I know, but I thought if anyone found out about you, then I would be sent away. A welfare home, someplace like that. Perhaps on a boat back to America. Christ, I don't know what I thought. I remember being scared that Julian would be punished. Sent to jail, even.'

Lauren reached for the coffee cup balanced on the arm of her chair. Drank. Two big gulps.

Sam looked at this passionate, articulate woman in her mid-thirties, tried to picture her bewildered, a child-mother. She's right, she realised with a shock. My imagination cannot take me so far.

'Anyhow . . .' she continued, her voice steadier now. 'When Pamela next came upstairs to see how I was doing, I told her I knew I couldn't keep my baby. She didn't say much – she could tell I'd been crying – just put her arms around me like Mom would have done and said that it was probably the wisest decision. That "probably" haunted me. Christ, how it haunted me . . .'

She paused, rubbed her eyes. For the first time, Sam could see her age etched on her face. Worn out, thought Sam with sympathy. Love tickled on the palms of her hands.

'One part of me was completely absorbed by you. The other part, well, was detached. Like I was watching it all happening to some other girl, not me. It was some other person, who looked just like me, agonising over what was best for her child. I was just a spectator.

'I'd seen how so-called decent society dealt with their unmarried mothers. They were treated as whores and their children were outcasts. Hey, there goes that whore's kid. I wasn't going to have that happen to you.'

Sam winced at the violence of Lauren's words. It seemed out of character.

'For eighteen years and ten months I have had to live with my decision, Sam. It's like an ache that never goes away. Barely a single day has gone without me thinking of you. But you know, it was the most unselfish act of my entire life. The most painful choice I ever made. But the most moral one. Believe me, I acted out of love. Not indifference.'

Lauren turned and looked Sam straight in the eye. She looked at peace.

'I'm not asking for your forgiveness, Sam,' she said strongly. 'I would do the same again. The question is, can you accept what I did?'

The direct appeal took Sam by surprise. In an instant, she had swapped her role as witness for that of judge. Her heart pumped absurdly as Lauren's words stretched taut between them.

One, two, three, four, five.

'I don't know,' Sam whispered. 'I want to . . .'

Lauren winced, as if her face had been slapped. But she carried on talking in her slow, measured way. As if she had not heard.

'All at once, the noise started. I felt marooned, hearing the commotion on the floor below. It seemed to go on forever. I could see it was dark outside. I'd managed to stagger out of bed and light some candles. Then Julian appeared with this tiny, tiny baby, asking if I could look after her. Telling me that things downstairs were bad.

'I made you a kind of snug in my bed – you were fast asleep – then took Anna from Julian's arms. She was so frail that it scared me. In the flickering light, her birthmark looked like a shadow. Gold rather than red.

'She was crying, this troubled, stuttering sound. I was scared she would wake you, so I did the only thing I could think of. I put her to my breast, just like Pamela had showed me with you, and nursed her. I felt so expert, so very powerful as Anna settled, then fell asleep too. It was so peaceful, just the three of us in that little attic room. It felt like a family . . .'

Lauren snorted at her choice of word, again tapping her fingers on the arms of her chair.

'Pamela reappeared in the doorway, bringing the smell of the world with her. I assumed she'd come to tell me that Gayle had given birth to the second twin. A boy or another girl? Pamela didn't answer my question, just said they had to go to the hospital straight away. Gayle's condition was very serious, she explained in this clipped, flat voice.

'I suddenly realised she'd come to take Anna. I was frightened. I couldn't help it. What's happened to the baby, I was asking, over and over. She didn't want to tell me. Probably thought I couldn't take it. Where's the other baby? Where's the other baby? In the end Pamela gave in, too worried to waste time. He was stillborn, she said. The baby was stillborn.

'In that split second, I made my decision. A crazy, crazy idea. The adoption people were expecting two babies, I knew that. There were two babies to give.'

'I didn't tell Pamela what I was thinking. In this robot voice I just said I was coming too. Somehow, adrenalin got me dressed and down the stairs, you curled in my right arm, Anna in my left. Julian and Pamela were too occupied with Gayle to ask what I was doing.

'It was icy outside and dark. Everything seemed to be flapping wild, trying to break loose in the wind. Between them, Julian and Pamela carried Gayle to the car, her hair whipping against their faces. Somehow, they got her into the back seat. I watched from the hall. In the weak glimmer from the old lightbulb in the porch, I could see the rain plunging down. Like snipers' bullets.

'What I remember most is the noise. The cracking wind and Gayle howling and the blood on the driveway. It was so luxurious, somehow. So very, very red on the gravel before the rain diluted it. Then Julian came back, took Anna from me, and we charged for the safety of the car. I had you tucked under my coat. He slammed my door, then ran round behind and threw himself into the driver's seat.

'The journey was scary. Those endless winding lanes, the headlamps barely picking out the black road ahead of us, and Gayle screaming and screaming that she was dying. Then the roads were orange and we hit the outskirts of Oxford. I remember I was surprised that the city looked the same as always. You know, the stores and restaurants, all in their usual places. Like any other Monday night.

'We reached the hospital. It was really busy. Every woman in Oxford seemed to be having her baby that night. Julian was calling for help and then Gayle was rushed away. Me and Pamela were taken in the opposite direction, crowded into this little annexe room.

It was so claustrophobic and hot. Paint peeling off the grey walls and wires and machines and the smell of disinfectant.

'If it had been quiet and ordered in the hospital, I don't know if I would've had the courage to go through with things. But doctors and midwives kept putting their heads round the door, apologising for the delay, then going out. Never the same face twice. Nobody seemed to know what was going on. Then this sweet nurse came in, sent to take some details from us and to start examining you and Anna. As she unwrapped you, I could tell she was really nervous. She was so gentle, though, and careful. I felt close to her for that. I didn't think about what I was saying, just let all this stuff come out of my mouth. Anna had been born first, I told her, then you afterwards. Wasn't it weird that you were so much bigger? Was that normal? She said she didn't know – she'd only started working on this ward a couple of weeks ago – but we could ask the doctor when he came.

'I was so convincing. I could feel Pamela tense beside me as it dawned on her what I was trying to do. She avoided my eye but said nothing. When the doctor came in to take over, she answered his questions about the labour and deliveries. Professional to professional. As I watched them put the pink tag round your wrist, I knew I'd got away with it. *Sam 12.11.62 5lbs 6oz.*'

Lauren stretched in her chair, invigorated by telling the story. She looked like a huge cat in her black woolly jumper.

'You were taken to a special bit of the nursery. Routine procedure, they told us, for premature babies. Then we were asked to leave. They will be reunited with their mother as soon as possible, the nurse said. There is no need for you to stay. Mr Driver is still with his wife. I suggest you go home. She sounded like a machine.

'Then suddenly I was outside getting soaked, feeling faint. Completely hollow. Not knowing what to do. I think I started crying. For you, for myself. For all of us, I guess. The whole bloody mess. I remember the firmness of Pamela's hand in the small of my back, helping me back into the car.'

She stopped, pierced by her memory of that bereaved midnight. The desolation, the realisation that nothing would ever be the same.

'It was still raining when I got home the next morning,' said Julian, bringing himself back into things. 'The most extraordinary thing is that after all that had gone on, I caught a bus. Maybe I didn't have enough money for a taxi, I can't remember. As I walked up the drive, I remember being amazed that Raphael House looked so completely unscathed in the grey morning light. It didn't seem possible it could have gone through the ordeal of the night before. No one was about, no signs of life. Just the sound of rain falling through the branches of the trees.

'You were sitting in silence in the kitchen listening to Dylan spouting on and on. You were so white, Laurie. You looked shell-shocked.'

'I hadn't been able to sleep,' she said, shaking her head. 'I felt lonely . . .'

'Where had Dylan been all this time?' asked Sam.

'It was extraordinary,' replied Julian. 'He had been in London for the weekend, then went straight to the art gallery on Monday morning. He didn't start work until twelve o'clock on Mondays. He'd knocked off at six, as usual, then met some friends at the Playhouse for a drink before the performance.'

'*The Just* by Camus,' snorted Lauren, gesturing wide with her hands. 'I can remember sitting like a dummy at the table watching his teeth as his mouth opened and closed, delivering his verdict on his night at the theatre. He had really crooked teeth, you know. He thought the play was absurd, too implausible to be taken seriously. Conspiracy theories, revolutionaries, fifth columnists, everything turning on unrealistic coincidences. And right above him was a floor covered with stained sheets and the tiny body of a stillborn baby. It was a moment of authentic surrealism.

'My eyes kept stealing up to the ceiling. I half-expected to see blood dripping scarlet through the plaster. A sort of stigmata as evidence. Dylan had noticed all the lights were on when he'd got in, he admitted, but hadn't really thought anything of it. He'd just gone to bed.'

She smoothed her hair across the top of her head. Cleaning away the cobwebs, like Peter did.

'Christ,' she added. 'Can you imagine if he had gone into the room . . . ?'

'Dylan walked around in a dream most of the time,' Julian admitted. 'He was just the same at college. It was only when I appeared in my outdoor clothes, looking like death warmed up, that it dawned on him that something must have happened. What was it he said?'

Lauren gave a snort of ironic laughter. 'Sorry I missed all the fun . . .'

Sam repeated the phrase like a spell in her head, like Dorothy's marching rhyme. Follow – the yellow – brick road. Boom, boom. Sorry – I missed all – the fun. Boom, boom. Sorry – I missed all – the fun. Hysteria grabbed her throat as images of gingham and plaits and sparkling ruby slippers bobbed up and down in her mind. She forced herself to focus on the reality in front of her. The cups, the tray, the table, the people.

'Did you ever tell your . . . the man about me?' she finally managed to ask, then immediately regretted it.

She didn't have to know everything, here and now. And it wasn't as if she really cared about her natural father, not any more. Sam was curious, of course she was. But he didn't matter, not like Lauren mattered. If the liaison had meant anything, then obviously Lauren would have told her.

'It was not a pregnancy that should have happened . . .' said Lauren quietly, looking down at her hands lying in her lap.

'I'm sorry,' Sam apologised, then took a gulp of coffee. It was tepid.

'What about our names?' she asked quickly, wanting to make up for her question. Julian smiled at her, as if he too was relieved to have the subject changed.

'This will sound ridiculous – Gayle certainly thought it was – but it felt important to me to give you names. The twins, I mean. As soon as I knew Gayle was pregnant I became obsessed with the whole business. I knew whoever adopted the babies would probably choose different names, but even so . . . It sort of became a private game between me and Laurie. I was convinced Gayle was having a girl and a boy, from the moment we were told it was twins. Somewhere along the line, the names Anna and Samuel became fixed in my head. Not very complicated, really. My middle name is Samuel and my grandmother was called Anna.'

'Some books of derivations list Anna as a corruption of the name Hannah,' expanded Lauren. 'By coincidence, my middle name is Hannah and, in the Bible, Hannah is the mother of Samuel. It all just fitted.'

She stretched.

'I don't know why Mom went for Hannah, but she called me Lauren for Lauren Bacall. The movies were her favourite thing.

She was such a romantic at heart, despite everything she'd been through.'

'What did Gayle think about you two having names for the babies?' asked Sam.

'It sounds awful, doesn't it?' replied Julian. 'As if we were going behind her back. But, you know, Gayle really never saw the twins as ours. She didn't seem to feel any emotional connection with them whatsoever. It was as if she saw herself as baby-sitting until she could hand them over to their real parents.'

'Like a surrogate mother,' said Sam.

'So when I was standing in the hospital,' continued Lauren, 'the names just came out naturally. At the time, it seemed to make a whole lot of sense. Looking back, I guess I hoped that if the nurses talked about the babies to Gayle – calling them Sam and Anna – then Gayle wouldn't realise anything had happened. I suppose, too, I hoped that if Gayle talked about a son and a daughter, then the nurses would put the confusion down to the trauma of her delivery and operation.'

'When my impulsive little sister here told me what she'd done,' said Julian, 'my immediate reaction was one of disbelief. Even though I'd been with Gayle and had seen how desperately ill she was, I didn't share Laurie's faith that Gayle wouldn't know her own child. Even though she'd not actually seen him. Pamela had made so many comments about the second baby being a boy during the delivery, well . . .

'But once it'd sunk in,' he continued, 'I saw the logic of what Laurie had done. Not only did it make everything less complicated, but emotionally . . . Well, it seemed right that you and Anna should stay together.'

Julian fell silent, thinking about just how much they'd staked on Gayle not being able to remember. So many lives hanging in the balance.

'Gayle nearly died that night,' he said, riddled with guilt at the knowledge of how little that death would have touched him.

'I never was sure how much she knew or didn't know about what happened,' he added in a low voice. 'I never was sure . . .'

'Well, we know now,' said Lauren firmly. 'However sick Gayle was, she was clear about giving birth to a girl and boy. Otherwise Sam wouldn't be sitting here with us now.'

Sam leaned forward in her chair, hands clasped, resting her lower arms on the bones of her knees.

'When we arrived at Gayle's house in Headington in July,' she said, 'Gayle thought Peter was Sam. She called him her little boy. That was the reason she let us in. She assumed I was his girlfriend. I mean, Sam's girlfriend . . .'

Lauren smiled as Sam tailed off, tangled up in mistaken identities.

'Only six weeks ago,' muttered Sam under her breath. 'Shit.'

'Do you think Gayle will do anything?'

Sam looked across at Julian's concerned face. She wanted to comfort him, say anything just to make him feel better. But she didn't want to lie. Not now they had all been through so much to get to the truth.

'I don't think so, no. I mean, Gayle was shocked. Very shocked. She didn't believe us at first. But she was more obsessed by the idea we'd been sent to hunt her down by this man, than bothered about something that'd happened eighteen years ago. Or, at least, that's how it seemed to me.

'Peter went back to see her on his own the next day. She hardly asked any questions at all, just wanted to go on about her problems. He reckoned she was the sort of person who was always drawing a line under her past. Her first marriage, her second marriage, Raphael House, everything. Like none of it had existed.'

'Well,' Julian said in a brisk voice. 'I hope you're right.'

'Hey, what can she do now?' said Lauren, then smiled at Sam. 'Come on, Julian. Let's finish this. We're all too tired to take much more.'

'Yes, of course,' Julian agreed. 'Yes. I went back to the hospital later that afternoon. The Tuesday, that is. I felt like a criminal, more and more apprehensive with every step. When I arrived at the ward where Gayle had been taken after surgery, the doctor came striding towards me. He looked like a turtle, I remember thinking that. All desiccated and sullen. I was convinced the game was up. Your wife has disappeared, Mr Driver. In a way, he was quite apologetic, even though he seemed to hold me responsible. He said they'd searched everywhere and had come to the conclusion that Gayle was, quote, "no longer on the premises".

'They were obviously worried about her state of health, both mental and physical, and wanted to call the police. I'm ashamed to say that I didn't take her disappearance seriously at this point. I thought it was another plea for attention. Utterly selfishly, I was more concerned about Laurie and you and Anna, and the deception being exposed.

'They must have thought me the lowest of the low. And of course, by now they'd checked their records and realised that we were the couple intending to offer their babies for adoption. Gayle had been booked at St Saviour's anyway, just for the beginning of December rather than mid-November. I could tell by the way they looked at me that they thought it was my fault. Assumed that I'd bullied my wife into giving up her children. *Her* children.'

Julian shook his head at the unfairness of it all. The wrong impressions, the damage done by so many little acts of betrayal and misunderstandings not put right.

'Anyway. We agreed that if Gayle hadn't reappeared by ten o'clock that evening, they would have to inform the authorities. I thanked them, said I would be back later, and pretended to leave. But I didn't. I felt my heart was bruising with this desperate need to see you and Anna again, just once. To say goodbye without anyone looking over my shoulder. It wasn't visiting time, but a sympathetic midwife let me in, just for five minutes. She was the only one who continued to treat me like a human being, even after she knew about the adoption.

'As I stood there, gazing down at those tiny cots, I fantasised about snatching you both in my arms and running. I didn't, of course. When I think back, it's unbelievable how indoctrinated we were about what was right and what was wrong. The experts said what was best for children and we took it, without questioning the sort of wisdom they were handing out. Stable families, mothers at home, fathers with respectable jobs. Everybody just the same, no variation. No backbone in the face of rules and regulations,' he added with disgust. 'Not one of us . . .

'Anyway, after that, I went to the Register Office. I didn't know what one was supposed to do. It was more that fear told me that once you and Anna were twins on paper, stamped and sealed, then we'd be home and dry. No going back. Looking back, I suspect subconsciously I was frightened that my heart would win out over my head if I delayed. That I might not be able to go through with the adoption.'

'What about the bracelets?' asked Sam. 'We – me, Anna and

Mum and Dad, that is – always thought they might be family heirlooms or something.'

'An impulse on my part,' replied Julian. 'I wanted you to have something concrete. Proof that we had existed, if you like. And that we loved you. Two silver christening bracelets . . . It seems an absurd gesture in the circumstances.'

'To have and to hold,' murmured Lauren.

Julian fell silent, as if he'd used up all the words he had ever known. Don't stop now, Sam shouted in her head. You're almost there. The image of runners pouring out of Greenwich Park suddenly came to mind. The first ever London Marathon. She'd watched it with Mum and Dad on the television. All those hopeful faces in the March drizzle, fresh and full of life. Then, hours later, the camera picking out the agonised mouths, the desperation writ large on those whose abused legs had carried them to within sight of the finishing line, before collapsing. The struggle to crawl just a few yards more.

'Julian?' she prompted.

He jumped.

'I'm sorry. From the Register Office, I rushed into the town centre. It was very cold again. I could see my breath, huffing white in the air. The man in the jeweller's was just turning the sign on his door from OPEN to CLOSED. I'm not normally very good at persuading people to do me favours. On this occasion, not only did I persuade him to let me in, but to engrave the bracelets for me right there. One each. *Sam 12 November 1962* and *Anna . . .*'

Sam stopped listening, as her mind added another sentence. ANNA WHITTAKER 12TH NOVEMBER 1962–9TH AUGUST 1979. The words on her gravestone.

'I must have looked quite mad, running back through Oxford to the hospital. This time, they wouldn't let me see either of you. But I tracked down the same kind midwife, who promised she would make sure the bracelets were passed on to the Adoption Society. How odd to know, after so long, that she kept her word.'

Sam felt drenched, as if her limbs had soaked up all they could and reached saturation point. There were hundreds more things she wanted to ask, thousands. But, now, all she wanted was to be a child again, to be lying curled up on the sofa at home listening to Mum making tea in the kitchen. Only one more question was still battering at her head. Just one more.

'What did happen to . . . to Sam?' she asked quietly.

'I buried him,' whispered Julian. 'I waited until Dylan had gone to work, then went down to the grove at the back of Raphael House. There was hardly any time. I was panicking about getting back to the hospital.'

Sam sat propped numbly in her chair. Lauren could sense the years dropping away from her daughter's face, watched Sam's fingers tiptoe unconsciously to her silver locket. The scales shifted again. No longer three equals sharing stories of the past. Instead, the room played host to two adults and their young English visitor.

'We should get you back,' said Lauren. 'Unless you'd like to stay, of course.'

Sam shook her head. Suddenly she cared deeply about what her parents would feel if they could see her, alone and exhausted in this Washington apartment. She wanted mental solitude and the comfort of Peter's familiar body.

Lauren quietly reached out her hand and laid it protectively on Sam's arm, just for an instant. Sam felt the coolness of her fingers through the grey sleeve of her jumper. Just the slightest of touches.

'I'll call you a cab,' she said softly.

CHAPTER 21

'Yes. Yes, I will. OK, then. See you tomorrow. Love you too, Dad.'

Sam put the receiver down. She'd had to conduct the entire transatlantic conversation with her parents *sotto voce*, perched on the edge of the bath with the heavy telephone balanced on her bare knees. At one point, her mother had asked her why she was whispering. A fair question, since Sam had shouted her way through every previous call as if she couldn't quite believe that they'd be able to hear her in England. But she could hardly explain she was trying not to wake Peter, without betraying the fact that he was in her bed, asleep, in the middle of the day. Too embarrassing. I'm not whispering, she'd hissed down the line. Must be a bad connection at your end.

Unjamming the phone wire from the gap between the bottom of the door and the cold tiled floor, Sam carefully emerged into the amethyst light of the room. Behind the drawn curtains, puffing out in the breeze, she could tell the sun was still warm. Peter was sprawled diagonally across the bed. Right leg bent, left leg straight and his crooked arms making the shape of a diamond above his head. He looked so secure, uninhibited. For a moment, Sam watched the near-imperceptible rising and falling of the thin sheet pulled up over his hips. She carefully put the phone back on the bedside table, then traced a line along the white skin of his arm, following a vein. Beautiful.

Leaving a kiss on his forehead, Sam padded over to the window. The carpet felt thick between her toes. Not wanting to spill light into the room, she hooked the curtains over her back like a purple cape, and stuck her head out. The street below was glorious, speckled golden with afternoon sun and shadows. Flaming virginia creeper and treacle-coloured leaves clustered among the green on the city trees, a reminder that this was an Indian summer, no longer the real thing.

For as long as she could remember, September had been Sam's favourite month. She'd been aroused, almost, by the coming of autumn. By a sense that life was there for the taking. All those back-to-schools, all those clean exercise books waiting to be filled. Until Anna had died and, with her, the possibility of new beginnings. Nothing left to hope for, no achievement worth the having.

It seems so soon, Sam muttered to herself, to be getting that familiar bubbling excitement in the pit of my stomach. Like I used to. Just one more milestone in learning to live without Anna, I suppose. She wrapped her bare arms around herself, thinking of her father getting ready for the start of his school year tomorrow.

Sam had found her daily calls to her parents a bit of a strain. In a way, they'd made her feel homesick. But they were also a reminder that Washington was time-out. Not real life. The Saturday morning conversation had been the worst. It had taken her ten minutes to pluck up the courage to pick up the phone, bracing herself to tell them about Lauren. That she was more than Julian's sister. From the way Tom had reacted, Sam had wondered if he was expecting news of that sort. He'd denied it when challenged, but there was something about his tone of voice that'd made Sam suspicious. Anyway, they'd been really good about it when she'd said she wanted to wait until she got home to tell them the full story. That she couldn't face going through it with a transatlantic echo.

After that, well . . . She hadn't lied about anything exactly, but she had skated over the fact that she'd been in Lauren and Julian's apartment on her own. Without Peter. And she had played down the intensity of things. When her mother had asked her how long she'd spent with them, she'd evaded the question. It all felt like a dream. Sam felt as if her brain had stalled, unable to sift through the mass of facts and motivations and emotions swirling round her mind and heart. She latched on to some of Lauren and Julian's words, others eluded her.

Sunday's call had been easier. Keeping to the bare bones of her itinerary, Sam had explained how they'd spent the weekend visiting monuments and landmarks. Tom had laughed at her description of the bug-eyed pigeons perched on the head of the nineteen-foot statue of Abraham Lincoln, then Helen had come on the line and listened in silence as Sam talked about how she'd been moved to tears at the Vietnam Memorial. The pair of old boots left propped up against the sweeping black granite, the bunches of flowers and the polythened poems, tributes to all the thousands of Americans who had died.

Not wanting to hurt her mother, Sam had not owned up to quite how comfortable she felt with Lauren herself. She did not hint at the bond she felt as she and Lauren had ambled arm-in-arm like old, old friends. She played down the similarities they discovered, the favourite foods they had in common, a taste in clothes, a sense of humour. Sam didn't admit how flattered she felt that Lauren talked to her as if they were contemporaries. About her mixed feelings on leaving England for America in 1968, with the newspapers full of Saigon and Hanoi and double-dealing. About how she and Julian had felt crazy returning to a country full of demonstrations and grey-white snow and the smell of civil war.

In fact, it was only at the tail-end of the phone conversation that Sam had come clean. No, Julian hadn't been with them on either day. Most of the antiquarian side of his bookselling business is done over the weekend, she'd explained. One-to-one clients, professional people unavailable during regular office hours, that sort of thing. No, Peter wasn't with us on Saturday, actually. He was more interested in the opening game of the football season for the Washington Redskins than playing tourist, she'd said, trying to make a joke of it. Helen's silence had made Sam feel both guilty and deceitful.

Oh well, she thought. It's Monday now. By this time tomorrow she would be back in Chichester, jet-lagged, sitting with Mum and Dad in the kitchen. Everything would be back to normal. Her little house, her room, just as she'd left them. The chink of the milk bottles on the early morning doorstep, the paper thudding on to the mat first thing. She'd go into town on Wednesday afternoon, to buy new pens and ring-binders ready for college on Thursday. Spending pounds rather than dollars.

Sam listened to the traffic roaring on New Hampshire. She knew she would return to Washington one day. She was bewitched by the place, wanted to belong to its wide streets and sidewalks. In her heart, though, she suspected she would not be back for some time. Three days ago, she and Lauren and Julian had shaken the past awake. The challenge now was to build a place for one another in their everyday lives. She and Lauren would have to get to know

227

each other long-distance before they could risk meeting face to face again. And what if it proved impossible to live up to the memory of this first, magical time? All those emotions. Curiosity and hope and catharsis and reconciliation, followed by what? Boredom? Disappointment? A gnawing sense of anti-climax?

Suddenly realising she was cold in nothing but a thin T-shirt, Sam looked down. Her skin was covered in goose-bumps and her naked feet felt numb. She ducked her head back under the curtains, scrambled in her bag for a cigarette, lit it, tossed the packet and matches on to the dressing-table, then sprinted for the warmth of the bed. Drawing her knees up to her chin, she rocked herself gently back and forwards. Thinking. Smoking in bed always made her feel sophisticated.

A warm hand on her cold leg made her jump.

'I didn't know you were awake,' she said, turning towards Peter.

'I wasn't,' he said in a languorous voice.

Sam shivered.

'How come you always sound so . . . well, you know.'

Propping himself up on his right elbow and shaking his hair loose, Peter raised his eyebrows at her.

'So what?'

'Well,' mumbled Sam, suddenly embarrassed. 'Well, like you're thinking about . . . making love.'

Peter flopped himself back against his pillow and laughed.

'Well, you do,' muttered Sam defensively.

'Cute,' he retorted, still laughing. 'And you don't? Is that it?'

Sam turned away in a huff. She'd meant it to sound seductive. An invitation, maybe. Instead, it'd come out like some sort of silly schoolgirl comment. And she loathed being teased. Loathed it. She stubbed out her cigarette in the ashtray, grinding it into the glass. Recognising the signs, Peter lassoed her from behind with his arms and squeezed her tight. Tucking her hair back behind her ears with his fingers, he felt her unwind a little. With slightly open lips, he started to nibble the back of her neck, coaxing her out of her bad mood.

'OK, you,' he said, 'we've gotta get going if we're to be outta here by six. Let's start with a shower.'

Sam shrugged her shoulders, disappointed. 'You can go first.'

'Nope,' he replied, swinging her across his naked lap. 'We'll share. Save on water . . .'

Struggling to his feet with Sam in his arms, Peter walked steadily across the darkening room towards the bathroom and kicked open the door with his heel.

'I'm like a heroine in a silent black-and-white film,' she giggled as he carried her over the threshold.

'Yeah, silent. Right! I don't think so . . .'

The waiter gathered up the menus, the business of reading, choosing and ordering over. We did it, sighed Sam, relaxing into her chair. Somehow, she and Peter had managed to shower, dress, check out of the hotel and still arrive at the apartment by six-thirty. Fucking amazing. The plan was that they would go back there after dinner to pick up their bags, then head straight for the airport for the red-eye home. Shower, she repeated to herself, then smugly at the euphemism.

They were all in their Monday best. Even Peter was more ironed than usual, black hair hanging loose like the glossy tail of an animal. A bottle of champagne slumped in a silver ice-bucket next to Julian's chair and the candles were lit, even though it was only twenty to seven. The restaurant staff had worked out it was a special evening.

Julian moved the vase of flowers from the middle of the table to the ledge behind his banquette so he could see Sam and Peter more clearly.

'Shall I propose a toast?'

The other three reached for their drinks.

'To us,' he said.

'To us.'

'And to those who can't be with us,' he added.

Silence. Stillness. Then the subtle chinking of glass against glass and four mouths opening to receive the ritual yellow fizz. The sombre moment dissolved and light-hearted conversation bubbled to the surface again.

Peter sat back in his chair and watched, his mind weaving easily from thought to thought. It was the first time he had been with all three of them since the initial meeting in the park. For Sam's sake, he was happy about how natural they all were together. He felt like a spectator, really. Enjoying the game, despite not knowing the rules. Peter fished his stash tin out of his pocket and started to unpack his tobacco and papers. The problem was that curiosity was burrowing under his skin like a splinter. Lauren and Julian were great, but there was an undercurrent. He couldn't quite put his finger on it, but something didn't add up. Maybe it was just that he'd been expecting them to seem more damaged. Lonely, maybe.

Licking the Rizla, Peter looked across at Julian from under his eyebrows. He looked pretty relaxed. Peter couldn't figure out what the guy might be feeling as he sat in this restaurant, drinking and talking to Sam. Knowing Anna had not even made it to her seventeenth birthday. Jesus, the man had buried his newborn son and lost his daughter. Wasn't he haunted by all the might-have-beens if only he'd had the guts to tear up the adoption papers?

And Lauren? She seemed a little jumpy. He surreptitiously watched her moulding her crumbs of bread into tiny balls and rolling them up and down the linen tablecloth. Like worry beads. She was quieter than he'd expected after spending time with her yesterday. He'd joined her and Sam on a trip to the Arlington National Cemetery on Sunday morning. It had been great. He'd really felt part of things, even talked about his family a little. When he'd confided that his mother Annette claimed to have been half in love with JFK, Lauren had put her arm around his waist. We all were, she'd smiled, with a touch of irony. That's the million-dollar question. Where were you on 22 November 1963? Peter had seen the happiness in Sam's face as she'd watched.

Peter lit his skinny cigarette, squeezing the comforting spent match between his fingers. Part of him wanted to lean across the table and shake Lauren. Ask if the sacrifice had been worth it, now she'd met Sam. In the twilight shades of the restaurant, her chestnut eyes looked almost brown. She was so attractive, so warm and sharp. Sam had snapped his head off earlier when he'd made the mistake of saying how odd it was that Lauren didn't appear to have a boyfriend. This, despite the fact that she'd spent the previous ten minutes inventing a secret lover stashed away for Julian. You're being sexist and homophobic, she'd shouted. As if a woman can't be happy without a man. Lauren might be gay. Had that even crossed your mind? Then she'd burst into tears.

Peter had felt pissed at himself for making her sad. But it had made him think again about how weird it was that Sam didn't want to pick over the bones of what Lauren and Julian had told her. Usually she was so curious, wanting to come at things from every angle, over and over until she'd exhausted the subject. Never letting go. But on Friday night, she had simply crawled exhausted into his arms and slept. And on Saturday morning – when the two of them had camped out in bed, picnicking on coffee and bagels – he'd had to encourage her to tell him what had happened. Questions and sparse answers, rather than her usual unstoppable stream of impression and opinion.

At first, Peter had put it down to tiredness. That, and Sam's wonderwoman ability to ignore anything that didn't fit in with the truth as she saw it. When he pushed, she did admit that a few half-questions had sneaked into her mind. But nothing major, as she put it. It's not an old-fashioned detective story, Peter. There's no cast of characters gathered around the fireplace for the dénouement. This is real. And I feel as if by dragging everything out into the open, we've put the subject off limits.

As they'd sat there in bed smoking the morning away, Peter had kept probing. Particularly on the issue of who her natural father was. It just no longer seems important, she'd said. When he challenged her definition of important, she'd accused him of being obsessed with all that, quote, "male bollocks about paternity". Peter smiled at the memory of Sam's fighting face. He was prepared to accept that there might be an element of justice in her comment, but even so . . . He couldn't imagine Tom letting the subject go either. Sam's refusal to think about it would irritate the hell out of him.

Peter brought his glass up to his lips and swallowed a mouthful of champagne. Then he set the glass back on the table in front of him and turned the stem round and round with his fingers. Over the past twenty-four hours, though, he realised he'd been coming round to the idea that Sam's refusal to analyse might be down to self-preservation rather than self-deception. Not exhaustion, not Sam's sheer bloody-mindedness, but instinct that there was no room in her scarred head for any more truths?

Jesus, thought Peter, pushing his fingers back through his hair. Trying to clear his head. What does it matter? He should be protecting Sam, not upsetting her with his buts and whys. What mattered was that Sam was OK and stayed OK. And she seemed fine tonight. Out of the corner of his eyes, he took her in. Her animated face, her confidence in her black velvet dress, the curve of low, scooped neck broken by her silver locket. Her hidden white skin. Lovely. A silk scarf was keeping her frizzy hair back behind her ears. He guessed she'd borrowed it from Lauren. It looked like something she would wear.

He suddenly realised the talking had stopped and everyone was looking at him.

'Excuse me?'

Julian smiled. 'I was only asking whether this trip had made you want to visit your home town again? San Diego, wasn't it?'

'San Diego,' Peter echoed, trying to shake the slippery thoughts from his head. 'Yeah . . . I mean, no. I've enjoyed being here, but it doesn't make me want to stay. I don't feel America's the place I want to be right now. It's so much easier living in somebody else's country. You don't feel so responsible for the mess.'

'It must be great living here in Washington,' said Sam. 'Just up the road from the President and the FBI and everything.' She shuddered theatrically and rubbed her hands together. 'All that power.'

'Actually, we don't really get involved much in politics,' admitted Julian. 'Having said that, I probably will go on the big rally in a couple of weeks' time.'

'What's it in aid of?'

'Against massive government cutbacks in health and education spending, I think. That's right, isn't it, Laurie?'

'Uh-huh. That's if we make it through this Miss America Pageant on Friday,' Lauren added sarcastically. 'Bathing suits and air-heads. Don't you love the fall . . . ?'

Sam was still laughing as the *hors d'oeuvre* arrived. All four of them leaned away from the table as the waiter darted from one side to the other. Back and forth, back and forth. Ladies first, gentlemen after.

The conversation flowed spontaneously as one set of plates was swapped for another. Oiled by champagne and emotion and a sense of occasion, their voices wound around one another, shot off at tangents, took a few bars' rest. Like a string quartet improvising.

Sam's last few American hours ticked by.

'Shall we get the bill, Laurie?'

Lauren tilted her head so she could see the hands on Julian's watch.

'Definitely. It's a quarter after nine already.'

'Do you know where the bathroom is?' asked Peter, pushing his chair back and standing up.

'Straight through the double doors with the circular windows,' replied Julian, indicating straight ahead. 'Then go down the stairs on your immediate right.'

'Thanks.'

Sam got up too, pulling her dress away from her sticky hot legs.

'Is the Ladies in the same place?'

'Just a different door at the bottom,' replied Lauren. 'So to speak.'

Sam laughed, one of her ear-splitting best, and followed Peter, hoping she didn't look too crumpled from behind.

Peter decided against waiting for Sam afterwards. He noticed she'd taken her bag with her, so guessed she was intending to fiddle with her scarf and her make-up. Once he'd snapped himself out of his over-reflective mood, he'd enjoyed the evening. He was tired now, though, and was not looking forward to seven hours on a cramped plane. Hopefully Sam would sleep rather than fidget . . .

At the top of the stairs, Peter put out his hand to swing the door open. Through the round glass panes he could see that neither Lauren nor Julian had moved from their seats. Julian was waving a plate around, trying to attract the attention of the *Maître d'*. Peter watched a waiter materialise from nowhere and take it.

As Julian lowered his arm, he tucked one of Lauren's long stray curls back behind her ear. An instinctive, automatic gesture, all over in the blinking of an eye. No. Surely no. Peter thumped his body back against the wall, his heart pumping in his chest. *Mierda.* How could he have been so blind?

'What's up?' asked Sam, walking up the stairs towards him.

'Nothing's up,' he replied quickly, taking her hand.

For a moment, Peter held it against his cheek. Then, kissing her palm, he pushed the swing-doors open and led her back into the restaurant to their table. Five minutes later, they were all on the pavement outside, the city air cool on their serious faces.

The silence was awkward. Peter could see that Lauren's eyes were wet, Sam's too. She looked washed out.

'One of my favourite restaurants,' said Julian, attempting to hold back the inevitable for just one second more.

The words of an old song were going round and round Sam's head. 'Fare-well, au revoir, auf Wieder-sehen, good-byeee.'

'I don't want to go . . .' she whispered.

The raw cry echoed in the mulberry night sky, then floated away up over the top of the buildings. Lauren opened her arms and Sam ran into them. Like two women drowning, they clung to one another. Sam was weeping with relief, not desperation. Because it hurt to part. And because she knew that, after so long, everything was going to be all right.

For a minute or two, the men stood quietly by. Irrelevant. Then Peter felt Julian tap him lightly on the shoulder.

'Shall we go inside and get the bags?'

His voice cracked, as if he was struggling not to cry too. The nakedness of the pain in his eyes touched Peter. He followed Julian silently into the lobby, into the elevator. The bright artificial light made their faces yellow, jaundiced in the mirrors. One floor, two floors, three. The doors swished open and they stepped out.

'This is it,' said Julian.

Peter felt he knew the apartment from Sam's infatuated description. The rugs, the vases, the walls of books. How everything led off the beautiful hallway, with its wall hangings and yellow paint. Their fluorescent pink and blue squidgy bags were stacked right next to the door.

'Sam said you had a great apartment. How long have you been here?'

'Nearly two years,' replied Julian.

'Can't it get rather awkward, living with your sister?'

Peter thought he saw alarm flash across Julian's face. An impression, then it was gone.

'It seemed sensible to pool our resources,' he replied in a steady voice, bending to pick up the luggage. 'It meant we could get something bigger.'

'But can't privacy be a problem?' Peter persisted. 'Girlfriends, boyfriends . . .'

Somewhere, hidden in the dark apartment, a clock chimed the half-hour.

'Not really,' Julian answered levelly, wrapping his fingers round the handles of one of the bags. 'In any case, neither of us is involved in a serious relationship at the moment.'

'Except that's not true,' said Peter quietly. 'Is it?'

Julian snapped his head up. Brown eyes stared into blue. Neither man looked away.

'What do you mean?'

'I think Sam's your daughter. Yours and Lauren's.'

It was as if the entire city had stopped breathing. Peter half-expected to feel Julian's fist smashing into his face, the taste of blood in his mouth. Instead, he watched defeated tears spill out of Julian's eyes and down his cheeks. Silent, like the rain in summer.

Peter bowed his head, immediately ashamed at what he had done.

'Jesus, I'm sorry,' he whispered. 'I had no right . . .'

He reached out for the bag in Julian's hand, let it drop back to the floor. The pattern on his Mexican bracelet matched perfectly the colours of the rugs hanging from the walls.

'We thought she'd be disgusted,' he murmured, his voice fading. 'You know . . .'

Julian rubbed the salty tears from the end of his nose.

'I fell in love with her the very first time I saw her. She was so alive, so perfect. She never felt like my sister, you know. Not ever.'

Peter ran his free fingers back through his hair. Forced himself to breathe calmly and to listen.

'We came here, to America, to try to live somehow. Not to forget. To crawl out from under the shadow of what had happened eighteen years ago. We thought it would be less painful not to be in England, always wondering. Then Pamela Greene rang, saying Sam wanted to meet. And all those memories came rolling back.

'Laurie wanted to tell her everything. No more hiding. But I persuaded her out of it. I didn't think we could survive losing her a second time . . . Can you understand?'

'Sure,' whispered Peter. 'Sure.'

Julian wiped his face with the flats of his hands. 'We never lied.'

'No.'

'Will you tell Sam?'

An image of her sparkling face stole into Peter's mind. He

thought of all she had been through, all the loss and doubt and searching. The grief that slept inside her, all the good blood and the bad.

Peter rested his head back against the wall. Sam was almost at peace with herself. This was the time to set the past behind her, where it belonged. To start living for today, rather than always glancing backwards, wondering who she was and where she'd come from. She'd been so elated over the past four days. How could he take that away from her?

He turned to look at the man standing next to him. Sam's father, waiting for him to play God. Peter felt turned inside out by his love for Sam. It was addictive and primitive, a passion that towered over every other feeling. This was what loving Lauren did to Julian. Bad luck? Maybe. But wrong? Who was to say?

'I think you will tell Sam the truth some day,' Peter said quietly. 'But not now. It's too soon.'

Sam and Peter sat bundled together in the back of the taxi, twisting round on the bench seat to wave out of the back window. Sam felt shattered, all her emotion spent. Turning back to face ahead, she hooked herself under Peter's arm.

'I'm glad to be going home,' she murmured.

He hugged her close, watching the figures on the pavement getting smaller and smaller and smaller. Just before the cab turned the corner, he thought he caught sight of Lauren and Julian with their arms around each other on the street. Still waving.

Peter caught his breath as desire filled his throat. He kissed the top of Sam's head, then looked out of the window at the Washington streets speeding by. Perhaps it was as much as anybody should hope for? For love to last. That he and Sam would be as happy together in twenty years' time as they were now. Like Lauren and Julian.

He turned back to Sam, leaning against his shoulder.

'I love you,' he whispered.

Sam didn't hear him. She had already fallen asleep, dreaming of home.

A November afternoon, murky and silent.

For two days and nights, unbroken rain had fallen from the flint sky and melted away like snow into the ground. England at its worst. More like a relentless April than the beginning of winter.

They were huddled in Peter's new rusty Morris Minor, somewhere on a country road in Oxfordshire. The car was at least as old as Sam herself. Nineteen years and four days old, as of today. 16 November 1981. The heater didn't work properly and their breath was steaming up the windscreen. Everything smelled damp and old.

Sam was regretting the impulse that had brought them to this cold and miserable impasse. She'd woken up earlier that morning feeling flat, still knackered from the excesses of her birthday a few days ago. Not hung over, as such, just foul-tempered and bored. Three cups of coffee at breakfast hadn't helped. She poked her toast, scowled at the clock and snapped at her parents.

At eight o'clock, the sound of the letter-box. A minute later, Tom had tossed a small package down on the plate in front of her without saying a word. She hadn't even bothered to say thank-you. Familiar handwriting, a Washington postmark. Sam had sat up and hungrily torn at the wrapping.

Lauren wrote she was fine and Julian was fine and they were both thinking of her. Sam shook the envelope and a pair of dangly twisted earrings had fallen out. Platinum shot through with blues and greens and purples. A tide-you-over birthday present, the letter said. Sam had put them on immediately, turning her head from side to side to feel them brushing the sides of her neck. Most exciting, though, was Lauren's confirmation that she could get over to England for a few days at the end of December. Paddington Bear birthday time. And could Sam thank her parents for their kind invitation? She was very much looking forward to meeting them.

Sam read the letter straight through again, energised by the thought of seeing Lauren. Then again to make sure she'd not missed anything. Shit. She couldn't just mope about the house all day, eating and drinking coffee, dreaming of Christmas and Lauren. She had to do something to celebrate. And it was so obvious. Today would be the day she would go to Raphael House. It had seemed like a good idea at the time . . .

Peter's voice, sounding a little ragged round the edges, cut into her thoughts.

'Do you have a clue where we are exactly?'

'I thought *you* knew . . .'

'Jesus, Sam. You're the one with the map.'

'I don't have the fucking map,' she muttered aggressively.

'It's there,' said Peter irritably, stabbing his finger at the floor between Sam's feet. 'Right there.'

'All right, all right,' snapped Sam. 'Stop, then. I can't read going along. I'll throw up.'

Resisting the temptation to slam the brakes on to shut Sam up, Peter slowed down. The old-fashioned indicator clicked loudly as he pulled the car into a lay-by and killed the engine. Next to him, Sam was wrestling with the razor-sharp folds of the Ordnance Survey and complaining.

Peter ignored her, doubling his arm back behind her seat and banging his cold fingers around on the floor, trying to find the cardboard of the silver Benson and Hedges packet wedged in her basket. Got it. He eased two cigarettes out, balanced them on the open ashtray, then started groping for the matches.

'They got wet,' said Sam, without looking up.

While he was waiting for the cigarette lighter in the dashboard to heat up, Peter fiddled with the antique radio. Squeaks and bleeps and whistles and snatches of music belched out as he turned the dial, station after station. The weather, Shirley Williams, gardening tips, Sting.

'Wait,' yelled Sam suddenly, grabbing Peter's hand. 'Leave it.'

A sombre and elegiac melody curled into the car, like a wraith of mist. Violins, desolate violas, cellos, building notes into music. Sam took his fingers and wound them around her own, as the sound drowned them in its sonorous arms. Chords to crack the heart.

'The *Adagio for Strings*,' announced the precise broadcasting voice, 'by the American composer Samuel Barber, who died earlier this year. Tomorrow's concert . . .'

Peter flicked the radio off.

'You OK?'

Sam didn't answer. The foggy air in the car reverberated in the heavy, damp silence.

'Sam?'

'That's what they played at the funeral,' she said quietly. 'I never knew what it was called.'

Peter watched the kaleidoscope of emotions turning across her face. Anna's grave in the Sussex churchyard, the plain white headstone telling inquisitive eyes everything they needed to know. A noisy place in summer, with the bees rummaging in the honeysuckle on the fence and the breaktime squeals from a nearby school playground. It was what had struck home the first time he had come with Sam. That it was good that Anna was in such a living place. There had been a time, he knew, when Sam had gone there every day.

Peter turned to look at her.

'I'm sorry,' she whispered. 'For being so grim . . .'

Peter cupped her face in his hands, pressed the end of his cold nose against hers. Eskimo kissing.

'You are a real pain in the ass, you know that? I just can't figure out why I love you . . .'

Sam twisted her body across and sketched a heart on his steamy window. SW 4 PN 4 EVER.

'Me neither,' she smiled sheepishly.

Peter laughed. Then, with his forefinger, he added the head and tail of an arrow to her glass heart.

'Shift yourself,' he said, heaving her off his lap and back upright into her seat. 'Have you figured out where we are yet?'

Sam hit him with the map.

The edges of the sign had all but rotted away. Furry olive moss was growing up the wooden support and over the board which was nailed halfway up. It looked like the rickety sails of an old windmill.

239

Sam wound down her window to get a better look.

'This is it,' she said, squinting at the letters. The ends were chewed off, but she could just make out HAEL HOU in the middle. It was no longer raining, but the world was still dripping from every branch and twig. Sam yelped as a huge raindrop bounced off the roof and down inside her collar.

'I thought Pamela said she had tenants,' she said, bobbing her head back inside the car.

'What are you talking about?'

'That sign doesn't create a very good impression.'

Peter laughed.

'Well, it doesn't,' insisted Sam indignantly.

'OK, OK,' he said, still chuckling. 'Anyhow. What do you want to do now we're here?'

Although Sam had been thinking about it all the way up, she still wasn't sure quite what she wanted from Raphael House. A spirit of place, perhaps? Just a glimpse of where the past had been played out? To see for herself the evergreen grove at the back of the house where Anna's little brother was buried? All of these things? None of them? What?

Sam tucked her hair back behind her ears, rocking her earrings. Now they had arrived, there was nothing for it but to trust in blind faith. An instinct that once she was looking up at the bricks and gables, she would understand why she had come.

'Can you drive up, please,' she croaked nervously.

Peter put the car into gear and slowly inched forward. The drive was narrow, flanked on either side by high hedges and fir trees. Sam could hear gravel scrunching beneath their slithery tyres as they crawled along. Daylight barely filtered through.

They rounded a bend and there, suddenly, was Raphael House. The four irregular walls, the complicated sloping roof, the porch and windows overlooking the lawns stretching away in all directions. There were lights on everywhere, as if the house was expecting them.

'What now?' he asked quietly.

'Just keep going,' she murmured under her breath, fiddling with the chain of her locket.

Peter followed the drive until they were right outside the front porch. He turned the engine off and, without a word, they both unclipped their seat-belts and stepped out of the car.

The slam of their doors echoed in the still afternoon, like shots from a gun.

'It looks friendly,' hissed Sam across the bonnet of the car. 'I thought it might be a sad place.'

Suddenly three pairs of bright wellington boots appeared round the corner of the house, two blue, one red. Three children, all bundled up against the damp November afternoon.

'Can I help you?'

Sam spun round in the direction of the voice to see a pleasant-looking woman in jeans and a jumper standing in the doorway, an inquisitive look on her face.

'Have you brought my bicycle?' demanded a child at Sam's knee.

She panicked, always ill at ease with children and their direct way of talking.

'Of course they haven't brought your bicycle, Lucy,' said the woman firmly. 'You can have five minutes more on the climbing-frame, then it's in. Go on. Scram.'

The three little girls let out a war-cry and galloped back the way they had come. Out of sight.

'I'm sorry about that,' she apologised, turning back to Sam and Peter. 'We're expecting her new bike to be delivered this afternoon. Anyway . . . are you lost?'

She left the question hanging.

Sam smiled, wondering where to begin.

'No. I'm not lost,' she said slowly. 'It's just that my sister was born here.'

And so was I, she whispered to herself. So was I.

ACKNOWLEDGEMENTS

First, my thanks to all those who shared with me their personal experiences of adoption – mothers and fathers, birth parents, sisters and brothers, as well as those who had been adopted.

I would also like to express my gratitude to the support group NORCAP (National Organisation for the Counselling of Adoptees and their Parents), to BAAF (British Agencies for Adoption and Fostering) and to staff at Somerset House, St Catherine's House and Lewisham Reference Library in London. In each case, my research was made simple by their efficiency, professionalism and interest.

Next, my thanks to my agent Mark Lucas, a deal-maker and telephone junkie without equal. And to everyone at Hodder & Stoughton, especially my editor, George Lucas. His trust and sensitivity and support made the vulnerable business of publishing a first novel much less painful than I'd anticipated . . .

My love, admiration and respect for my parents, Richard and Barbara Mosse. It is their pride and faith in me – throughout my childhood and beyond – that has always given me the confidence to try my hand at anything.

My gratitude to friends who put up with months of obsessive rambling, questions, unsociability and food-cravings while I was writing *Eskimo Kissing*. Special thanks to Rosie Turner, for her generosity with Carcassonne and – more importantly – her inspired and enthusiastic grannying. She is very much appreciated.

Finally – as always – to Greg. With every book it gets harder to think of new ways to say the same thing: how everything is only made possible because of his never-ending enthusiasm, practical support, love and belief in me.

The best I can do here is to repeat that without Greg – and our children Martha and Felix – there would be no point to anything.

Kate Mosse
London, 1996

USEFUL ADDRESSES

BAAF
(British Agencies for Adoption and Fostering)
11 Southwark Street
LONDON
SE1 1RQ
Tel: (0171) 407 8800

NORCAP
(National Organisation for the Counselling of Adoptees and
their Parents)
3 New High Street
Headington
OXFORD
OX3 7AJ
Tel: (01865) 750554
10 a.m. to 4 p.m., Monday, Wednesday and Friday

GENERAL REGISTER OFFICES

For England and Wales:
The General Register Office
St Catherine's House (formerly Somerset House)
10 Kingsway
LONDON
WC2 6JP
8.30 a.m. to 4.30 p.m., Monday to Friday

For Scotland:
The General Register Office
New Register House
EDINBURGH
EH1 3YT

For Northern Ireland:
Registrar General
Oxford House
49–55 Chichester Street
BELFAST
BT1 4HL

Republic of Ireland:
The General Register Office
8–11 Lombard Street East
DUBLIN 2